# And Then She Kissed Me

# HARPER BLISS

# And Then She Kissed Me

ladylit_ publishing

## OTHER HARPER BLISS NOVELS

That Woman Next Door
About That Kiss
At Your Most Beautiful
A Breathless Place
If You Kiss Me Like That
Two Hearts Trilogy
Next in Line for Love
A Lesson in Love
Life in Bits (with T.B. Markinson)
A Swing at Love (with Caroline Bliss)
Once Upon a Princess (with Clare Lydon)
In the Distance There Is Light
The Road to You
Far from the World We Know
Seasons of Love
Release the Stars
At the Water's Edge
High Rise (The Complete Collection)

## THE PINK BEAN SERIES
## THE FRENCH KISSING SERIES

## CHAPTER 1

# Sadie

"Look what the cat dragged in." My brother grins at me from behind the bar. "If it isn't Hollywood's finest TV cop."

"Happy birthday, Sam." I head toward him with widespread arms. "It's good to see you."

"Ditto and ditto." Sam gathers me in his arms. "Are you ready for an epic party?"

I want to shake my head. I'm tired after having finished the relentless, against-the-clock period of shooting that always happens before the yearly hiatus of our show. I'd much rather have a quiet drink with my twin brother to celebrate our fortieth birthday, but that's not Sam's style and I don't want to be a downer from the get-go.

"Sure." I step back to get a good look at him. Owning The Bay beach bar doesn't seem to have affected his wholesome North-Cali surfer boy looks. His skin is golden brown, his hair streaked with sunlit blond highlights, and his body looks as trim as it was when we were in our senior year of high school.

The door to the back room swings open and a blonde girl

who doesn't look a day over twenty-one walks out. My mind races to what has always been the obvious conclusion—that she's my brother's latest age-inappropriate conquest—but Sam swiftly puts me straight.

"This is Cassidy, my most valued employee."

Cassidy brings her hands to her mouth. "Wow. Sadie Ireland in the flesh. It's such an honor." She holds out her hand. "I adore *King & Prince*. I watch it all the time."

I'm of half a mind to tell her that the very last scenes with both King and Prince were shot last week, but I'm contractually forbidden from doing so.

"Thank you." Since Cassidy is my brother's employee—and possibly more than that—I shake her hand warmly.

"Will you be in town a while?" Cassidy asks.

"I might very well be." I catch my brother's gaze. I'll be staying with him to recover from what has been an emotionally draining ten months of divorcing my co-star while simultaneously shooting a show together.

"I'll see you around then." Cassidy isn't the lingering type of fangirl, then. She disappears into the back room again.

I shoot my brother a look that can't be misinterpreted.

"It's not what you think," he says. "She's the best employee I've ever had and I'm not about to mess that up."

"How old is she?"

"Old enough to work in a bar," is all he says.

Noise comes from the back. A car door slams shut, and I hear animated voices.

"That must be the caterers," Sam says. "You relax with a beer on the deck. Look out over the ocean and contemplate the first forty years of your life." He runs a hand through his thick hair. The man doesn't look a day over thirty.

He reaches into the fridge behind him, takes out a bottle, twists off the cap, and hands it to me.

"Do you honestly believe that anyone who works on-screen in Hollywood actually drinks beer?" We've had this conversation many times.

"You're forty today and recently divorced. Have the beer. Take all the comfort you can find."

"Sam!" someone shouts from the back.

"I know I'm only twenty minutes older than you, but do as I say, anyway." With that, he turns around and disappears through the door to the back, leaving me alone in the bar.

I head out, beer in hand, and take a seat on a stool lining the deck, overlooking the waves. I drag my gaze away from the sea for a minute to study the bottle I'm holding. The beer is called Surfer Juice IPA, which probably means it sells well in these parts. I scan the label to see if any new local breweries have sprouted up since I last visited. Lennox Breweries. Not a small-batch local brew then.

I take a sip. I haven't had a beer in months—not since Sam came to Los Angeles for a few weeks last March to support me through the worst of the fall-out after my divorce from Mike. Sometimes, when you're being chased by paps, you need your twin brother's ridiculously muscular arm around you to shield you from the never-ending scrutiny.

The beer tastes crisp and light and I feel myself relax. It's hard not to with this view. It's quiet on the boardwalk between the bar and the beach—the calm before the big birthday storm Sam has planned, no doubt.

It suddenly hits me that I didn't offer to help Sam and Cassidy set up for the party. I'm about to go back in to offer my services when I hear footsteps approach.

"I came straight from work," Suzy, my older sister, says, followed by a shriek worthy of a teenage girl at a boy band concert.

I get up to hug her, using the time it takes to throw my

arms around her to remember what Suzy's current job is. Even though we speak on the phone several times a week, it's hard to keep up with my sister's employment—a bit like Sam and his women. My sister's quest for the ultimate professional fulfillment has had her job-hopping for decades.

"I did my first solo coaching call," Suzy says as I sink into her embrace.

Oh, yes. She works as some sort of life coach on the internet.

"I knocked it out of the park with my quick thinking skills. My boss was so complimentary after, I could hardly believe it."

I let my sister rattle on for as long as she likes. It's her thing. The first ten minutes of any conversation between us are spent exactly like this until she's gotten everything that's on her mind off her chest. After which she fixes her gaze on me, and asks me, the way I imagine she asks her clients, how I'm doing and what I'm struggling with these days. Come to think of it, maybe life coach is a great profession for Suzy.

"We are complete." Sam has ventured outside.

"Oh, Sam," Suzy says. "I invited Devon last-minute. I hope that's okay."

"The more, the merrier," Sam says. "You know that."

"Sam's convinced tonight will be epic," Suzy says.

"You only turn forty once," Sam replies. "And I'm not the only one."

I missed our joint thirtieth birthday party because of reshoots that couldn't possibly be rescheduled and our thirty-fifth because, that season, a few episodes of *King & Prince* were shot on location in Mexico. But fifteen years on the same prime-time TV show have earned me, alongside the habitual executive producer credit, a bit more say over my schedule. I made it abundantly clear I wouldn't miss another big birthday party because of the show's shooting schedule.

"To an epic party with my two favorite people in the world." I hold up my half-empty beer.

I let my gaze glide over Suzy and Sam. They fall into their easy brother-sister banter. I lean against the railing and, with the ocean behind me and my brother and sister within touching distance in front of me, I revel in the soothing sensation of coming home.

I need it now more than ever.

## CHAPTER 2

## *Devon*

am and Sadie's party is in full swing when I arrive. I spot a lot of familiar faces, but I'm here for one face in particular. I can see Sadie on my TV screen whenever I want these days, but it's been years since I've seen her in the flesh. When Suzy invited me earlier today, I didn't have to think twice about accepting. I consider myself a down-to-earth person—you have to be in my profession—but Sadie Ireland has always been the exception to any rule I've ever set myself.

I make my way through the throng of people on the deck. I hear two guys I know talking about catching some waves in the morning. I give them a nod of recognition. I try to ignore the coil of nerves in my stomach, even though I know better than most how futile it is to try not to feel your feelings. But again—Sadie's the exception to everything.

I spot Suzy first. She's part of a circle of people that have gathered around Sam and Sadie, as if they're holding court. Suzy's usually the center of every circle, but maybe she's happy to surrender the spotlight to her siblings on their birthday. I know all three Irelands and it has always struck me as odd that, out of the three of them, Sadie ended up the TV star.

Not that she doesn't have the looks for it—she always had. I lock my gaze on her and it all comes back to me, engulfing me like a dream I'm not sure I ever want to wake up from.

We're both twenty-four years older now, but the slant of Sadie's nose and the shape of her eyes are as familiar to me now as they were then.

Sadie has spotted me. She does that thing with her eyes when she glances away at first before her gaze is pulled back, as though she has no other choice but to look at me again.

"Devon!" Suzy must have seen something on her sister's face because she has turned around and is pulling me toward them. "So glad you came."

"Happy birthday, Irelands." I stand around awkwardly because I don't know whether to kiss them or hug them or, more than anything else, how to behave around Sadie.

Sam opens his arms wide and draws me into a bear hug. I'm not a regular at his bar, but I stop by here often enough, usually for a post-surf morning coffee.

"Happy you could make it," he mumbles, his words slurring a touch already.

"Thank you so much for having me. I'm sorry I didn't bring a gift. It was all a bit last minute, but it's definitely forthcoming."

"Your presence is your gift." Sam steps back and I have a full view of Sadie again. Does she even remember that day? Probably not. It meant different things to us. That has always been clear.

"Devon!" Sadie sounds surprised to see me. "Oh, my god!" She opens her arms to me and I walk into her embrace.

"Wow," Sadie whispers when her lips are close to my ear. "What a trip down memory lane."

I'm partial to tight hugs full of intention, but I only manage a limp pat on Sadie's shoulders.

"I know." I send her a smile after I've stepped back. "It's been a minute." I regroup and turn it on in a way that fools even myself.

Sadie arches up her eyebrows and brings a fingertip to my left arm. "Wow," she says again. "Those are so incredibly cool."

"Devon's the most tattooed life coach around," Suzy says. "Sadie's right, by the way. You're such a cool chick, Dev."

I chuckle heartily. "Cool is the very last thing I'm feeling right now." I give Sadie a look so she knows I'm referring to her presence.

"Don't tell me Sadie's fame impresses the likes of you." Suzy brings her hands to her hips, as though scolding me. "That's not what I signed up for when I hired you as my coach."

We all have our weaknesses, I think, but can't possibly say out loud. "It's not so much the fame that impresses me, but that the girl I used to sit next to in class is now on my television every time I turn it on."

"Professional hazard," Sadie says.

"Here." Sam offers me a bottle of beer. I'm not much of a drinker, but tonight, in the presence of Sadie Ireland, I may very well indulge.

"Here's to you two." I hold up the bottle and both Sam and Sadie clink theirs against it. I try to catch Sadie's gaze as we toast, but it skitters away. Maybe a flash of memory surprised her, too.

"You must have turned forty recently?" Sadie inquires.

"A few months ago."

9

"Here's to you as well, then." She lifts her bottle again, and this time, she returns my gaze for a split second. Her eyes still have the same bottomless darkness to them. Her smile is still as lopsidedly gorgeous as ever. "You look really good, Devon."

Heat flashes up my neck. Thank goodness the light is dimmed in the bar. Damn you, fair complexion. Unlike the surfer dudes on the deck, and despite all the time I spend in the water and underneath the California sun, my skin only knows two tones: alabaster white and lobster red.

"Thank you." More people arrive and want a piece of Sam and especially Sadie. According to Suzy, even though LA is only a six-hour drive south, Sadie doesn't make it back to Clearwater Bay very often. Also, according to Suzy, Sam is the luckiest of the three Ireland siblings because Sadie bought him a beach house and a bar in his beloved hometown, and he gets to enjoy the fruits of their sister's labor the most.

"I hope we get to talk some more later," Sadie says, before she's swallowed up by a group of people I'm not familiar with.

I lean against the bar and cast my gaze about the place. I see plenty of people I know and should chat with, but my eyes are drawn back to Sadie time and time again. I'd best get a grip. I look away and think of my son, Finn, who should be fast asleep right now at his dad's. It's easy enough to picture him in a funny, haphazard sleeping position, which is exactly what I need to pull me out of my Sadie Ireland induced trance.

When I scan the bar again, it's with different intentions. I fully acknowledge that I have some residual feelings left for Sadie, while I also know that twenty-four years later, they no longer hold any meaning. It's more nostalgia than anything else. Perhaps mixed with a touch of loneliness. I won't wallow in either, which is why I decide there and then, as my gaze scours the women in The Bay, to kill two birds with one stone —if I feel less lonely, nostalgia won't stand much chance either.

As if on cue, the music is turned up. Suzy's the first to start dancing, pulling her reluctant brother and sister along with her. Both Sam and Sadie retreat to the bar, while Suzy is quickly surrounded by other people more than willing to dance.

A woman I don't know catches my eyes. She has a few tattoos of her own, which is always a way in. I try to focus on her, but it's as though an invisible force field radiates from farther down the bar, where Sadie's standing. I can't help but look—and I can't help but melt a little more either. Damn you, nostalgia.

## CHAPTER 3
## Sadie

Devon Douglas looks mighty fine in that orange top. It brings out the fire in her hair. Even though I could tell that seeing me rattled her for a moment, she looks like she has it all together. Like she has it all figured out. She has that healthy glow about her that comes with successfully keeping existential dread at bay. I suppose it's a minimum requirement when you claim you can coach other people at 'life.'

When Suzy mentioned that she'd invited Devon to the party, I had no idea she was referring to *the* Devon Douglas. For a while in high school, we were inseparable, until we weren't. Because that's how things can go at that age.

I smile at her before taking another swig of beer. I don't remember how many I've had. As soon as I finish one, Sam is there to put another in my hand. I should talk to him about that. But not tonight.

Devon smiles back, and I take it as my cue to walk toward her. By now, most people at the party are over the fact that Sadie Ireland is here. I'm just a TV actor. I'm no Ida Burton or Faye Fleming. People get over being starstruck pretty quickly when they meet me in the flesh—look at Cassidy. Devon's attention didn't fade though—but she knew me a long time before there was any talk of *King & Prince*.

"Hey." I can't help but giggle like the teenagers we once were. "Are you having fun?"

"It sure is a trip seeing you again, Sadie."

"Yeah?"

"Of course." Devon stares intensely into my eyes.

I know I should say something, but I don't know what. It's as if my mind has gone blank. The only other time that happened to me was when I had to act opposite Mike again after we separated. Sometimes, emotions catch up with you despite your rational mind's best intentions.

"Are you okay?" Devon points to the beer bottle in my hand.

"Sam," I say, as though that should make it all perfectly clear.

"Want me to finish that for you?" Devon holds out her hand. "It might make for less of a headache in the morning."

"Sure." I give Devon my beer and watch how she brings it to her lips and tips the bottle back. For some reason, probably severe inebriation, my gaze is glued to her neck as she swallows.

"How long are you in town for?" Devon asks.

"For the entire hiatus of the show. I'm not doing anything else. Just retreating to my home base and licking my post-divorce wounds."

"I'd love to meet for coffee sometime. Catch up."

"I'd love that very much, too." I tilt my head. "You look... I don't know. Like the opposite of how I feel. Happy. Like everything is as it should be in your world."

"Looks can be deceiving. You should know that."

"Oh, I do. But..."

"It's okay. Whether you're Sadie Ireland living it up in Hollywood or Devon Douglas enjoying a quiet life in Clearwater Bay, we all go through good and bad times. It doesn't matter where you live or what you do for a living."

"That's deep for a birthday party." I've drunk too much to come up with even the slightest witty repartee.

"Yeah, I'm sorry." Everything Devon says sounds so heartfelt. "And I'm sorry you're going through a tough time."

Of course, she knows all about my divorce. The entire world knows. By lying low, I hope the attention on my former marriage will die down soon.

"I'm here now, with my family." Suzy has somehow convinced Sam to stay on the makeshift dance floor—The Bay isn't exactly a clubbing hotspot. My brother has many talents but moving his body in synch with a musical beat is not one of them. He seems to be having a blast, however. So much so it's infectious, and I feel like I'm missing out—kind of how I've felt about their lives since *King & Prince* took off and I had less and less time to come home.

"Do you want to dance?" Suddenly, I'm curious to see how Devon moves to the beat. If she can maintain that cool demeanor on the dance floor.

"How can I say no to Sadie Ireland?" She leads the way and, as these things can go at a boozy party, one moment I find myself lamenting my private life, while the next I'm going bananas to a Tina Turner song.

Suzy curls her arm around me and pulls me near. "I'm so glad you're home, little sis," she yells in my ear. "I missed you so much."

"I missed you too, Suze." My eyes go watery as I look at her. That must be the beer as well.

"I know what we need." Sam has approached us.

I groan in anticipation.

"Shots!"

"Shots! Shots! Shots!" Suzy joins in.

I'm having too much fun with my siblings to put up much of a fight. And it's not as if I have to be on set tomorrow. I'll have two months to recover from what will be a heinous hangover.

Sam orders shots with a few well-practiced hand gestures and next thing I know, liquor is burning down my throat. So much for letting Devon finish my beer earlier. Speaking of, where is she? She doesn't seem to partake in the reckless knocking back of shots. She's moved away from where we are clumsily swaying to the music and is talking to a woman I don't recognize. Devon's smiling and the other woman is peering intently at the tattoo sleeves on Devon's arms.

Next thing I know, I'm being lifted in the air, my legs swinging in front of me.

"Put me down, Sam," I yell. "I'm forty years old, for crying out loud."

"Only if you do another shot with me."

"Oh, what the hell." Thankfully, he releases me from his hold. My legs wobble when my feet touch back down on solid ground. "I might as well."

"To you and me, sis." Sam offers me another shot. "I promise I'll be on my best behavior while you're staying with me."

"Big words, bro. Big words."

"I'll try to remember to put the toilet seat down." He grins at me.

"That's it?"

"Some other things as well."

"How about you try not to bring a new woman home every other night? I would really appreciate that."

"That's not a promise I can make." He pulls his face into a forced scowl.

"Of course you can! We can agree on one night a week and I'll make sure I'm elsewhere. I'll stay at Suzy's or Dad's."

Sam shakes his head, then his eyes grow wide. I follow the path of his gaze.

"Someone's getting lucky tonight," he says.

Devon and the woman are standing very close but it's not as though they're doing anything that might indicate they're 'getting lucky.'

"They're just talking."

"Yeah right. And I'm a virgin." Sam elbows me in the biceps. "Maybe you've been out of flirting practice for too long, but I certainly know it when I see it. Anyway, good for them."

I stare at Devon and the woman she's talking to. Are they flirting? And does it matter whether they are? If so, why does it seem to bother me to the extent that I find it hard to look away because I want to see how it ends?

Is it because Devon Douglas isn't just a girl I went to school with? She's also the girl who kissed me, out of the blue, on a sunny Wednesday afternoon.

## CHAPTER 4

### Devon

I t's a challenge to focus on what Zara is saying with Sadie's gaze burning a hole in the back of my head. I removed myself from the situation as soon as Sam mentioned the word shots. I want to be present for my son tomorrow, not wallowing in the throes of a completely avoidable hangover.

I could only rely on my gaydar when I walked up to Zara, who owns the bakery Suzy used to work for a few years ago—long enough ago for Suzy to never have mentioned to me whether her old boss is gay and single. We seem to bond mainly through our mutual love for body ink, and although I'm getting some signals, I can't be sure.

"Gosh," Zara says. "That Sadie Ireland is one attractive woman."

There's another clue right there, although I wish it didn't have to include Sadie.

"She keeps staring our way. Although I'm flattered, it's a little unsettling."

"I think all the Irelands have had a bit too much to

19

drink." I cast a quick glance in Sadie's direction. She looks more out of it than intently focused on us.

"Speaking of," Zara says. "Can I get you another?"

I nod. "Just a soda water with lime for me, please." Someone needs to keep a clear head.

"Coming right up."

I sit on a chair by the window while I wait for Zara to return. It's almost fully dark, but I can still make out the ocean. The tide is low and the beach wide and inviting. I hope no one gets any silly ideas before the sun rises again. The allure of the water can be hard to resist, especially when you feel invincible after having a few too many shots.

Zara has struck up a conversation at the bar and it takes a while before she returns. Sadie has gone back to dancing with her brother and sister and a small group of other people. Since having Finn, I've become the opposite of a party person and I've always, happily, volunteered to babysit him even on weekends when he's with his dad—whose party days seem to have decreased considerably this past year, since he met Bobby.

I've had a chat with Sadie. We have tentative plans to go for coffee soon. I got what I came here for. But there's the promise of Zara, of course.

"Sorry it took a while." Zara has returned with two glasses of soda water. "This place is filled with people I used to know."

"Same here." I down my water.

"So you're Suzy's new boss. Does that mean you're well acquainted with her sister?"

I chuckle. "I used to be. A long time ago. We went to school together." For a while there, we were best friends in high school, until my teenage brain read a situation entirely wrong and I ruined everything.

"Technically, I'm only at this party because I'm friends

with Suzy. She didn't work for me for very long and I never got the chance to meet Sam and Sadie. But you know what Suzy's like."

"Suzy likes to invite the whole town to everything," I say.

"As long as she doesn't have to clean up the day after."

"Speak of the she-devil."

Suzy's dancing her way toward us, holding out her arms. "Come on, you two. And I'm not taking no for an answer. If only for the next five minutes. For the duration of one single song." She angles her head and pouts.

"I guess we have no choice." Zara shoots out of her chair and lets herself be dragged onto the dance floor while holding out her free arm to me. I take it, because I might as well. Now that I am at a party, I should make the most of it. And it brings me a little closer to Sadie again — my eternal weakness.

Her dancing is much sloppier than before, her arms flailing wildly. This might be her birthday party, but I don't think Sadie's going to make it to the end. In fact, I think someone should walk her home sooner rather than later. Perhaps I can volunteer.

"Do you want to go for a drink somewhere a bit quieter some time?" Zara suddenly shouts into my ear. She has sidled up to me and is gyrating her hips, making it very hard to say no. Not that I have any reason to decline her offer.

"I'd love that." I send her a wide smile.

"Shall I put my number in your phone?"

I nod and give it to her.

"There you go." When she hands it back to me, she plants the lightest of kisses on my cheek, making all my previous doubts evaporate. "I can't stay much longer. Bakers don't have the luxury of Sunday morning lie-ins."

I nod my understanding.

"Which is why, for the next ten minutes, I'm going to

21

dance like there's no tomorrow." Zara flashes me a toothy grin. "I hope you'll join me."

My hips feel a touch rusty when I take it up a notch, but dancing is so inherent to being human that I lose myself in the rhythm in no time. Zara and I give it all we have for the next three songs and the abandon and joy radiating from the dance floor soon has me in a state much like intoxication, minus the alcohol consumption.

Zara and I say our goodbyes and I watch her bid adieu to Suzy, Sam, and then, hesitantly, Sadie, who has drifted to the edge of the dance floor.

I find Suzy, and say, "Maybe you should take Sadie out for some air. She looks like she needs it."

"Why don't you take her outside," Suzy says, the mumbling of her words indicating she could do with some fresh air and a few gallons of water as well.

"Okay. I will." I'm not about to argue with a drunken Ireland.

I walk over to Sadie and start with a warm smile. "Hey."

"Oh, hi, Devon. Sam and I were convinced you were about to get lucky."

I laugh off her comment. I might drop by Zara's bakery tomorrow. I'm sure Finn will be up for a cupcake. "Looks like I didn't."

Sadie sways and, instinctively, I bring my hand to the small of her back to steady her. "How about we go for a little stroll on the beach?" I ask.

Sadie squints at me, then just nods.

On the way out, I ask the man behind the bar for a large bottle of water. Then I join Sadie and we cross the boardwalk to head onto the beach. A few other partygoers have drifted there and are dotted in small groups around us.

I give her the bottle of water and she drinks from it as though she has just completed a marathon through the desert.

"Jesus. Sam and his fucking shots." We walk closer to the shoreline. "I can't handle my liquor the way he does. I'm a Hollywood lightweight. I have no choice."

I don't really know what that means, but I give Sadie an encouraging nod.

She stops in her tracks and takes a deep breath. "I live in Malibu, but the beach feels different here. The air smells better. The ocean..." She hands me the bottle and lets herself fall backward onto her behind.

I sit next to her and give her the bottle of water to finish. It will take more than a bit of water to sober her up, but at least it's a start.

"It's because you're home," I offer. "Everything feels and smells different at home."

"Where do you live?" She turns her head and looks at me. It's fully dark now, but her eyes still shine bright.

"Just a few blocks away from the beach."

Sadie screws the bottle into the sand and leans back on her elbows. "I could never be without the ocean. Long before I could afford my house in Malibu, I drove to Santa Monica almost every day, no matter the ghastly LA traffic, to get a whiff of sea air. When you grow up here, it's hard to be without..."

"I totally agree." I know what she means. We have the ocean in our bones. The sound of the waves is part of our DNA. "Do you still surf?"

"How dare you even suggest that I wouldn't?" She smiles up at me.

"I don't know. I hear Hollywood's a crazy place. Surfing's never without risk. The show must want some assurances about your off-set activities."

She turns on her side. "God, Dev, you haven't changed a bit. You're still the ever-practical, thinking-three-steps-ahead girl you were in high school."

"I've changed plenty." I draw up my eyebrows.

"Yeah, time tends to do that." She twists herself away from me and sits up, cross-legged, looking into the dark expanse of ocean in front of us. "Can't wait to catch some waves."

"I'm curious to see your moves."

"I am forty now, of course. I'm not as flexible as I was when I was sixteen, but I have much more experience, which should make up for that." She turns to me again. "Shall we go out together sometime this week? I can't wait to see your moves either."

Because I can't help myself when it comes to Sadie, my heart does a crazy pitter-patter beneath my rib cage.

"If you're not too busy with the woman who gave you her number."

"Here I was convinced you were way too drunk to notice."

"Yet, I did." She flashes me a smile, then her face scrunches up. "I think all this water is having an adverse effect on my stomach."

I'm sure it's the water, I think, as I leap to my feet and help her up. "Shall I walk you home?"

Sadie doesn't move and swallows hard a few times. Then she shakes her head. "I don't want to go to Sam's. I know my brother better than any other person on this earth and chances are he's going to arrive home at the crack of dawn, blind drunk, with a twenty-something girl in tow. I don't want to wake up to that." She takes a deep breath.

"Surely he will take into account that you're staying with him."

"He won't. Not tonight. He's completely wasted already and will not get any less drunk as the night goes on."

"Shall I take you to Suzy's? I'll run back inside to get her keys."

Sadie stands there swaying in the gentle midnight breeze. She scratches her head. "Do you have a spare room?" she asks.

"Me?" If Sadie stays at my house, I probably won't be able to sleep a wink. On the other hand, the thought of her being there in the morning, all sober again, is quite exciting. It is, in fact, an irresistible prospect. "Sure. Yeah, you can stay at my house. No problem."

"Thank you so much."

"Are you okay to walk? It's less than ten minutes from the beach, even when carrying a surfboard."

"Yes, but can I?" She holds out her arm and I offer her mine to hook it through. Arm in arm, we amble off the beach, as though we've wound back the clock twenty-four years, and we're still best friends who've sneaked a few secret beers out into the night.

"Good thing you didn't get lucky," Sadie says once we're on the boardwalk. The music from the party blares loudly.

I text Suzy and Sam to tell them Sadie's in safe hands with me and not to worry about her. "Who says I didn't?"

Luckily, the booze hasn't made Sadie's sense of humor disappear and we both giggle as we make our way to my house.

## CHAPTER 5

*Sadie*

When I wake up, I have no idea where I am. My head throbs and my stomach feels tender. I throw the covers off and check the clothes I'm wearing. Panties and a faded gray T-shirt I don't recognize. Panicked, I turn my head, but the other side of the bed is empty. I rack my brain and the memory of Suzy shouting, 'Shots! Shots! Shots!' comes back to me, followed by me walking somewhere on Devon's arm, the two of us giggling like the schoolgirls we once were. Devon. I'm at her place. I take a breath. Even though I haven't seen Devon in years, I still trust her to take care of me when I need it. Perhaps I shouldn't, yet here I am. In her guest room. I listen for sounds outside the bedroom door. I hear a shriek followed by quick footsteps. What the—?

The bedroom door swings open and a child rushes in.

"Finn! Stop that!" Devon yells.

What the hell is happening? Who is this child?

"Who are you and what are you doing in Mom's bed?" the child fires at me.

"I'm sorry." Devon appears in the doorway. "He had a

doughnut at Hunter's and he's so hyper, he's unmanageable." She puts an arm around the child's shoulder. "Sweetie, why don't you go back to your dad's for a while. I'll come get you later. I'm sure Spencer could do with some extra playtime."

Hunter? Spencer? My hungover brain can't process any of these things. Who is Devon talking about? Is this child hers?

Then the fog in my head starts to clear and I remember Dad mentioning a few years ago that Devon had had a child.

"Come on." Devon puts a little more force into her tone and the child seems to listen. "But first, apologize to Sadie for barging into her room like that."

"But, it's *your* room—"

"Finn." Devon's tone of voice not only seems to have an effect on Finn. It does something to me too.

"I'm sorry," Finn says. "Have a nice day." With that, he turns on his heels and sprints off.

"I'll be right back," Devon says before she closes the doors behind her.

Jesus, Mary, and Joseph. To think I asked to stay at Devon's—which, in hindsight, I should probably not have done—so I could wake up quietly, without whomever my brother brought home with him asking me awkward questions.

I try to recall any information Dad gave me about this child at the time, but draw a blank. Who's the dad Devon was referring to? I thought she was a lesbian. In fact, I was the first person to know that about her. Maybe now I'm the last to be informed about the fluidity of her sexuality. Everything's possible, of course, and I'm dying to find out.

My head still reminding me of why I need to have a stern talking-to with my brother, I swing my legs out of bed. My jeans are folded neatly over a chair. There's no way I did that in the state I was in. Devon must have helped me undress. What a way to return to my hometown.

I hear a soft knock on the door. "Sadie? Can I come in?"

"I'll be out in a few minutes."

"Okay. A fresh pot of coffee awaits you."

Ten minutes later, I find myself on Devon's back porch with a steaming mug of strong coffee in my hands.

"I wasn't sure if you knew about my son, but you sure do now." Devon has pulled her hair back, and she looks positively radiant in the morning sun.

"He's hard to miss."

"Finn's five. They have so much energy at that age. It baffles me every single day."

"You mentioned his dad?"

Devon pulls her lips into a smile. "My best friend, Hunter." She cocks her head. "He's gay. We both wanted a child, and we figured that, between us, we had all the equipment necessary to make that happen."

My eyes grow wide. "Wow."

"We didn't conceive the natural way, in case you're wondering." The blissful expression on Devon's face says it all.

"My brain's slow this morning, that's all."

"Hunter lives next door, and Finn mostly comes and goes as he pleases, especially during the weekend. Hence the noisy morning surprise for you." She chuckles. "I can imagine you're shocked by all of this." She locks her gaze on mine. "And I guess it was quite confusing for him that you were in my bedroom instead of the guest room." She smiles apologetically. "I wasn't expecting guests and the room wasn't exactly ready to be used. I slept in Finn's room."

"Oh, gosh, I'm so sorry. If it's any consolation, you look

surprisingly well rested for someone who hasn't slept in her own bed."

Devon's cheeks pink up. She always was quick to blush. I'd forgotten about that—I've forgotten about so many things.

"And had to walk home a scandalously drunk woman," I add, to ease the tension.

"How are you feeling?" Devon hides one flushed cheek behind her cup of coffee.

"Could be much worse. If I had stayed at the party and hadn't downed that bottle of water. Thank you for taking care of me like that, Devon. That's very kind of you."

"What are old friends for?"

"But, still. I'm really grateful. I look forward to seeing the state of my brother and sister this morning."

"Best give them some time before you check up on them." The color of Devon's cheeks has gone back to normal. "I texted both Sam and Suzy last night so they knew not to worry about you, by the way."

"By the time that *epic* party was over, I'm sure they'd both forgotten I was even there in the first place."

"Surely not. Suzy talks about you all the time. Maybe she got a bit carried away because she's so happy you're back. At least for a while."

"I worry about them sometimes," I say. "It's like all three of us missed out on the successful long-term relationship gene."

"You were married for quite some time, though?"

"Seven years. It's longer than any affair Sam and Suzy have ever had, but, at the ripe old age of forty, it hardly makes for an exemplary track record in relationships."

"As far as I know, Suzy's very happy. I don't know Sam that well."

"I sometimes wonder if Sam's really happy. Isn't he getting a little old for that surfer-playboy thing he's got going?"

"Only he knows the answer to that," Devon says.

I want to say I'm pretty convinced it's because we grew up without a mother, but I don't want to spoil the mood, nor do I feel like my brain is operating well enough to start a conversation about my long-absent parent.

"You're single?" I glance at Devon over the rim of my cup.

"Very much so. Dating hasn't been my priority since I had Finn. The first three years with a baby are absolutely bat-shit crazy, even if the father lives next door. Although Hunter basically lived at my house back then, so I could at least get some sleep even when Finn was awake."

"Can't wait to meet this Hunter," I blurt out.

"I'm sure he can't wait to meet you, either. If he finds out *Leona King* slept at my house, he'll be beside himself. He might demand the sheets you slept in."

I quirk up my eyebrows.

Devon bursts into a chuckle. "You must be aware that Mike is quite, um, popular with the gay community, and so are you."

"I'm popular by association with my ex-husband's impressive biceps?"

"Well, truth be told, your character has always appealed much more to the lesbian viewership. Funnily enough, Hunter, Bobby, and I had a conversation about this just the other day. We believe that's why *King & Prince* has such longevity. All target groups are accounted for. There's something for everyone."

My turn to chuckle. "If you put it like that."

Devon's expression becomes more solemn again. "How are things between you and Mike? It can't be easy working together after going through such a highly publicized divorce."

"First of all, I know I'm in an extremely privileged position." I wrap my hands around my now empty cup of coffee, but some of the warmth lingers in the porcelain. "But yes, it's been hard. We're not at each other's throats, but being on set with him is like this constant reminder of all the things that went wrong between us."

I hope Devon doesn't start probing into exactly what went wrong between Mike and me. That's not a conversation to have on a hungover Sunday morning.

"Maybe you can tell me about it sometime." She holds up the pot of coffee. "More?"

"I should probably go. Your son's waiting for you."

"He's fine with his dad. Judging by the absence of noise next door, they've probably taken Spencer out for a walk." Devon refills my cup. "Spencer is their dog, by the way. Bobby is Hunter's partner."

"Oh, there's a partner as well."

"A quite recent addition to our extended family." Do I detect a hint of tension in Devon's tone?

"So Hunter has gone back to dating."

Devon gives a terse nod. "It's been quite an... adjustment for me, to be honest. For four years, it was just Finn, Hunter, and me in our little bubble. Then this guy comes along and, well, Bobby is no quiet wallflower. He has an opinion on every little thing and he can't go to bed without having voiced it in a loud, booming voice. I always knew Hunter had a thing for guys like that, but now that guy is a big part of our son's life, and it's not always as smooth sailing as I'd like it to be. But I'm working on it."

"Isn't that your specialty? Being a life coach and all?"

Devon paints on a knowing smile. "Sure." She takes

another sip. "Does this mean we won't be going for coffee anymore? Because we're drinking some already."

"We can skip the coffee date and go straight to surfing."

"Deal. I look forward to teaching you some tricks."

"You think you can teach me something I don't already know?"

Devon nods slowly, her brown-eyed gaze pinned on me.

"Challenge accepted."

"On Sundays, Finn and I usually go out at sunset. Feel free to come check us out."

"As much as I would love to, I'm going to see my dad. I haven't seen him yet since I arrived." But there will be plenty of other sunsets.

"How's Jack?"

"Spritely for a man in his late sixties, or at least so he tells me when we talk on the phone. I can't wait to see for myself."

"He made Finn's new surfboard. He has a pair of golden hands when it comes to craftsmanship like that."

I nod. Suzy, Sam, and I have only ever used boards made by dad. "Last night's indiscretions notwithstanding, I didn't think coming home would feel so good." Or maybe it's because sitting across from my old friend brings back such sunny memories from our high school days. Of course, life was complicated because we had raging hormones to negotiate. I had a jacked-up jock of a twin brother to tolerate. We were moody teenagers for a lot of the time, except for the times when, after school, we'd go straight to the beach, get out our boards, and hit the waves. More often than not, Devon and I were the only girls in the lineup, but we didn't care one bit.

A few months after I turned sixteen, it became very clear to me why Devon cared so little about boys in general.

"Must have been that—" What Devon says next is

drowned out by a child screaming next door. Are all of them so loud? How do parents cope with that? It must be my hangover and my increased sensitivity to disturbing noises. "They're back. It's very convenient living next door. When I want to know what's going on, all I have to do is go outside."

"Mom! Moooom!" Finn shouts from next door. "Can I come home now?"

Devon buries her face in her hands. "I don't know what's gotten into that boy. He's usually much better behaved. Too much time at his dad's," she mumbles, before removing her hands and sending me a close-lipped smile.

"In a minute," Devon shouts back to Finn.

"Thank you once again for your hospitality." I push my chair away from the table, suppressing a sigh. I could have stayed out here in the shade, drinking coffee with Devon a good while longer. There are far worse things to do on a hungover Sunday morning. "I'll leave you to it. Time to see how my brother's recovery is going."

"You don't have to go, Sadie. Finn's fine."

"It's okay." I push my chair underneath the table. "That's some damn good coffee, by the way."

"You're welcome to come over for a cup any time."

"I might take you up on that."

"I hope you will." Devon's smile reaches all the way to the corners of her eyes now. "Say hi to all the members of your family from me."

"I will. Thanks again, Devon." When we're at her front door, I'm unsure what to do. Hug her goodbye? Kiss her on the cheek? Pat her on the arm?

Devon solves my conundrum for me. She puts her hand on my upper arm, leans in, and kisses me on the cheek. "It's been a real pleasure seeing you again."

## CHAPTER 6

*Devon*

Bobby covers Finn's ears with his hands. "But what was Sadie Ireland doing in *your* bedroom?" He's gone into overdrive already, rivaling Finn's uncontrolled energy.

"I couldn't let her sleep in the guest room between Finn's toys and the mountain of ironing I never get to."

Bobby releases Finn from his grasp. He runs off, Spencer chasing behind him.

"I slept in Finn's room," I clarify.

"Still, my head's spinning." Bobby is such a drama queen. It's just like him to make a thing out of absolutely nothing. He slaps my knee playfully. "Why didn't you introduce us? Oh my gosh, to sit beside the likes of Sadie Ireland."

"I always thought you were much more interested in Michael Morales."

"I am, but, you know, one degree of separation and all that."

Hunter walks out with a tray of tacos. "Lunch is served. Finn, come and get some."

"Did she give you any juicy details about the divorce?"

"Not really." Even if Sadie had, I wouldn't be sharing them with you, I think, but smile at Bobby nonetheless. For all our sakes, it's important that we get along. "But she will be in town for a while. A few months, I reckon. There's plenty of time for you and Sadie to meet and hit it off like a house on fire."

"I wonder what will happen to the show now its two leads are no longer married. Acting is such a vulnerable thing," Bobby muses like he does sometimes. Hunter advised me to not always reply.

"Is that lady going to live with us like Bobby lives with Daddy?" Finn asks, out of the blue.

I nearly choke on my taco. "No, sweetie. Sadie's just a friend. She's Suzy's sister."

"Okay." When it comes to certain things, my son's still easy to placate, although he is in that phase where his favorite word to utter is 'why.' He goes back to eating his taco. Spencer sits patiently beside him, looking up with begging eyes, waiting for a scrap of food to fall to the floor.

"You're too young to watch her show, but that lady's on TV every week," Bobby says to Finn.

Hunter and I exchange a look.

"Can I watch it?" Finn asks.

"No, sweetie," Hunter says. "Only when you're older."

Finn's only five. He probably doesn't yet grasp the difference between people he sees on TV and in real life.

"We're hitting the waves later, you and me," I change the subject. "You'd better rest up a little this afternoon so you can keep up with me."

"But I'm not tired." One of the other most spoken sentences in his repertoire.

"If you don't nap, you'll be tired when we go surfing and

I won't be able to teach you what comes after the bottom turn."

Finn's eyes grow wide. "I'll take a nap with Spencer."

Spencer gives a little yelp at the mention of his name.

"Good."

Finn finishes his taco. "Can I be excused?"

Because we're at Hunter's, I let him reply. "Sure."

"Come on, Spence." Finn leads the dog inside.

Bobby claps his hands together dramatically. "Neat trick, Mama," he says.

"How was the party?" Hunter asks.

"Great." Seeing Sadie again and subsequently taking her home with me was the highlight of my evening, but I'm not going to tell Hunter and Bobby that. "I met someone, actually."

Bobby lets his mouth fall open, then clasps his hands in front of it. "Sweet baby Jesus, say it ain't so." He crosses himself and looks upward.

Both me and Hunter can't help but burst into a fit of giggles.

"Do tell," Hunter says.

"There's not that much to tell yet. Her name's Zara and she runs a bakery in Pinecliff Bay. She had to get up early, so she couldn't stay long. But I promised I'd drop by the bakery sometime this week." I vividly remember the impressive design of the tattoos that were visible on her arm. I'd love to study them in detail, with some more light to take in their intricacies. "Suzy used to work for her."

"Ooh," they both coo, because my ongoing spinster status has been the source of much delight for Hunter and Bobby—like I'm some silly lesbian cliché while they're living it up as fabulous gay men who can really have it all.

"What a night for you." Hunter grins at me. "I hope you still like her in the daylight."

"We'll see."

"When are you going to her bakery?" Bobby asks. "If you want to look keen, go today. If you want to play it more aloof, give it at least two if not three days."

I contemplate driving over to Pinecliff Bay today. I have plenty of time before I take Finn surfing.

"We can take Finn to the movies on our own just fine," Hunter says. "In case you want to go on a little adventure this afternoon."

Oops. I forgot about that. Must be the effect of sitting across from Sadie earlier today. And my night of not-so-good sleep in Finn's too-small bed.

"I think I'll sleep on it." If I'm being perfectly honest, which I can be with myself but not with Bobby and Hunter right now, I'd much rather spend the afternoon with Sadie— just for old times' sake. But Sadie's with her family and, as far as I know, she's still as straight as she was when I decided to ignore the odds all those years ago and recklessly kissed her lips. "Too much excitement for me for one weekend. A post-lunch nap is what I need." While we carry the dishes inside, I thank Hunter and Bobby for the food before heading back to my house.

Without changing the sheets, I slip into the bed Sadie slept in. It reminds me of all the times when we were in high school and had a sleepover at my house. Because my mom felt overprotective of Sadie after her mother left, she stayed at our house at least one night most weekends.

One particular night, I had lain awake next to Sadie, my body feverish with a desire I couldn't even name back then. I had no idea what was happening to me, all I knew was that I wanted to kiss Sadie the same way Sam had tried to kiss me a few months prior—an overture I brusquely put an end to as soon as he leaned toward me. Because Sam was a boy, he could try to kiss me all he wanted. It was different for me and Sadie because we were two girls.

This was not long before I got my heart broken into a thousand pieces for the very first time—by the girl who would become the woman who slept in my bed last night. If only I could go back in time and tell my sixteen-year-old self that it would all work out well. That Sadie Ireland would not be the only woman I would ever love. That a much bigger, but very different love was on the cards for me at the age of thirty-five, when my son would be born. That lovers would come and go, but friends and family would always be there, and that would be perfectly all right. That life would be lovely, with ups and downs, but there would always be the ocean and surfing and the boost of energy from meeting someone new and interesting.

I don't have a time machine and I can't change the past. Come to think of it, I wouldn't even try if I could. Because kissing Sadie on the beach that afternoon is part of my history, my story of how I became who I am today. When she rejected me—and acted as though she was utterly disgusted by me—it was devastating in the moment, but it also set things in motion for me that otherwise might not have happened for years.

I had to tell my mom why Sadie wasn't coming around anymore—and why I was so sad all the time. I could have lied, but I told her the truth instead. She's the one who held me in her arms, let me cry on her shoulder, and told me that everything would be all right. That it might hurt a lot now, but Sadie was not the only girl on this planet I would fall in love with—far from it.

To this day, as a matter of principle, my mother changes

the channel when an episode of *King & Prince* comes on, claiming there are far too many crime shows on TV, and can't we have some more good comedies instead? Not because Sadie couldn't reciprocate my feelings at the time—no one could ever hold that against her—but because she stopped being my best friend that day.

For all of those reasons, and also because I don't want to risk developing a crush on Sadie all over again, as a means of self-protection, I jump out of bed, strip the sheets, put them in the washing machine, and drive to Pinecliff Bay.

## CHAPTER 7
# *Sadie*

**J**ust like my brother on a good day, my father looks at least ten years younger than his actual age. I must take after my mother in seeing my exact age reflected in the mirror, although I will never know.

Dad's waxing a surfboard when I arrive, etching my most precious memories of him a little deeper into my brain. Every time we came home from school, or from anywhere else, we would always find him in his workshop, working on a surfboard. Or as Sam sometimes puts it, "after Mom left, he married his workshop."

"Sadie," he states matter-of-factly, when he sees me, as though I was just here yesterday.

"Dad." A smile blooms in my chest and works its way to my mouth at the sight of him.

He puts away his materials and opens his arms to me. He smells like he always has, of sweat and wax and another note of something I've never been able to define.

"Happy birthday, kiddo. It's good to have you home." His voice is low and gruff. What remains of his hair blows behind his head in the breeze.

41

"It's good to be here."

"Let's go to the deck." He winks at me, and more warmth engulfs me. I should really drive up more, no matter the shooting schedule of *King & Prince*. But time hasn't been the only reason for my prolonged absence from Clearwater Bay. I chose to go through my divorce away from my hometown, because I didn't want to associate that kind of pain with the place I grew up—or so I'd like to tell myself. As though my childhood here was pain-free. As though anyone's anywhere ever is.

For a man who loves the ocean so much—he still surfs every day—my father has always lived in this house on the edge of the forest.

"I'll have both," he's always said. "You can't ask a man to choose between the woods and the sea."

So when we sit on the deck, it's a vastly different view than from Sam's beach house. It's green and lush and noisy with bird song instead of the sound of the surf.

Dad goes inside and walks back out with a pitcher of homemade lemonade and two glasses.

"How was the party? I haven't heard from Suzy or Sam yet."

"I left earlier than they did." I pour us each a glass of lemonade and we sit side by side in two Adirondack chairs facing the forest. "But it was good."

I always wonder, when Sam and I celebrate our birthday and when Suzy celebrates hers, if it reminds him of when we were born—and the woman who gave birth to us.

"I'm making your favorite for dinner." He reaches over and gives my knee a quick squeeze.

"Meatloaf and mash potatoes it is." The carb hangover I will have when I go back to LA will be mighty, but none of that matters now. I'm here for nothing but comfort and my dad's food is a big part of that.

"And a green salad, of course," he adds. "How are you, kiddo?" He looks at me and I can see his eyes are a touch watery.

"I'm good, now that I'm here."

"When things end, it can be tough for a while, but it always gets better. That's my promise to you."

"Thanks, Dad." I smile to assure him I'm fine. "How are you?"

"I'm great, as ever. Doing what I've always done."

Our quiet moment together is interrupted by the sound of a car in the driveway.

"Sam," Dad says, recognizing the sound of his car, no doubt.

My brother looks his age today. The wrinkles in his skin seem to have deepened overnight and he has purple bags underneath his eyes.

Sam and I head inside the house together to fetch more glasses.

"Color me surprised when I saw a text from Devon on my phone this morning." He purses his lips. "If I remember correctly, the last I saw of her, she was chatting up Suzy's ex-boss."

"Yeah, well, with the number of shots you were knocking back, I thought it safer to find refuge for the night elsewhere."

Sam rubs his temples. "Damn. It was an epic night, though. Pity you left so early."

"I can't keep up with you and Suzy like that."

"What's that about Suzy?" Our sister has arrived. "You like shots just as much as Sam does."

Suzy walks straight toward me and throws her arms around me. "Are you all right? I knew you'd be in super-safe hands with Devon, but still. I feel a bit guilty for leaving you in her care in the state you were in."

"A state this one put me in." I point a finger at Sam.

"You only turn forty once."

Suzy releases me from her embrace and gives me a once-over. "You look way too good for an off-the-clock TV star the day after her birthday party."

"It's the gloss from seeing me again. It hasn't worn off yet. Give it a day or two."

"What was it like seeing Devon again after all these years? You two were pretty tight in high school, weren't you?"

Suzy was in college when Devon and I fell out—trying for one of the many degrees she never got. She doesn't know the details of what happened back then. Neither does Sam, for that matter. When I was sixteen, I hated my brother much more than I loved him.

"It was a bit of a shock to be woken by a five-year-old barging into my room. That has never happened to me before."

"Finn," Sam says. "That boy has the makings of a surfing legend. I offered my services to Devon to teach him, but she told me she had that all under control."

"She basically told you to get lost, Sam," Suzy says. "You think you're a better teacher just because you're a man."

"All right. All right." Sam holds up his hands in supplication. "You know what we should do later? Catch the sunset surf. The three of us together."

"What about Dad?" I ask.

"Dad's a morning guy," Sam says matter-of-factly.

"I haven't been on a surfboard in years," Suzy says.

"High time to get back on one, then." It's as though Sam's complexion brightens as he hatches this plan for us.

"What do you say, Sadie?" He's already holding up his hand for one of his annoying high-fives.

Devon said she'd go surfing with Finn tonight. I wouldn't mind seeing her in action.

"You're on, bro." I slap my palm against his because I know it makes him happy.

"I have no choice, then, I guess," Suzy acquiesces. "I'm not being left out of any twin activities any longer."

"We can pretend we're triplets, like we used to," Sam teases her. "Just to make Suzy feel better."

"We should at least ask Dad if he wants to join us."

"Sure," Sam says.

We all head outside again. Dad's sitting in silence gazing into the treetops.

"Dad, do you want to go surfing with us later?"

"Surfing after dinner? Have you lost your mind?"

Sam shoots me an I-told-you-so look.

"Speaking of dinner." Dad starts pushing himself out of his chair. "Let me get on with that."

"We'll take care of it, Dad," Sam says.

"Not a chance in hell. You're my kids. All three of you are here. There's no way I'm not feeding you myself."

I touch him gently on the shoulder as he walks past me. If it felt good to be with my brother and sister at the party last night, it feels a million times better still today, to have all four of us together again in our childhood home.

CHAPTER 8

## Devon

A slew of butterflies flutter in my belly as I open the door to the bakery. Zara is busy with a customer and I take the time to look around. Half the wares on sale are gluten-free; the other half sugar-free, some both. That's how things are in California now, especially in the long-reaching shadow of Silicon Valley.

"Hey." She beams me a wide smile. "Just a second." She tells the other man behind the counter she'll be taking a break, then heads toward me. "You came." She looks a touch surprised.

"I was overcome with an unquenchable need for a sugar-free cupcake."

"I have plenty of those. Let me grab some and we'll sit out front. Do you want some coffee or tea with that? Anything else?"

"Some iced tea would be lovely."

"Coming right up. Make yourself comfortable." I watch her scurry off. I didn't notice last night, but there's something homely about her. Something instantly comforting and nurturing. Or maybe it's just the simple fact that another person is fetching me a cupcake for once—and is asking me to make myself comfortable. I should probably tell her about Finn first thing, which is never a hardship, because my son is always at the forefront of my mind.

I take a seat outside and the weather's perfect. Not too cold and not too warm, with a lovely breeze coming from the Pacific. Sadie picked a good time to come home—*damn it*. I'm not meant to be thinking about Sadie. That's the whole reason I'm here in the first place.

Zara sits with me and offers me a raspberry and vanilla cupcake and a tall glass of iced tea.

"Thank you so much." I tuck right in.

"Late night? In need of some faux-sugar?"

"It wasn't that late and I'm not much of a drinker."

"So I didn't miss much? Suzy didn't dance on the tables half-naked or anything else outrageous like that?"

"If she did, it was long after I left." I find Zara's gaze. "I have a little boy who wakes up early." It's always a gamble how a woman will react. Because of my training, I'm pretty good at deciphering non-verbal clues.

"Oh. Really?" Zara's smile is genuine enough, albeit a bit shocked—again. "What's his name?"

"Finn. He's five. He would love these, by the way. And avoiding the sugar rush he usually gets from cupcakes would be great."

Zara laughs. "I bet." She sinks her teeth into her bottom lip for a moment, as though deeply contemplating something before continuing. "It was really lovely meeting you last night. On the way home, I kept wondering where Suzy had been hiding you all this time." Her smile is soft, her expression inviting. "Did Suzy tell you anything about me after I left?"

"Suzy was much too busy doing shots to tell me anything about you." Getting herself and her sister very drunk. I wonder what Suzy should have told me. For a split second, I wonder if Suzy and Zara had more than a professional relationship, but as far as I know, Suzy doesn't date women—she doesn't date anyone, really.

"Okay, well, I like to be upfront about this." Zara's dark gaze rests on me. "I'm in a long-term relationship, but we're open. As in both my partner and I believe that one monogamous relationship is not enough to fulfill all of a person's needs. We're poly. We date other people."

It couldn't be more of a West Coast moment, I think, as I try not to choke on my sugar-free cupcake, which is delicious nonetheless.

"Oh." My turn to try and hide my surprise. For the better part of my life, my best friend has been a gay man who firmly believed monogamy was a false construct no one in their right mind should ever abide by—until he became a father; and met Bobby. "Okay."

"If you're not familiar with this lifestyle, it might be a lot to process, but it wouldn't feel right continuing this conversation without telling you first."

"I appreciate you telling me." I'm no prude and I like Zara, but none of this sits quite right with me. But I know I need to check myself. Just like any other female on this planet, I've been influenced by the insidiousness of the patriarchy and its archaic institutions like marriage and monogamy. I teach classes on this very subject. Many of the people I interact with in my line of work started practicing non-monogamy once they stopped caring what other people thought about them. But none of them are semi-single mothers to a five-year-old boy—and I always put Finn first.

"I understand if it's a dealbreaker. That's why I'm telling you now. With a young son in your care, I'm sure you want to keep your energy focused." What Zara's confession tells me about her is that she's most likely not someone who gets off on judging others; that she's skilled at open communication; and probably has more experience than most in the bedroom. All of these things do appeal to me.

"It doesn't have to be." I pull my lips into an encouraging smile. Only time will tell if that is actually true.

"Great." A minivan pulls up the road and half a dozen people jump out. "Tourist season has well and truly begun," Zara says. "I'm going to have to help Ziggy out with this."

"Of course."

"Can you stick around for a bit? I'll be back as soon as I can."

"Sure." I eat the rest of the cupcake as I contemplate what Zara has just said. My train of thought is interrupted by three cars parking to my left in quick succession, swiftly followed by two cyclists, and another minivan. I don't think I'll get to see a lot more of Zara this afternoon—I did drop by unannounced.

After she has settled some people on the patio, she rushes over to me. "We're swamped this afternoon. How about dinner tonight?"

I promised Finn I'd go surfing with him and I have an early morning call tomorrow.

"I have my son tonight. Sometime this week, perhaps?"

Zara glances inside. "How about you give me a call? You have my number. We'll work it out under different circumstances."

"Deal."

Zara bends and gives me a quick kiss on the cheek. "I hope to see you very soon," she whispers in my ear.

I introduced Finn to a surfboard when he was only three years old. As a consequence, he can do what not many five-year-olds can do in the water. Most of all, he loves being in the ocean more than anything else. As do I, especially with my son next to me.

We watch a group of regulars wait for the perfect wave to roll around. For an incessant chatterbox, Finn's always serenely quiet in the water, as though a different part of him comes out when we go surfing. An added advantage of a sunset surf is that, as soon as I take him home, he'll fall asleep, without his usual whining for another story or to go over to Hunter's for one last cuddle with Spencer.

Because Finn and I have magical times like these together, it's easy enough to lure myself into believing I don't need anything or anyone else in my life. And I don't *need* anyone as such, but, on the other hand, there's nothing wrong with admitting it might make for a nice change. Truth be told, I'd settle for something easy with no strings attached to ease back into things, and maybe Zara is the perfect person for that.

"What are you looking at, Mom?" Finn asks.

"Nothing, sweetie." I catch myself peering in the direction of Sam's house, which sits right opposite Clearwater Bay's prime surfing spot—which is why he lives there, of course. All he has to do is walk outside and he's ready to catch some waves. But Sadie said the Irelands were having a family dinner tonight. "Let's have another go."

Finn and I paddle to a spot where the waves have already broken and are less forceful and imposing. I watch him as he tries to ride a few small waves to the shoreline. Every time he paddles back into the water with his bright-orange life vest strapped over his chest, I'm engulfed with a hit of warmth, because he's so utterly adorable and mine but also not mine. I see a lot of Hunter in him, but he has my freckles and my red hair, and he can most certainly surf better than Hunter, who didn't grow up on the coast, and for most, that makes all the difference.

From the corner of my eye, while keeping most of my attention on Finn, I see movement at Sam's house. Three figures in wetsuits descend the stairs to the beach. They stop at Sam's beach hut and he distributes boards. Damn it. My heart is already beating double-time.

"Come here a minute, sweetie." I beckon Finn over so I can get a closer look—so I can check whether one of those three people is Sadie.

Like in some romantic family saga, all three Irelands walk toward me, boards made by their father tucked under their arms.

"It's that the lady from this morning," Finn says.

"It sure is," I reply.

# CHAPTER 9
## Sadie

"Hey, champ!" Sam heads straight for Devon's son and gives him a high-five. Earlier, at dinner, when I talked about meeting Finn, to my utter surprise, my brother announced his new life goal, now that he's in his forties, is to become a father. All of us did a double-take, Dad included.

We exchange hellos, and Sam asks if he can take Finn to a perfect spot for awesome five-year-old surfer dudes a little farther down the cove. Of course, Devon can't say no when Sam puts it like that and Finn looks up at her with begging eyes as large as some of the massive seashells crunching under our feet. I assume that Devon knows very well she can trust my brother with her boy when it comes to the ocean.

"Sam's feeling broody," Suzy blurts out, as she is wont to do.

"Really?"

"Oh yes, as of today, he's on the lookout for a wife to impregnate." Suzy stares into the middle distance. She's not even trying to be funny. This is just how she talks—how she is. Or maybe I'm giggling because I'm seeing Devon again. On the way over, I was hoping she'd still be here, although I suppose Finn needs to be in bed by a certain time.

"He might have to cast a wide net around Clearwater Bay," Devon says, "because it kind of looks as though that's exactly what he's been trying to do since he turned eighteen."

We all laugh now and it's hard to keep my eyes off Devon in her wetsuit. Her hair is slicked back and much darker because it's wet and the setting sun illuminates her freckles. She looks like some ocean goddess that just emerged from the waves.

"I get to see your tricks already," Devon addresses me.

"Come on then," I challenge her.

She looks around for Finn.

"I'll keep an eye on him," Suzy says. "And watch you two for a bit first. I'm a bit rusty."

"Not for lack of my encouragement," Devon says.

"True, boss. True." She nods in the direction of the water. "Go."

"I'm sure Finn's safe with Sam. He's been teaching kids for two decades," I say.

"You're right. Let's do this." Devon extends her arm in front of her. "After you, Miss Hollywood."

"Gladly." As I head into the water, it's as though time recedes, and Devon and I are fifteen again—that magical year of surfing, when we still had lots to learn but were already good enough to attempt some advanced tricks. I lie down on my board—it's identical to the one I have at home, but with less wear-and-tear because it doesn't get used that often. Sam and Suzy know not to use my board, nor would I ever use theirs—and paddle to the lineup.

It's strange to feel Devon's presence behind me again. Surfing has always been there for me, because of my family, because of where I grew up, because the ocean is always honest and demands my full attention. Out of all of the mindfulness activities I've tried, nothing even comes close to surfing for clearing my head. But today, my attention on the waves is different. I'm not surfing to clear my head tonight. I'm surfing to impress Devon.

The first surfer in line jumps to his feet and rides the wave. At the crest, he attempts a 360, but is swallowed by the water midway.

"Nice try, Hank," Devon shouts, when the surfer emerges from the water.

When I surf in the bay at the back of my house in Malibu, I never feel like one of the locals, even though I've lived, and surfed, there for ten years. It's never exactly the same as where you grew up, where everybody knows your name because you live there, not because you're on TV

We watch three more surfers ride the next waves, then it's my turn. Then I have no choice but to clear my head and focus on what comes next. On getting my feet on the board. On crouching down at the right angle. On keeping the board flat while I ride it to the top. At the crest, I do what comes naturally to me. I twist my board, lean backward, and rotate my body with the wave. Pure exhilaration shoots through me as I ride it out.

"Show-off," I hear Devon shout from the line.

A big smile breaks on my face. I hurry out of the way so I can see which trick she has up her sleeve. I find myself much more enthralled by her easy grace in the water than the reverse 360 she attempts and effortlessly succeeds at.

"Not bad," I say when she has reached me. "Do you want to go again?" I say, because, already, I can't get enough of this.

"I should check on Finn." Devon says, in contrast to when we were teens, and her sole focus was always on me— until I didn't want that any longer.

"Sure. Let me try to get Suzy into the water. She has a severe case of cold surfer feet."

We head to the shore, where Suzy is watching Sam and Finn bounce up and down the waves rolling onto the shore.

"So from now on I can call your brother to babysit Finn?" Devon jokes.

"Best give it some time." It's probably not rocket science why none of us have any children. When your mother leaves you when you're ten in Sam's and my case, and thirteen in Suzy's case, and you never hear from her again, it tends to leave some emotional scars. "See how his resolution shakes out."

"I think he'd make a great dad. Finn adores him. Well, he adores any man who can hold his own in the waves. His dad will forever be jealous of that. I offered to teach Hunter, but he much prefers getting a tan on the beach than actually venturing into the water."

I really can't wait to meet this Hunter guy. As far as I can tell, Finn is all Devon, but maybe I'm suffering from a case of tunnel vision due to severe nostalgia.

"Did you see that, Mom?" Finn rushes toward Devon, his tiny life vest bopping and the strap of his helmet bouncing against his chin.

"That was amazing, sweetie." The smile she sends her son is so dazzling, so loving, it pries at an old hurt inside of me. This is how mothers love their children. Why didn't our mother love us like that? I ignore the thought and don't let it develop into something bigger. I've had years of therapy to discuss my mommy issues. Instead, I enjoy the energy between Devon and Finn, this passion they share, which I can empathize with easily, because it's the same passion Sam, Suzy, and I share with our father.

The sun is dropping lower into the ocean, painting it the

same gorgeous deep-orange of Devon's hair on a summer afternoon.

"It's going to be dark soon. I need to get this champ to bed," Devon says. "But it was great seeing all of you."

"No, Mom, one more time in the water," Finn says, but even I can tell his heart's not in it. Sam must have tired him out. Once I was in the water with Devon, I stopped paying attention to what they were doing.

"It's a school night, Finn." Devon's voice has dipped into strict mom register again. "But maybe we can meet up with Sam for some more surfing next week."

Sam drops to one knee, and says, "It would be my pleasure, little dude. Knock on my door any time. When I'm not at the house, I'm at the bar. Always easy to find and always up for a surf." He tips a finger against his forehead then offers his fist to Finn for a bump. Maybe he would make a great dad. I've never given it much thought because the notion of my brother with a family is simply too foreign to even entertain.

"Let's go, buddy." Devon takes Finn's surfboard and tucks it under her other arm. "Have fun, Irelands. See you around."

"Talk tomorrow, boss," Suzy says. Her wetsuit is still dry.

As Devon walks away, I simply can't resist the urge. "Hey, Devon," I call after her. I take a few steps away from Sam and Suzy. "Is it okay if I stop by later? Just for a, um, little talk?"

She narrows her eyes but it's still easy to see their sparkle as the setting sun reflects in them. "Sure. Give me an hour for bath-and-bed."

"Okay. See you later. Bye, Finn." I give them a quick wave before turning around.

"What was that all about?" Suzy asks.

"Nothing. We're old friends, that's all." I give her a stare

57

that can't be misinterpreted. "Come on. Time for all three Irelands to ride side by side."

"Okay." She nods, her face full of intention.

"It's the golden hour, when the ocean's at its most beautiful," Sam says. He must feel it, too. The power of the three of us being here together, for a sunset surf.

"Let's do it, suckers." We wade into the water and for the next hour, as we do what we do best, it feels like everything everywhere will be okay forever.

## CHAPTER 10

## *Devon*

Sadie's hair is still wet when she arrives. She looks very down-to-earth and human-like-the-rest-of-us, without a hint of makeup and in a simple pair of jeans and a loose-fitting sweater for the after-dark chill in the air. Yet, there's still something magical about her. Something glamorous that comes through her girl-next-door surfer vibe. I can't help but wonder if that's always been there, but I'm the wrong person to ask. Sadie was, and will probably always be, my blind spot. My eternal weakness.

"I was just making tea," I say, once I've ushered her to the back porch where we had coffee this morning. It feels like a lifetime ago. "Do you want some?"

"Yes, please."

When I come back out, Sadie has slipped off her flip-flops and is sitting with her legs drawn up and her arms curled around them.

"Good surf?"

"Oh my god." She tilts her head back. "It was like I'd died and gone to heaven. To surf with Sam and Suzy like that. It felt like going back to the best time I've ever had. Plus, we had a really good laugh at Suzy simply trying to balance on her board. My sister's a good sport, though."

I pour us some green tea and push the cup in her direction.

"Did Finn go down well?" Sadie asks.

"Always after we've been out on the water."

"It's so wonderful to see a kid enjoy it so much."

I nod. Even though surfing requires a lot of energy, it gives me back so much. I always feel supercharged after I've ridden some waves. "You haven't lost your touch."

"Neither have you, Dev. You're like a goddess in the water."

I chuckle because I don't know what else to do. "Let's not get carried away."

"Sorry. In LA everything is said in superlatives. Something can't just simply be 'good'; it always has to be 'amazing' or at the very least 'great.'"

"You may still be in California, but you're no longer in LA."

"Thank goodness for that."

"Any juicy celebrity gossip you can share with me?"

Just watching Sadie drink tea is a feast for my eyes. I much prefer her like this, barefoot, de-glammed, and relaxed.

"Well, if you can keep a secret, because I'm not supposed to share this with anyone yet..." She quirks up the side of her mouth.

"Of course."

She exhales dramatically—must be the actor in her. "Mike's leaving the show. His character's being killed off in the season finale."

"Oh gosh." I guess it figures that one of them had to leave after the divorce, although I don't know the ins and outs of

Hollywood and I don't really know how these things usually work out. "No more *King & Prince*?"

"He's being replaced with a female actor almost half his and my age."

"At least they've gone for a female character." Because Sadie's character, Leona King, is a tough police detective who is always dressed in either tight blazers or leather jackets, she has a wide and passionate lesbian following. If her future co-star is going to be female, some places on the internet—which, admittedly, I too have frequented—will go berserk with speculation and explode with erotic fan fiction. "Who will be playing her?"

"Valentina Leon. Not a big name—yet." Sadie smiles. "She's lovely, though. And she has big shoes to fill."

"What about the name of the show? How can it still be called *King & Prince* if Prince is dead?"

"Because the new character is Prince's niece, of course." Sadie sits there grinning. "The wonders of network TV never cease."

"Thank you for sharing this exclusive piece of information with me. I shall keep it in the strictest confidence." Why does it feel so right to sit here with a person I haven't seen in so many years? A person I have every right to hold a grudge against for the rest of my life, no less.

"Hey... Can I... say something?" Sadie starts.

"Of course."

Sadie gazes into her cup of tea. When she looks back up, her expression is different. "I'm sorry for what happened between us. When you, um, you know... I shouldn't have reacted that way and I most certainly shouldn't have treated you as someone with an infectious disease for the rest of our senior year. That you're so kind to me now, is beyond words.

I didn't deserve your hospitality last night, yet you gave it to me, anyway."

"Sadie..." I wasn't expecting this. "It was such a long time ago. We were kids, really."

"We were sixteen."

"And sixteen-year-old girls are the absolute worst."

"Maybe, but it's still no excuse."

"You don't need an excuse, Sadie." Without thinking, I lean over the table and put my hand over hers. "I forgave you a long time ago."

"Thank you." She doesn't remove her hand. "I'm sorry for hurting you, because it must have hurt so much."

*Fuck, yes.* "I—" I clear my throat. "I was in love with you, like you were in love with Dylan Petrowski in our sophomore year. It happens to every teenager."

"Dylan Petrowski wasn't my best friend and favorite surfer buddy, though."

She has a point. "Thank you for apologizing. I do appreciate it." I stare at our hands. I seem to be having some trouble retracting mine. "If anything, I shouldn't have kissed you."

Sadie chuckles. "If you're going to apologize for that, we'll be stuck in a merry-go-round of apologies all night." Our eyes meet and it's as though I can catch a glimpse of the girl I fell in love with—the one I never stood a chance against.

"Let's close the subject then." I do remove my hand now. It feels out of place now that the apologies have been dealt with. If I leave it, it might come to mean something else— something *I* might have to apologize for later.

"You're very gracious."

"I am now. Back then, I really hated you." *And I loved you; the worst possible combination.*

"I probably hated myself as well." She rolls her eyes.

"Compared to what you went through as a teenager, an unreciprocated crush on my best friend was really nothing."

"It wasn't nothing, Dev." She manages a smile. "It's so great to see you with Finn. There's just something so right about it. I don't know how else to put it."

That moves me much more than anything else that's been said already. "Becoming a mother is the most profound and earth-shattering thing to have ever happened to me. It changes everything, instantly. It's a constant challenge, but all the love I feel for Finn has made me a different person."

"I can tell. I mean, not that I know you. Or know the adult version of you. It just really suits you, that much I can tell."

"Thank you."

"There was no one special around, apart from your gay best friend, to have a child with? Not that you're exactly a single parent, but it can't be easy."

"Raising a child is never easy, but... yeah, the woman I was supposed to have a child with turned out not to want a child any longer when it came down to it."

"And your clock was ticking?"

"If you want to put it like that. Having a child was never going to be dependent on me being in a relationship, anyway." It no longer hurts to think of Ayesha, because I have Finn now. Not that one person you love can be replaced with another—and I loved Ayesha very much. But no matter how much it hurt to break up with her, the choice was always clear. "Then Hunter started talking about kids and we were off to the races."

"You split up with your partner because she didn't want a child?" Sadie asks.

"Yes, and I haven't regretted it for one single second."

"Are you still in touch?"

"God, no. Sometimes you just need a clean break. I loved Ayesha to bits. We were very well suited and I genuinely believed we'd grow old together, but she just didn't have that same urge to become a mother. A child is not something you can force on another person, nor is it something to deny the person who wants it. It's simple, but pretty damn cruel when faced with the choice."

"Fuck." Sadie stares into the distance. "I'm no expert on mothers, but I believe you."

"I didn't mean to bring up anything for you."

"No, no. It's fine. My mother didn't want to be a mother anymore. She gave it a good go, but it wasn't her thing, so..." Her voice is coated in sarcasm. Maybe your mother leaving you as a child is something you never fully recover from.

"You and Mike never wanted children?"

She expels some air and drinks some more tea. "We talked about it, but... if we did, we would've really had to plan it to a t. And I probably would've had to take a year off from the show. Let's just say there was always a reason not to go for it and, in hindsight, I'm glad that it never happened." She pauses. "I'm sorry. Did that sound harsh?"

I shake my head. "Everyone's circumstances are different."

Sadie emits a strange-sounding giggle. "The problem with Mike and me is that we just grew so incredibly bored with each other." She laughs as though she has just told a hilarious joke. "We were always together. At home. On set. At events and galas. On vacation. It was just too much."

"I'd feel the same if I had to spend that much time with a guy," I blurt out.

Sadie laughs again, but is quick to say, "That wasn't really the issue."

"I was just kidding."

"I know." She squints as though studying my face for an

answer to a very deep question. "Have you ever been with a man?"

"Heavens no. Why would I do that?"

Sadie erupts into laughter, then covers her mouth. "Sorry. I don't want to wake your son."

"He's out like a light. Don't worry about that."

"I'm sorry. That was a bad question, wasn't it?" Sadie says. "It's like you asking me if I've ever slept with a woman."

"Have you?" Two can play that game.

"No. Although my character has kissed a woman on the show. Ten years ago, when it was still edgy to do something like that on prime-time network TV."

I've personally contributed many views to the millions the video of that kiss has garnered on YouTube, but I'm not going to tell Sadie that.

## CHAPTER 11

# *Sadie*

I don't even know why I'm here with Devon instead of with my family. All I know is I was pulled here by the invisible threads of nostalgia. Because my bond with Devon dates back to a time before I was Sadie Ireland from TV, when my life seemed so much simpler and, despite glaring evidence to the contrary, I still believed, without a shadow of a doubt, that relationships could work out beautifully.

I certainly don't know why we're talking about me kissing another woman. I do know it was important to say I'm sorry about what happened. Because I am. Because I know very well how much I hurt Devon that day and even though it happened a very long time ago, in another lifetime, it still needed to be said out loud.

"Anyone new on the horizon?" I ask Devon. "How about that woman from the party?"

Devon nods and her face lights up a little. "Zara. Yeah. I went to see her at her bakery today."

"How did it go?"

"It wasn't the best timing. She was a bit swamped, and we

didn't really get to talk much. But a proper date is in the cards for this week."

"How exciting." I'm genuinely happy for Devon.

"We'll see." Devon looks as though she just remembered something about Zara she isn't too fond of. "I have very low expectations. As I said this morning, I haven't really dated since Finn."

"Not at all? He's five, right?"

"Hunter set me up on a blind date last year and it was atrocious. We had nothing in common, except for the fact that we were lesbians and we had children. As though that's all it takes." She runs a hand through her hair. It falls to her shoulders. My gaze is drawn to her tattooed arms again. It's hard not to look at arms like that. "As though putting two touch-starved, desperate lesbians together will just do the trick."

"Don't you all know each other as well?" Oh, god. And the award for lamest lesbian joke goes to...

"Sure." Devon doesn't even do me the courtesy of laughing. When it isn't funny, it isn't funny. "I did date someone briefly last year. Long enough to, you know..."

"End up between the sheets?" I'd do anything to make Devon blush again like she did this morning, although it's dark outside and the backyard lamps don't shed enough light on her face for my liking.

"Yes. I don't know why I have so much trouble saying that out loud."

"We're not exactly friends." Yet, I think. "More like old acquaintances."

"It's so strange with you, Sadie. You're so easy to talk to. Why is that?" She runs her fingers through her hair again, but not all the way, and rests her head against her palm, looking at me.

"Because we have history and some things just never fade."

She quirks up her eyebrows. "Maybe."

A silence falls. Perhaps we're both contemplating why it's so easy to pick up a friendship that was so rudely interrupted all those years ago. Perhaps an explanation is not required. It can just be what it is, which is also how it is when you're a child and you don't have an agenda apart from having the most fun possible. And Devon and I, especially on our surfboards, had a world of fun.

"Do you want to come to dinner sometime this week? Hunter and Bobby would be ecstatic." Devon asks.

"I would like that very much."

"Maybe bring Sam? He can babysit Finn."

"I'll ask him. Let me know when. I'm pretty free." The prospect of having an empty calendar is so relaxing, I sink into my chair a little deeper. I could sit here with Devon all night long, catching up, reminiscing, getting to know her all over again. But she's not on vacation like me. "I should probably get going. Do you have an early start tomorrow?"

"Fairly. I have clients in all time zones, and I do have an early appointment every Monday."

"Maybe next time you can tell me all about your business. I've heard good things from Suzy."

"Suzy's a real gem. I can only hope she sticks around."

"Me too, but my sister is a restless soul. She needs constant change. She's addicted to it."

"Yet, she has always stuck around in Clearwater Bay."

"Yeah. It seems like a hard place to tear yourself away from." I hold out my palm to Devon. "Case in point." I smile and she returns it. Devon's not a wide smiler, yet there's something so genuine about her face when she does. "Suzy and Dad are very close, and I honestly don't think she ever wanted to leave him behind. Not without a very compelling reason, anyway."

"Like landing one of the leads in a massive TV production, you mean?"

"Something like that." I nod. "Suzy's very independent, though. She has never accepted any money from me. She doesn't want it. It doesn't interest her. Whereas Sam..."

"Sam likes living in a swanky beach house."

"It impresses the ladies no end. His words, not mine."

"So you bought him the perfect bachelor pad."

"It's not going to be a bachelor pad for the next two months, I'll tell you that. Although I, too, am single now, of course."

"You won't be starved of male attention while you're in Clearwater Bay, that's a given. I bet some of the men are even willing to leave their wives for a night with Sadie Ireland."

I can only groan. "Even the notion. A man is the last thing I want right now, least of all a married one. I just want to be like my sister. And like my dad. He's been single for thirty years. Of course, I don't know everything, but the man has never as much as looked at another woman since Mom left—not as far as I know, anyway." I study Devon's face. Maybe she knows more about my father on that front than I or any of my siblings do. "Have you ever seen him with someone?"

"Never," Devon confirms. "Even though, according to my mom, it doesn't have to be that way for a man like him."

"How's Brenda? And Clint?"

"They're fine. Delighted to be grandparents. They spoil Finn rotten, especially my dad. His biggest regret is that he can't take Finn surfing. He's not like Jack—up at the crack of dawn and into the ocean at first light. He doesn't have the physical ability any longer. Mom comes with us once in a while, but my family was never as surf-mad as yours."

"Apart from you."

"Apart from me."

"Give my best to your parents, if that's appropriate." I don't really know if it is. I broke their daughter's fragile teenage heart, after all. I make to get up.

"Will do."

"Thank you so much for letting me invite myself over."

"You're welcome any time, Sadie."

While Devon walks me to the door, it hits me that I've seen more of her than of anyone in my family since I've arrived. Today alone, I've spent time with her on three different occasions.

"Sweet dreams." I open my arms to her because it feels like this evening—and this day—can only properly end with a hug. She walks into my embrace, and we hold each other tight. I inhale the scent of her hair and it's impossible to remember whether it still smells the same as when we were girls, but details like that are of no importance, because she still very much smells like home.

---

I find Sam in his reading chair, an open book on his chest, but his eyes firmly shut. I try to be quiet and tiptoe around the house, but my presence soon wakes him up.

"Hey, sis." He blinks a few times.

"The party finally caught up with you, huh?"

"I'm not thirty-nine anymore, am I?" He sits up and rubs his eyes. "No sunrise surf for me in the morning."

"I'll be quiet as a mouse if I venture out."

"Thanks. Did you have fun at Devon's?"

"Yeah. She's inviting us to dinner this week, by the way. Let me know when you're free."

"Okay. Sure." He scratches his full head of hair—the kind my ex-husband would sell a kidney for. "Suzy and I were asking ourselves when you and Devon got so tight again? If I remember correctly, you and she weren't friends any longer when you left for college. Have you been in touch with her all this time?"

I jut out my lip and shake my head. "No. Not at all. It's just good to see her again. It's like...we've clicked all over again, the way we did when we were in school."

"Okay. Just checking whether you've switched teams. Not that that would be an issue, of course. The Irelands are *hella woke* like that."

I roll my eyes at him. "Oh, please." I pretend-smack him around the head. Sam pretends it's very painful. "You know we were best friends in high school."

"That I do. What I've never known is why Devon all of a sudden stopped being your best friend."

"Because you were way too busy chasing girls to notice."

"That's hardly fair. I asked you like a million times and you never said."

"It's no longer important. It was a silly teenage thing that could have been avoided, but it wasn't. It was my fault. I was being stupid."

"No news there, then." He nudges me in the ankle with his toe. "Devon's kid's got the makings of a pro surfer. I can tell. He's got his mother's genes when it comes to that. Devon can rip with the best of them."

"She sure can." The memory of Devon in her wetsuit, hair slicked back, face so satisfied after a successful trick, comes back to me. That Zara she mentioned is one lucky woman. I wonder if she surfs. Not being any good at it doesn't have to be a dealbreaker, of course, especially at our age. Mike spent more time next to his board than on it when we took to the ocean together, and it never bothered me, but someone who can hold their own on the water does hold a certain appeal.

"I'm going to hit the hay. I'm absolutely knackered." Sam gets up.

"A million shots will do that to you, bro."

"Jibe accepted." He gives me a quick pat on the back and heads upstairs.

I'm pretty exhausted myself, but I need some time to unwind after my visit to Devon. I go out onto the deck and stare at the black mass of ocean in front of me. I take a few deep breaths. For a brief moment, I wonder what Mike is doing now. He's contracted to shoot a movie in New York and he mentioned something about going to Europe with his brother and nieces. Then I push the thought of him from my brain, which seems to become easier as the days pass. Being home, I'm sure, will make it easier still.

Besides, it's not missing my ex-husband that hurts. It's the fact that I had to walk away from my marriage—that I had to turn into my mother and leave someone I was supposed to love forever.

CHAPTER 12

## *Devon*

Every Monday after school, Finn goes to his grandparents, and I pick him up there. Dad and Finn are making meatballs when I arrive. As usual, his opening line is to tell me where my mother is.

"She's celebrating wine o'clock in the backyard," Dad says.

After I've kissed my son and my father hello, I go to find my mother whom I consider to be one of my best friends. Ever since I came out of the closet at the tender age of sixteen, there isn't a thing I haven't confided in her.

"Mrs. Douglas," I greet her.

"Ms. Douglas. Do sit." She beams me a wide smile. "It's lovely to see you, sweetie."

An empty glass waits for me. Because she knows I'm not nearly as fond of pre-dinner wine as she is, my mother pours in only a finger.

"Has Finn been good?"

"Manageable. He left his jacket at school again, but your dad went back to pick it up. He's been exemplary since they started cooking." She holds up her glass of wine. "And you can't teach them to cook young enough."

If it were up to my mother, Finn would already be vacuuming the house with her. I guess my dad's too old to be taught that particular skill. He does do all the grocery shopping and cooking, though, and has done so for as long as I can remember. For the sanity of everyone in my family, I stopped giving lectures on the furtive effects of the patriarchy to my parents a while ago.

"How was your weekend?" Mom asks.

I don't even know where to begin. "Guess who's back in town?"

"Sadie Ireland. That's all over the grapevine."

I nod and take a tiny sip of wine. Maybe I'll drink more than I'm used to tonight—and the reasons why are obvious. I'd only be doing it not to feel a certain feeling. But I don't care. Seeing Sadie again has been too much of an emotional avalanche, especially seeing so much of her.

"How do you feel about that?" My mother paints a quizzical expression on her face.

"Pretty good. We spent a lot of time together the last couple of days. We even surfed together last night." The memory is coated in the warm orange glow of the sunset we surfed in.

"Finn did say something about surfing with Sam," my mother says matter-of-factly.

I tell her about the party and how I ended up taking Sadie home because she didn't want to go back to Sam's and how she came over to my house again last night.

"What's that all about then?" She peers at me over the rim of her glass.

"I don't really know. It's just so... easy with her." On the way over, I was thinking about this, and the best I could come up with is that Sadie and I were always meant to be friends, but certain things that happened got in the way of us continuing our friendship in our teens. Now time has passed and, because we've always seen something very specific in each other, we can tap right back into that. Although it's different now, of course, because we're not teenagers anymore. "Anyway." Maybe I should've led with this. "At the party on Saturday, I met someone..."

My mother's face lights up as it always does at even a hint of possible romance. Even though we've talked about this extensively and I've explained all the reasons why I don't need to be in a relationship to be happy, my mother's default stance stubbornly remains the same. I can theorize about it all I want, and show up single and happy as a clam on her doorstep every day, but her subconscious programming won't allow her to accept that my life is complete without the addition of a partner. I've given up on that particular discussion with my parents as well, because some generational disagreements are too futile to fight. Having been single for six years, I'm hoping I'm getting my point across just by living my life and showing them—especially my mother.

I tell her about Zara, leaving out her poly lifestyle, because that's none of my mother's business.

"Have you called her yet?" Mom asks.

"Hm. No."

"What's stopping you?" She uses the tone of voice I sometimes use with Finn when he's not listening and I really need him to.

"Sleep. Work. Being here with my family."

"As long as it's not because of Sadie Ireland," she says, baffling me.

"What does Sadie have to do with anything?"

"Beats me." She holds up her hands trying to look all innocent as though she didn't just imply what she did.

"I got over Sadie a long time ago. You know that."

"Sure, but Sadie wasn't in town, then. You didn't surf into the sunset with her, then."

"Sadie's straight, Mom. We're just friends."

"Okay, well, it'll be ages before those two"—She nods her head at the kitchen door—"are done fixing dinner. Why don't you give Zara a call now? Set up that date? Why wait?"

"Jesus, Mom. She's not going anywhere. I'll call her later, after I've put Finn to bed."

Mom chuckles. "I'm sorry, darling. When you're a mother, you never stop worrying, even if your child is in her forties. It never goes away."

"There's nothing to worry about."

"You let me be the judge of that," my mother says, and purses her lips to take another sip of wine.

---

Two days later, all my mother's wishes have come true, because I'm sitting across from Zara in a candlelit restaurant in Pinecliff Bay.

"I was so glad you actually called," Zara says. "It can really put people off when you tell them about being poly."

I don't really know what to say to that. "I appreciate your honesty."

"I suppose you have a ton of questions." Zara has a very disarming way about her. It's also difficult to keep from staring at the gorgeous tattoos on her arms. They make me want to go through the long, painful ordeal of getting another really big one, maybe on my back.

"Maybe a few."

"Okay. Ask me anything. Really. I'm an open book."

"I figured I would learn as we go along..."

"But?" Zara's eyes sparkle. Is she getting off on this? Every first date is full of unknowns, but this one is filled to the brim with them.

"So, you have your primary relationship." I did a bit of Google research before coming here tonight.

Zara nods.

"And then you have a bunch of other, um, lovers?"

"Some are just lovers; a select few are much more than that."

My main goal for this evening is to figure out whether my initial attraction to Zara is still there, but also, as always, I'm thinking about Finn's best interests. Can I bring him into a world—a lifestyle, if you will—like that? My first instinct is to say no, but then again, I don't have to bring him into anything. Perhaps I can just be Zara's secondary lover for one night.

"Do you fall in love with other women?" I ask.

"Of course, I do. All the time. That's the beauty of it. Who doesn't adore that heady sensation of falling in love? And why do so many people in monogamous long-term relationships deprive themselves of that deliciousness?"

"I don't fall in love that easily. That's probably my issue."

"Maybe you're afraid to." Her thick eyebrows are arched all the way up. "Did someone hurt you?"

I huff out some air. "Sure, but not a disproportionate amount. My ex and I split because I wanted a child and she didn't."

"Ah. That must have been pretty damn painful."

"It was, especially because she'd given me the impression, for years, that we were on the same page about having children."

79

"Did she think that you would change your mind for her?"

I nod. "I think so. Yes." The other night, when I was talking about this with Sadie, I probably made it sound easier than it has been. Maybe I wanted to paint a prettier picture for Sadie because of who she is—or because of who we used to be to each other. "I like to tell myself that we had a clean, easy enough break-up, but I also know those don't really exist. When profound feelings are involved, it's always messy, and it always hurts so much. When it comes down to it, Ayesha hadn't been completely honest with me for a long time."

"That's tough. It must have been hard for her as well."

"Yes, it must have." Most of all, it was complicated and dreadful to walk away from someone I loved so much and had so many amazing adventures with.

"How did we get to exes so quickly?" Zara's eyes are soft as she smiles at me. "I was only hoping for some mild flirting, really."

"Me too, actually."

"Some mild flirting coming right up." Zara cocks her head. "I'm sorry, but I can't help myself. Do you know Sadie Ireland well? Dani and I have had a TV crush on her for the entire time she's been on *King & Prince*." That'll be fifteen years, then. "Even though Suzy used to work for me, Dani could not believe I was actually at a party with her sister—and that I left without talking to her! All I managed was a rather awkward goodbye as I left."

Oh, great. A Sadie fangirl. It's not that I can't relate, although I do have different reasons to adore Sadie. And did Zara just mention the name of her partner, Dani? Twice?

"Sadie and I were in school together and I guess, for some people, that can create a lifelong bond." What am I even talking about?

"Sure." Zara nods excitedly. "I still have friends I was in high school with." She narrows her eyes. "Were you close?"

I nod, because it's true. "Pretty much inseparable from when we were twelve to when we were sixteen. Apart from being in school together, we surfed together almost every day."

"Wow." She scrunches up her lips. "What happened when you turned sixteen?"

I scoff. In the past years, I've barely given a thought to me recklessly trying to kiss Sadie when we were sixteen, but this weekend, that event is catching up with me double-time.

"I was deeply, madly in love with her. It wasn't mutual."

"Oh, damn. Your first girl crush was on Sadie Ireland?"

I nod slowly. Back then, Sadie was just Sadie, not Sadie Ireland from the TV,

"Was she nasty to you?"

"Let's not go there." I shouldn't be talking about this with someone who is still mostly a stranger to me. "It happened a long time ago and I think Sadie and I are well on the way to becoming friends again." Are we? *Yes.* That much I know. That much I feel in every cell of my body.

"That's wonderful." There's something a little fake in the smile Zara sends me next—something I'm not too fond of. "Maybe we can all have dinner together some time?"

"Do you mean, um, *Dani* included?"

Zara shrugs. "Why not?"

In that moment, when panic shivers through me at the prospect of having to deal with my date's partner, of having to take someone else into account from the very beginning, I know this is not going to work out for me. Instead of sitting with my discomfort about this and just letting it be what it is, I'm judging. I know I shouldn't, because nothing good ever came from judging—that much I do know—but I can't help myself. Or maybe it's the image of 'all of us' that is projected into my brain. Some kind of bizarre double date situation where Sadie is the only single person at the table. My brain can't really compute.

I navigate my way through the rest of the date politely, but end it as soon as I can. On the way home, I realize that my most prevalent thought is not concern for my own emotional well-being or even Finn's, but that I could never put Sadie in a situation like that.

## CHAPTER 13

# Sadie

"You didn't know Devon Douglas in her party days," Hunter says. "She wasn't always this shining example of a mother with the glow of an angel about her, you know."

I like Hunter. A lot.

"Will you please shut up." Devon's cheeks are so deliciously pink, I feel like pinching them. "Finn's just over there."

Devon wasn't kidding about Sam babysitting Finn. They're building an elaborate fort out of couch cushions in the living room.

Hunter waves her off. "Finn's way too busy to listen to any of this." He does lower his voice a fraction.

"Tell me more, please," I insist.

"We met on a dance floor in San Francisco. You have to picture the scene. Y Bar was still pretty much exclusively gay back then, but Devon didn't care one bit about that. She didn't have as many tattoos yet, but enough to draw the eye, especially when barely dressed." He fixes Devon with a stare.

"I expect this level of exaggeration from your better half,"

Devon says. "But not from you, Hunter. Besides, you may act the part of the buttoned-up, wholesome daddy all you want, you were no stranger to those clubs yourself back in the day."

"What are you insinuating?" Bobby brings a hand to his chest, his voice all drama. "That I have a tendency to overstate the facts?"

Devon just rolls her eyes at him.

"I don't know why they're being like this." Devon rests her gaze on me. "It must be some sort of ploy to impress you, Sadie, but I personally don't really get it."

"Oh, I am very impressed." I missed all the juicy bits of Devon's life. I could have been there with her when she painted the town red in San Francisco. I could have been her friend through all of this if I hadn't been a typical, selfish, torn up sixteen-year-old girl. Maybe if I'd had a mother like Devon's to run to at the time. Someone to confide in who could tell me, in no uncertain terms, that you don't blow a friendship like ours over something as silly as an attempted kiss. "Your ploy is working, boys. Give me more."

Sam's head sticks out of the fort he's been building with Finn. "Someone just fell asleep much against his will."

"I'll put him to bed." Hunter gets up. "Give Dev a little breather."

Devon gives him an almost imperceptible nod—of appreciation, I assume. It's revealing to see them together. The silent understanding between them and the obvious warmth of their friendship, and being Finn's parents, is like a soothing balm to the soul.

Sam joins us, and I see how Bobby's gaze lingers on my brother's chest.

"I'm going to need to know much more about those party days of yours," I say to Devon.

"Hunter has loads of photographic evidence," Bobby says, then rakes his gaze over my brother again.

"All in good time," Devon says.

As though he needs to actively engage his brain with something else, Bobby turns away from Sam, and looks straight at Devon. "Now that the little man's off to bed, give us the nitty-gritty on your date."

Poor Devon. She's really not getting a break tonight. These gays are relentless. Or maybe they are, somehow, trying to impress me, although I don't see how they can achieve that by grilling Devon.

Devon groans in response. "I need to check on dinner."

"I'll give you a hand." I follow her into the kitchen.

"Are you okay?" I watch Devon as she peers through the oven window. She's dressed in a denim shirt with the sleeves rolled up all the way to her biceps and it makes her look so damn cool, I don't know how she does it. "Bad date?"

"It just..." She turns away from the oven, toward me. "It wasn't bad per se, but I stumbled on a few dealbreakers very early into the evening and then I couldn't get back into it anymore. The spell had been broken."

"I take it you don't want to talk about it."

"I don't need to talk about it." Her smile is as confident as ever. "But Hunter and Bobby are so hyper tonight." She blows some air through gritted teeth.

"That must be down to me. I have that effect on people sometimes. If you want, I can easily freeze them out." But then I wouldn't be finding out about those two decades and a half without you, I think.

"It's okay. They're just beside themselves at meeting you. I can't hold that against them." The smile Devon shoots me is close-lipped, again, but also full of warmth, her eyes perhaps conveying what her lips are reluctant to do.

"I suppose I'd best prepare for some questions about Mike sooner rather than later."

Devon nods. "Once they start feeling comfortable around you, you won't be spared from their inquisitive ways."

"The season finale of the show is airing next week. Even though I'll be here, I suspect I still might have to go into hiding."

"You can stay with me. I'll stow you away." Devon's gaze lingers on me. I don't mind because her eyes are so kind and warm.

"I wouldn't want you to have to sleep in your son's bed again."

"I'll make sure the guest room is useable. Next week, you said? I can make that work."

"Thanks, Dev." Without thinking, I reach out my hand and touch her forearm.

Raucous laughter from the dining room spills over into the kitchen. I retract my hand while thinking that, just maybe, Devon and I can become the best of friends again.

"This should be ready. I'll be right out." Is it the heat from the oven making Devon's cheeks flush, or something else?

I head back to the dining room, Devon right behind me. I watch Devon as she dishes out dinner, a pasta bake that looks delicious.

"Do you have a chef?" Bobby asks. Clearly, he's reached the stage of feeling comfortable around me already.

"Most of the time, I do. When we're shooting the show, I don't have time to cook." I know how this sounds, especially to parents of young children with full-time jobs, but that's how it is. I'm aware of my immense privilege, but I can't change it, nor should I have to.

"Mike didn't cook either?" Bobby continues.

"What's with the twenty questions?" Devon shoots him a rather menacing look. It warms my heart that she's so protective of me.

"Twenty? Who's exaggerating now? I've only asked two."

"I'd rather not talk about my ex-husband tonight, if that's okay with you." I flash Bobby my TV smile.

"Of course. I get it. Apologies." He elbows Hunter in the arm. "It just dawned on me that Hunter and I are the only ones at this table in a long-term, monogamous relationship, defying all gay stereotypes."

"How long have you been together?" I ask.

"Almost thirteen months." Bobby sits there beaming as though he just climbed Mount Everest in record time.

"Congrats, man," Sam says. To him, it's probably a lifetime.

"That's the equivalent of about thirteen years in hetero time." Hunter chuckles and puts an arm around Bobby's shoulder. "But trust me, once I became a dad, it was suddenly so much harder to get a second date with a guy, let alone a third."

"I think what you've done is awesome," Sam says. "This whole arrangement raising Finn. Hats off."

"Don't go getting any ideas in your head," I say to my brother.

"I have so many ideas in my head." Sam sounds a little wistful. Maybe he is really serious about becoming a parent. Turning forty can do that you—although it hasn't had the same effect on me. But I'm still licking the wounds of my divorce. "Adoption is out of the question for a single parent, especially a man," he says, as though he has already done his research. "Maybe surrogacy is an option."

"Or marriage?" I offer, more teasing than anything else.

"Or marriage. Yeah." He grimaces as though that would be the greatest sacrifice of all time. "I don't know."

"Or how we did it," Hunter says. "This arrangement can work for straight people as well."

"I've considered that, but I can't think of a female friend I would be able to do that with." Sam scratches his five o'clock shadow.

"Because you've slept with all of them already," I tease.

Sam's gaze on me is a touch thunderous. "I don't sleep with every woman I meet."

"Could have fooled me."

He shakes his head. Maybe I'm not being entirely fair on my brother.

"You haven't exactly been around that much, Sadie." His voice has a slight tremor to it. Did I just hit a nerve I didn't know my Casanova brother had? Maybe he is ready for a change in his life.

"But, Sam," Devon interjects, "you have to admit that you do have a certain reputation. I know that much and I have been around."

"Sure." Non-siblings can get away with saying so much more. "But I want more now." He turns to me again. "And I would very much like for my twin sister to take that seriously."

"Fine, bro. I get it. You're finally ready to grow up."

"Thank you." He blows me a kiss. "I knew you would understand."

"That's what you get for spending all those months in the womb together. Infinite understanding of each other."

"What's it like being Sadie Ireland's twin brother?" Bobby has scraped his courage together again after Devon's shut-down earlier. Come to think of it, Devon's stood up for me twice now in the span of about fifteen minutes. Clearly she's feeling more protective of me than my own twin brother is.

"Let's just say it has its advantages." Sam paints on a disgusting smirk.

"Oh, Christ," I groan and hold up my hand. "I don't want to hear it. Okay?"

Bobby nods as though he understands exactly what Sam means by that.

Sam's phone beeps in his back pocket.

"I bet that's a booty call." I make sure the sarcasm in my voice can't be ignored.

"You don't know that. It might be something at the bar. Cassidy's alone tonight."

Sam reads the message. "Turns out you were right, sis. It is very much a booty call."

"It's like we've all jumped into a time machine and are back in high school," Devon says. "Sam's captain of the football team again and, for some reason I will forever fail to understand, girls keep throwing themselves at him."

"If only I'd known when I tried to kiss you that time," Sam says. "That my efforts were futile and it wasn't me; it was you."

"Don't be such a dick." I might be overreacting, but what my brother just said got all the way under my skin.

"What?" He sits there smiling his stupid boyish smile. "It's true, isn't it?"

"You tried to kiss Devon but you didn't know she was into girls?" Hunter asks.

"This was in the late nineties," I say, even though it's really not my place to explain. I might be suffering from some residual guilt and using my brother to assuage it. "Kids weren't coming out in droves while they were in high school yet."

89

"You're telling me, girl?" Hunter lifts his eyebrows.

"I'm sorry. You're right."

Hunter waves off my apology. "Did you give him a good slap across the face, Dev?"

"If memory serves, I didn't have to." Suddenly, all signs of joy leave Devon's face. Oh, fuck. I remember now—and maybe so does she.

She might not have had to slap my brother away, but I slapped her on the cheek when she tried to kiss me.

I wish I could crawl under the table and hide until this feeling of utter embarrassment passes. I must have pushed all memories of that shameful slap into the deepest recesses of my mind, hoping to never be reminded of it again. I can't hide, so I try to find Devon's gaze instead, but she has turned away and is looking at everything and anything but me.

"Excuse me," Sam says. "I just have to make a quick call."

"What? The eggplant emoji doesn't work anymore?" Bobby asks, completely oblivious to the shift in temperature at the table.

"I need to check on dessert." Devon gets up as well and hurries into the kitchen.

I want to follow her, but I'm not sure it's a good idea. I decide to give her some time.

"I'm just going to check on Finn." Bobby leaves the table as well.

Hunter and I are the only two people left. "Do you think Devon's okay?"

"Why wouldn't she be?"

He's oblivious as well. Maybe I'm the only one who notices. Maybe I'm the only one who knows.

## CHAPTER 14

# Devon

Sam's left Sadie behind to attend to his booty call and we've said goodbye to Hunter and Bobby. It's just Sadie and me in the kitchen. She's handing me dirty plates and I'm stacking the dishwasher. For some reason, we're not chitchatting. The only sound is the thud of crockery meeting the inside of the dishwasher.

"All done." I switch it on and glance at Sadie. "What do you think of Hunter and Bobby?"

"They have a lot of interesting information about you." Sadie grins at me. "So I like them." Her face straightens. "On a more serious note, they seem like really great guys."

"They are." I rinse my hands and dry them on a dish towel. "Do you want a cup of tea for the road?"

"Sure or... I could use something stronger if you have it."

"I happen to have a very exclusive bottle of Japanese whisky. A gift from a client."

"Sounds absolutely wonderful."

I get two glasses out of the cupboard and hand the bottle to Sadie to carry outside. Instead of sitting at the patio table, I sink onto the step of the back door. I pat the spot next to me.

"I like to sit here for a bit before I go to bed. Take stock of the day." I hold up the empty glasses. Sadie takes my cue and pours us each a generous measure of whisky.

"Was today a good day?" Sadie lightly tilts her glass toward me.

"I've had far, far worse." We gently clink rims "Thank you for making my baby-daddy and his boyfriend's day." I tilt my head. "Finn's completely smitten with Sam, so there's that, too."

Sadie takes a sip from her drink. Her face softens—this is some damn good whisky, very mellow with a hint of chocolate underneath the honey and floral notes.

"Yum," she says. "That client must have been very grateful."

"Most are when I do my job right."

"Look, um, Dev," Sadie starts. Sitting on my back porch seems to have a contemplative effect on her. "About earlier and what Sam said about trying to kiss you. It reminded me of, um, something I did. I don't know if you remember?"

"I remember." I peer into my glass. It was a shock to be reminded of Sadie striking me like that—as though I could feel it all over again. Her cold, hard fingers against my cheek, leaving a red mark. The blemish on my cheek disappeared within minutes, but the scar on my heart remained for years. It might still be there.

"I'm so sorry," Sadie says.

I smile but don't look at her. It somehow feels too hard to look at her right now. "It's okay. I told you. You're forgiven."

"I forgot I did that. How awful is that? I completely forgot about it, probably because it made things a lot easier for me not to remember."

"It might not have been your finest moment, but you're

not an awful person, Sadie. I know that much. You wouldn't be sitting here with me now if you were."

"I'm just..." From the corner of my eye, I see her raise her hand, and then hesitate. "I just want you to know that I'm sorry and that I should never have done that." I can't help but look at her now, my eyes drawn to the movement of her hand. Ever so gently, she brings it to my cheek. "I feel like I need to apologize to your cheek as well." She caresses me below the cheekbone with the back of her fingers.

"Don't be silly," I whisper. I look into her eyes. Are they a bit watery? She's only had one sip of whisky so it can't be that.

"Dev, I... I'm so drawn to you," she whispers back. "It's like, since I've come back, I can't stay away from you."

I indulge myself and lean into the soft, delightful caress of her fingers a little. "Maybe what we promised each other all those years ago, before we fell out, is true. Maybe we will find a way to be friends forever."

Sadie nods slowly, then fixes her gaze on me again. Her fingers slide down my cheek until her thumb rests under my chin. She tilts my head toward hers.

What is she doing? This can't be happening.

Next thing I know, my face is so close to Sadie's I can't even see her eyes any longer. I can only feel her breath on me. And then, her lips on mine. The kiss only lasts a fraction of a second. It's flimsy and furtive, yet I feel it everywhere—I feel it as though it's all I've ever wanted in my life.

"What are you doing?" I pull back so I can look her in the eye again.

"I have no idea." She briefly sucks her lips into her mouth, as though wanting to savor the taste of what might linger there. "Going with my gut, because..." Her fingers are still on my chin. "You are so incredibly beautiful. It's like I can't resist you." With a subtle flick of her wrist, she tilts me toward her. She leans in again, but I'm not sure I can do this. Yet, I do. Because this is Sadie. My Sadie. I've only dreamed of a moment like this a billion times. I close my eyes and I let her kiss me. I open my lips to her and let her tongue inside. I give myself the gift of this impossible moment, even though it's really, actually happening. Sadie's hand slips down my neck, her fingers resting on my throat.

When we break from the kiss, its intensity—its effect on me—has left me slightly breathless.

"What is this?" I ask.

"Two people kissing on the doorstep." Sadie's grin is so seductive, so everything I want.

But I shake my head, because like all those times when we were teenagers, this means something entirely different to me than it does to her and I'm not doing that again. I'm forty and I have enough self-respect to not let Sadie happen to me all over again.

"Two *women* kissing on the doorstep."

"Two old friends kissing on the doorstep," Sadie counters.

"Sadie." I pull farther back. Her hand slides off my neck. "I feel things too, but I'm not doing this. I'm not going to be the absolution you seek for something that happened light-years ago. Nor am I going to be some rebound experiment for you after your divorce. Believe me, part of me very much wishes I could be that for you, but I really can't."

"Dev, you're none of those things to me."

"Then what am I?"

"I don't know." There's a hint of desperation in her voice. She probably has no clue. "You feel like... home. Like..." She must be lost for words because none follow for a few moments. "When you just said you feel things too, what did you mean by that?"

I scoff. "Come on, Sadie. We have history. You were the first girl I loved. You were the first girl that hurt me. I came out to my mother because of that kiss. You will always mean a lot to me. But as I just said, that's in the past. You can't just turn up again, after all those years, and start kissing me. That's hardly fair. How is it supposed to make me feel?"

"I didn't come here to kiss you. That was never my intention."

I'm aware of the outside of our thighs touching.

"It was a spur of the moment thing, although, somehow, it doesn't really surprise me that I did it."

She's so fucking beautiful and she's saying things that might not make full sense to me but still sound like the most harmonious symphony to my ears. But I have to protect myself. She's been back in town for less than a week and I already know I'd fall back in love with her in one wretched heartbeat, for all the wrong reasons—and I'm not having my heart broken by Sadie Ireland again. It takes too long to mend. The price is too high.

I don't know where exactly I find the strength to speak the words, yet I do, "I think that maybe you should leave now."

"Oh, yes. Okay." Sadie's demeanor changes instantly. "God, something more to apologize for. I didn't mean to—" Again, no more words follow. She's probably even more confused than I am. She pushes herself up. She's still holding the whisky glass. We barely drank. She puts it on the nearby table.

I rise but hold on to my glass. I may need its contents soon. "Maybe we should just forget this ever happened."

"If that's what you want." She looks around frantically, as though suddenly realizing she forgot something. "I'll just leave through there." She's been here a few times and knows where the door in the backyard fence is. "Um, thank you for dinner." She gives a tight nod and rushes to the door. It falls shut behind her with a soft thud that reverberates inside me like the loudest bang.

What just happened? Was this even real? But the glass in my hands is real; the amber liquid inside smells real. I can still smell Sadie. I can still taste her on my lips. Why, oh why did I not just let her kiss me until she got tired of doing so? Asking the question is answering it, of course. Because Sadie would have grown tired of it long before I ever would.

How long did she say she would be in town for? Two months? I sink back onto the doorstep and finish my drink, after which I finish Sadie's.

I want her and I don't want her. It takes me right back to that grueling senior year when I both loved and hated her with a vengeance. And I know very well that neither one of us is still the same person we were then, but I'm still gay and she's still straight. That much I do know.

I pour myself more whisky because I need something to calm myself down. All the processes I taught myself over the years, all the thought work, all the models, all the inner strength and resilience I've gathered, it's all out of the window in the face of this. I need another drink because I need to ask myself a very serious question: would I say yes to a one-night stand with Sadie? To get her out of my system once and for all. Even just so she could find out that it's not her thing. That what she believed was attraction to me was just nostalgia mixed with a friendship blossoming again. None of those reasons are valid nor strong enough.

It's not my responsibility to remind Sadie that she's straight. It is very much my responsibility to not let any out-of-control lust for her cloud my judgment about that. I asked her point-blank the other night and her answer was loud and clear—and I was glad of it.

I'm happy. My life's going well. I have a lovely son. Business is great. I don't need a complication like Sadie turning everything upside down. Sure, I'd like to date. I'd like to find someone—someone to have a serious, long-term, monogamous relationship with. Sadie's not going to be that person. She can't be. It's simply not an option.

As I drain the last of my glass, I erase the possibility of a one-night stand with Sadie from my mind and I pretend the idea was never there in the first place. I try to erase the memory of that kiss from my mind as well, of her soft lips against mine making a lot of my dreams come true, but that's going to take a bit more effort and time—I can only hope less than the last time we kissed.

## CHAPTER 15
## *Sadie*

I know I shouldn't have done it. I shouldn't have kissed Devon, yet I don't regret it. Because, in the moment, I really wanted to kiss her. I may not know exactly why, but sometimes, the why comes after. The reason is still buried beneath the instinct to just do it. And I wanted to do it. The moment was right. The vibe was a touch sultry. The air was full of possibility. Or maybe I just read it wrong. It sure seemed to surprise Devon when I touched my lips to hers. And yes, she's a woman, but she's also Devon.

Instead of walking home to Sam's house I make a detour via his bar. God knows what he's doing at the house with the woman who texted him, anyway.

"Hi, Sadie." Cassidy is all alone in the bar. "I just kicked everyone out. I'm about to close, but I'm sure the boss won't mind me making an exception for you."

"Never mind Sam. As long as you don't mind."

"It would be my pleasure to have a drink with you." Cassidy is all wholesome California vibes with her tan skin and blonde hair. "What will it be?"

"Do you have any Japanese whisky?" I never got to finish the drink Devon poured me.

"Japanese whisky? I have no idea. No one's ever asked for that, to be honest."

"Any whisky's fine. And a very expensive drink for yourself, of course."

"Why, thank you." She narrows her eyes. "Any reason you're out after closing time? Did Sam kick you out of the house you so generously bought for him?" She doesn't look as though she's actually expecting a reply and promptly turns around.

I gather my thoughts as Cassidy finds a suitable bottle of whisky. "It's not Japanese, but it's the most expensive one we stock." She grabs two glasses. "Rocks or neat?"

"Neat, please." I take a breath. "I had dinner at an old friend's and I didn't want to go straight home," I say truthfully.

"Wanting to linger in the vibe of a lovely evening a little longer?" Cassidy slides the glass my way.

"Something like that." Before I drink, I run my tongue over my lips. I understand why Devon reacted the way she did. Of course I do. Who do I think I am, anyway? To waltz into town like this after all these years, cozy up to her as if nothing ever happened between us, and go about kissing her like that in the darkness of her porch? "It's been rather eventful. Lots of reminiscing."

"I bet." Cassidy tips the glass to her mouth and sips. "Damn, that's hella good stuff."

"Is my brother a good boss?" I figure I can ask that question freely seeing as I own most of this bar and that technically makes me Sam's boss.

"Sam's the best. He's very laid-back, you know. And very sweet. Just a good, kind man in general."

"Wow." That's not usually how women talk about my brother. "Such high praise."

"I know he has this reputation and I've seen him put the moves on a few women in here, of course. But that's never the vibe he puts out to me. He's much more respectful than most men, trust me."

"That's good to know."

Cassidy takes another sip. "More often than not, it's women coming up to him. And good for them, you know? Why wouldn't they. He's really *very* dishy." She giggles, betraying her young age.

"I can't see my brother that way, but I'll take your word for it." She wouldn't be the first girl I've sat across from who has a huge crush on my brother—it was what a lot of my life consisted of all throughout high school.

"I like working for him." She suddenly sounds much older, less like a smitten schoolgirl.

"Do you have any other plans for your life apart from serving drinks in my brother's bar?"

"Not right now."

I just sounded so condescending. "I get it. There are worse places to be than Clearwater Bay."

"You bet." Cassidy's gone all silent.

"I'm sorry if I just offended you. It wasn't my intention. I was just being an entitled Hollywood brat." Saying sorry seems to be trending in my life today. Sorry for slapping Devon twenty-four years ago. Sorry for kissing her in the moonlight earlier.

"You're not the first to ask, but I'm perfectly happy with how my life is now." That's all Cassidy gives me and rightly so. She doesn't owe me any further details. I can see why Sam likes her—only not in that way, or so he claims. Moreover, I never asked Sam or Suzy if they wanted something different from their lives than sticking around where we grew up—where we were fortunate to grow up because of its proximity to the ocean and endless opportunities to surf—because they wanted to stay close to dad. Whereas I needed to venture out. I needed to get my face on TV so that my mother could see me and know that her deserting us didn't crush us—not for too long, anyway. Someone in the family had to do it. I did it for all of us, not that our mother has ever been in touch because of it, but, if she's still alive, which we silently assume she is because we've never found any evidence of her being dead, she must have seen me on *King & Prince*.

"You're miles away," Cassidy says.

"It's coming back here. It's a bit of a trip, you know? I've been back before, but not like this. I never stayed long enough for anything to get under my skin. I've always been far too busy for that. Far too married. Far too full of other plans. Far too reluctant to look back on certain things." I stare into my almost empty glass of whisky. It reminds me of Devon.

"It must be weird for you, being who you are. Is everyone all over you all the time?"

"Not excessively, although it does happen." Wait until the finale of the show airs, I think. "I'm used to it. It's part of the job." At least when I'm out in the ocean, no one asks me for a selfie. I knock back the last of the whisky. It burns as it slides down my throat and I must be a little tipsy because I suddenly have a very pertinent question for Cassidy. "Can I ask you something personal?" She belongs to the generation that's very open and liberal about all this stuff.

"Depends." She swirls the liquid around in her glass. "But you can try."

I chuckle and almost shy away from asking the question, but my inhibitions are down and I feel safe here with her in my brother's bar. "Have you ever kissed a girl?"

"Sure." Cassidy doesn't even bat an eyelid, as though she gets asked this question regularly.

"Are you bi?" I can probably learn a lot from today's youth. I'd best prepare myself because my new co-star will be Cassidy's age.

"Sure. I don't really stick a label on it, though. I don't feel like I need to. I just like who I like. Sometimes it's a woman; sometimes it's a man. It depends on the person, really."

"And you like Sam?"

"Well, yeah, but he's my boss and um, yeah." When her cheeks flush like that, she doesn't look older than a high school senior.

"He said you're the best employee he's ever had."

Cassidy smiles. "Well, then. I'm golden."

"Oh, damn. Are you, like, really in love with him?"

"A little bit, but it will pass, I guess."

"Does he know that you have feelings for him?"

She shakes her head. "Please, don't tell him. I know you're close. He's always going Sadie-this and Sadie-that."

Is he? And didn't Devon say something similar about Suzy?

"Your secret's safe with me, but have you considered telling him?"

"Not really. It's such a cliché. Don't you think?"

I huff out some air. "Maybe we need another one of these." While Cassidy pours us another, I consider that I would definitely think of my brother as a big fat cliché if he were to take up with Cassidy. But now that I've spoken to her, I already feel a little differently about it. She's no longer just the young girl working in my brother's bar. She's kind and much more confident than I was at her age—although I still haven't determined how old she actually is—and the best employee Sam's ever had, which is probably most telling of all. He frequently regales me with tales of woe about how difficult it is to find good and trustworthy people to hire—although Sam can be a bit of a drama queen like that.

"It doesn't have to be a cliché." I hold up my glass to her. "Anything's possible, really."

Cassidy smiles at me. "Maybe this should be your last one, Sadie. You might own this place, but I'll have to cut you off soon."

"Fair enough."

"Why did you ask me about kissing girls earlier?"

"No reason. Just curious." Despite the whisky, I manage to keep a little bit of my guard up.

There's stumbling outside and then Sam walks in. "I was on my way home and noticed the lights were still on." He eyes my glass, then the open bottle on the bar. "On to the good stuff, are we?"

"Would you rather I drink your inferior booze?"

"You usually don't drink much at all, sis. And we had all that wine at Devon's earlier."

"What are you doing here, anyway?" I'm not going to take a lecture from my brother. Not tonight. "I thought you were"—I'm trying to be sensitive for Cassidy's sake—"called away."

"I'll have one of those as well, Cass, please." He sends her his roguish smile. No wonder the girl's got the hots for him. Sam just can't help himself.

While she puts an empty glass on the counter, Sam continues, "Why don't you go home? I'll lock up."

From what I can read on Cassidy's face, that's not what she wants to hear at all.

"Oh, come on. Stay, Cass. We'll all lock up together," I say, slurring my words. Maybe it's about time Sam carried me home, not that I would let him.

Unexpectedly, she shoots me a wink. "I'm a little tired. I'll see you tomorrow, boss." She finishes her drink and disappears through the back door.

"Let's take this onto the deck. Get you some fresh air." Before we head outside, Sam pours me a large glass of water. It's like déjà vu from the party; only then, it was Devon leading me outside and taking me home. I wish she were here again tonight. I wish I could kiss her again.

"What's going on?" Sam asks.

"Says the guy who couldn't stop forcing shots on me only last weekend," I counter.

"That was different. That was a one-off at our fortieth birthday party. This is just an ordinary Thursday night."

"Maybe I figured I'd try alcoholism for a while." Christ. I nearly make myself vomit with my obnoxiousness.

"Talk to me. Come on." Because he's my twin, Sam has a way with me that can't be explained with words. We have this invisible but unbreakable connection. He knows something's going on.

I take a deep breath. "I kissed Devon," I whisper, because it doesn't feel like something I can say out loud.

Sam goes totally silent. When I look at him, his eyebrows are nearly touching his hairline. "I'm sorry. I'm very confused. Did I hear that correctly?"

"I kissed Devon," I repeat.

"And?"

"And... she said we should just pretend it never happened."

"But why did you kiss her?" He bumps his knee into mine. "What am I missing here, because I feel like there's a crucial piece of information that I don't have."

"I don't know why I did it. We were having a moment

and it was special and... I don't know. I just really felt like kissing her."

"But... are you attracted to her? To women?"

"To women?" I shrug. "No. I don't know."

"Only to Devon?"

"Fuck, Sam. I can't analyze this right now. I don't know what I feel."

"Okay." He nods slowly, sipping his whisky. "It must be messing with your head if you came to the bar to drink my best stuff."

"I didn't want to go home. I thought you might be there with someone."

"What? No, I told you I was going to Mandy's place."

"You did?"

"Yes, positive, but you must have been too busy plotting to kiss Devon to hear."

"I really wasn't. I didn't plan it. It just happened." I look at him again. "You didn't want to stay the night at Mandy's?"

"I shouldn't have gone over there in the first place. It reminded me of the person I don't want to be anymore. This... man-whore who will sleep with anyone who crosses his path."

"You're meant to say sex worker instead of whore."

He bumps his knee against mine again. "You know what I mean."

I kind of do and don't at the same time. My brother has the same wounds from our childhood as I do, but he has dealt with his in another way. "You want to become a daddy."

"Yes, but I don't just want a child, Sadie. I want a family. I want the family you and I never had." Did his voice just break a little? "Mom was our age when she left. I always figured if I waited until I was forty, I would be safe. I would never feel the urge to do that to my family."

"Oh, my god, Sam." I'm the one who's breaking a little bit. I blame the whisky—Japanese or not. "Fuck. That woman messed us up well and good."

"We turned out all right, though." His voice is steady as a rock.

"Kind of."

"Let's go home. I'm beat."

"Yeah."

He puts his arm around me. "Looks like you've kissed more girls than I have today, sis." Sam thinks this is very funny and he's still laughing when he goes inside to lock up the bar.

CHAPTER 16

*Devon*

"When are we having dinner with Sadie again?" Hunter asks as soon as I walk into his house. Finn rushes to Spencer and they almost tumble over each other as they run outside.

"Not anytime soon." I pull my hand through my hair.

"Do I detect a vibe?" Hunter leads me into the den. "Bobby's out. You can speak freely. Tell me all your secrets, Mama."

"Oh, fuck, Hunter." Maybe I shouldn't talk about this with anyone because of who Sadie is. Maybe she should never have kissed me, then. Although I was the one who suggested we just forget it ever happened, but I need to tell someone. "I loved her for such a long time. I know I was only a teenager and I didn't really know what love was back then and blah-blah-blah, but to me, it felt very real. She was everything to me. She was my life. We did everything together until..."

"Back up a little, Dev." Hunter stares at me wide-eyed. "What are you saying?"

Sadie's been on the forefront of my mind so much since she got back to town, I just assumed Hunter knew. But he

109

doesn't, because how could he? He's my best friend, but I never told him, because by the time I met Hunter, I was more than ready to forget about all things Sadie and what happened between us. I only told him what I told everyone else: that we were in school together. Like Sam and I were in school together. Nothing special.

I swallow hard. Sadie's kiss left me so shaken, I barely slept. With every hour that went by, I spiraled through a different emotion. I've been angry with her for being so reckless, so callous. I've been smitten with her because of the girls we once were. I've felt sorry for Sadie because she must be so confused if she goes around kissing the likes of me—kissing other women. I know she's hurting, that much is obvious. But that doesn't give her the right to abruptly kiss me. Anyone, just not me. It carries too much weight and racks up too many unprocessed emotions.

"Sadie and I weren't just classmates. We were best friends. Thick as thieves. Out surfing together every chance we got. Her mom left when she was ten and she kind of clung to me, I guess." I don't know that for sure, but it's how I like to explain it to myself. "And I... I was in love with her. I must have been in love with her for years, but I was too young to realize. Until I wasn't. Until it hit me with such force. Fuck, I loved her so much. Like only teenagers can, you know? Most days, it was like Sadie was the only thing in my tunnel-visioned world." I blow out some air. It feels good to talk about it, to let it out.

"Until one day, I just couldn't take it anymore. I had just turned sixteen and I knew what I felt and I knew what I wanted. Oh, how I knew. And my enthusiasm, and hormones, no doubt, made me go a little crazy. Made me a little reckless." I can still remember as if it were yesterday. I can still feel the heat of the sun. I can still hear the roar of the ocean we'd just walked out of. I can still see the drops of water rolling down Sadie's golden-brown shoulders. Although I'm probably just imagining it all, painting it in the sentimental light of memory.

"I kissed her. Well, I tried to kiss her. Our lips barely touched. The look she gave me when she pulled away said it all. And then..." I bring my thumb to my cheek, to the spot where Sadie caressed it last night. "She slapped me across the face. It was an instinctive reaction. Her body saying no loud and clear." I rest my chin against my palm. "We barely spoke after that. I tried, but she wouldn't see me. I surfed on my own for the rest of the school year while she joined Sam and his friends, whereas before, it had always kind of been us versus them." No tears, please, I tell myself. This happened too long ago for me to spill any tears over now. Yet, something pricks behind my eyes, for the girl I once was. For the foolish mistake I made. For how Sadie treated me. "It hurt me so much at a time when things like that really leave an impression. And I couldn't tell anyone. I mean, I told my mom. I came out to her because I didn't really have much choice and I had to talk to someone."

"But, Dev... if all that happened, why did you invite her to dinner? Why did it feel, to Bobby and me, like you were just two old friends reminiscing?"

"Because, in the end, that's what we are—two old friends." I understand the confusion on Hunter's face. "She came over to apologize on Sunday, for what happened. She apologized again last night, after you guys left." I run my fingertip over my lips. "Then she kissed me and I've basically been in tatters since. I don't know what to do with myself. There's this force inside me that's stronger than any willpower I have. Than the hours of brain management I've put myself through. But it's ridiculous. It's based on nothing.

On a memory. Or maybe even on some twisted subconscious desire to... I don't know... atone for kissing her in the first place. I don't know what it is, but Sadie still does something to me. A lot, actually. I don't really know what to do with that."

Hunter's jaw drops. "Sadie kissed you?" He slants forward a bit, as though engrossed by the most sordid of tales. "Did you kiss her back?"

"No. Yes. A little bit, I guess."

"Holy mother of Jay-sus." He all but crosses himself. "But she's... she's not... I mean, I've fooled around with many a 'straight' boy"—he curls his fingers into air quotes—"in my time, but this is Sadie Ireland we're talking about here. Is that why she and Michael Morales divorced? She's into the muff?"

I have to laugh. This is why I had to tell Hunter, so we could have a good old laugh about it. How else can I release this wretched tension in my body and, worst of all, these cobwebs from my mind?

"I really don't think she is. As far as I know, that's not the reason for their divorce." But what do I really know? Although Sadie told me the reason why they separated. She was very frank about that.

"Knock, knock!" Suzy's voice comes from the kitchen. "I thought I'd find you here, boss."

I completely forgot about our meeting. We're meant to prepare the coaching call Suzy's leading tomorrow.

"Suzy Ireland." Hunter adores Suzy. He jumps out of his seat to greet her as elaborately as he always does—as though they haven't seen each other in months instead of days.

"Everything okay here?" Her voice stiffens. She must be picking up on a vibe as well. "Finn's okay?"

"Finn's outside torturing Spencer," Hunter says.

"Good." Even when Suzy became my client, a few years

ago now, I never allowed my mind to drift back to the time when her sister and I were so close. When she talked about Sadie, I somehow tricked myself into thinking about her solely as the Sadie Ireland she had become—the TV star living in Hollywood. It worked. For the longest time, I could see it for exactly what it was: a teenage indiscretion made futile by the passing of time. Until Sadie returned and Suzy invited me to her birthday party. I should never have gone, but with Sadie actually in town, it was hard to resist. Not all dams hold forever.

"Hi, Suze." I get up so we can go back to my house for our meeting.

"Must have been some dinner party last night. Neither Sam nor Sadie have responded to any of my messages. What did you give them?"

"Nothing out of the ordinary." I try to keep my voice level. At least Sadie hasn't talked to her sister about what happened. She was always good at keeping silent about certain things. As far as I know, she never told anyone about me trying to kiss her that day.

Hunter distracts Suzy with a couple of questions, then ushers us out. "I'll stop by later," he whispers in my ear as I say goodbye.

Alone with Suzy, going over the submissions the members of my online community have sent in, I feel out of sorts. Suzy doesn't even particularly look like her sister. Before last weekend, I never much thought of Suzy as Sadie's sister. She was just Suzy. But today, it's all I can think about.

More than another chat with Hunter, I need to go out into the ocean. Once I was able to divorce that activity from spending time with Sadie and it could just become the gloriousness of surfing again, it saved me. It gave me joy again even when I saw Sadie out there, performing a new trick she'd learned without me. The weather seems good for it tonight.

"I was thinking of organizing a viewing party of *King & Prince*'s big season finale next Tuesday," Suzy says, out of the blue. "Are you down? I hear something big is going to happen."

"Oh, I don't know. I'll have Finn and he can't watch that show yet."

"We'll do it somewhere he can sleep. It's no biggie. I'm sure Hunter would be a very willing co-organizer."

"You shouldn't count on me being there. I have too much going on."

"Oh." Suzy's eyes narrow. "Is it Zara? Bring her. The more, the merrier."

"What do you actually know about Zara?"

"All I need to know." She cocks her head. "You did see her again, didn't you?"

"Yeah, but Zara and I are not going to be a thing. It's not a good match, what with Finn and everything."

"Okay. Sure." Suzy doesn't push, probably because she has an inkling of why Zara and I aren't suited for each other. "What's the problem, then? I thought you and Sadie were getting along swimmingly?"

"Can I just say no? Isn't that a valid option to any invitation, without having to give a reason?"

"Yes, of course." Suzy seems genuinely taken aback. None of this is her fault. She just really likes inviting people to events. "Sorry."

"No, I'm sorry, Suze. I'm going through something and I need a bit of me time to sort it out. That's all. Nothing major. Certainly nothing to worry about. But it's personal."

"All right. Shall we finish this meeting, then? Or do you

want me to handle the submissions on my own? For the record, boss, I think I'm perfectly capable of doing so."

"Are you sure?"

"Of course, I'm sure. You're my teacher and you're the best." Damned Irelands with all their effortless charm. "Tell you what. I'll email you my notes for the call so you can look them over tomorrow morning."

"That sounds absolutely wonderful."

"I'll leave you to deal with whatever it is you're dealing with, but, Dev." She pins her dark Ireland gaze on me—all three of them have the same set of soulful dark brown eyes. "If you want to talk, I'm here. Okay?"

"I know. Thank you."

As soon as Suzy's left, I put on my wetsuit and head out to catch some waves.

## CHAPTER 17

# Sadie

The sunset surf is gorgeous this evening. The only thing missing, the only thing that would make it infinitely better, is if Devon were here. But I could hardly text her and ask if she was up for it. Or maybe I should have. I'd only be doing what she asked me to do: pretend that kiss never happened. But my gut instinct is telling me to leave whatever the next step is up to her, whatever it takes to put that kiss sufficiently in the past. If that's what she wants.

It's almost my turn. There's only one person in front of me in the line. A young girl who reminds me of myself when I was her age. Eager and a little rash—until my dad set me straight.

"You don't have to do more dangerous tricks because you're a girl," he would say. "It doesn't make any difference and, besides, you're already better than most. No need to push it."

I wish I could say that to this girl. That she'll be fine even if she just goes with the flow, if she doesn't try to show off for the boys. Or maybe that's just my memory playing tricks on me. There are far more women out here tonight than there were when I lived in Clearwater Bay. It's almost fifty-fifty. I'm probably just projecting my old insecurities onto this girl.

I watch her as she tries to climb over the foamy crest of the wave but loses her balance. She'll learn. Then it's my turn and, despite the advice I would have given to the girl, it's always been in my nature to put on a show. In the water, I'm pretty unrecognizable, although some of my fellow surfers must know who I am. I was surfing alongside some of them decades ago. And I can't help myself. As I approach and gauge the upcoming wave, I decide to go for a tube ride. My bottom turn is pretty decent and I make it underneath the curl of the wave and start gliding, start riding it out. But my focus must have slipped—I'm not as clearheaded as I'd like to be after last night's whisky—and I'm not low enough on my board. I get caught in the swell and, for all the line to see, tumble off my board. Thank goodness Sam isn't here. He wouldn't let me hear the end of it for the rest of the weekend.

Thankfully, my dad taught me well. The very first thing he taught us was that surfing pretty much equals falling off your board most of the time.

"A bit like life," he used to say in his more philosophical, or perhaps downbeat, moments.

So I dust myself off and join the end of the line so I can have another go. When I reach the line, the figure in front of me is unmistakable. I don't even know how I know, because Devon and I have only surfed together once since we were sixteen—and her body, although already strong from growing up in the ocean, looked so different then. We were so different then. Or maybe we're still pretty much the same, because some things never change.

She turns around. "Nasty tumble," she says, flashing me one of her close-lipped half-smiles. "Off your game today?"

Damn it. She saw me fall. Even though it's part of it and

all we did when we were learning how to surf was tumble into the water together for hours on end, it stings. "A bit, but I'm regrouping."

"Can't wait to see what you have in store. I'd even let you cut in front of me to witness your comeback."

"Ah, no. I can't break the code. That wouldn't be fair."

"I'm sure you've cut many a line in your life," Devon says.

"Many," I confirm, because it would be foolish to deny that having your face on TV every week for years doesn't open many doors that would otherwise remain closed. "But I'm not cutting this one."

It's not busy in the cove today and Devon's turn is fast approaching.

"All right. I'll show you how to ride that tube then. Looks like you need a refresher."

With utter delight, I watch Devon do her thing. She rides the wave flawlessly and I'm so entranced that the guy behind me has to nudge me to take my turn. Wisely, I don't attempt the same trick. I just do a simple bottom turn because my mind's too preoccupied with how casually Devon teased me. Maybe she has forgotten about last night already, as she urged me to do.

We take a few more turns, but it's not my day in the water. Yet it still feels good to be here with Devon as the sun sets behind us. She's clearly not suffering from whatever I am, because every single move she makes on her board impresses the hell out of me.

As though agreed upon beforehand, we walk out of the water together.

"Do you want to come back to the house?" I ask, because I'd like to spend some more time with her—and I need to know if a bout of surfing is enough to take us back to where

119

we were before I kissed her. Back to being old friends. "It's Friday so Sam's at the bar."

"Oh." She stands there dripping water, shielding her eyes from the setting sun with her hand. "I don't have any clothes with me. I wasn't—"

"You can borrow some of mine. We'll put your board in our shed."

"Hm. Yeah. Okay, I guess."

"I'll even rinse your board for you."

"Wow. A Hollywood star rinse. That's an offer I can't refuse."

We walk to the shed beneath Sam's house. I start rinsing my board but, just like in the old days, I can't help but, very much on purpose, splash some water onto Devon. It's stronger than myself when I'm with her. It's like I want to go back to that time, to that glorious year before everything changed. Because I might have been the bitch who slapped Devon. The insecure girl who felt like she couldn't spend any more time with her best friend because she'd tried to kiss her. But I lost her, too. Despite my behavior, I missed her terribly. And I never told anyone, not one single person, why I stopped hanging out with Devon that day.

"I'll get you back for that."

"I was just trying to wash your board for you, Dev." I paint on an innocent smirk as I hose the salt water off her surfboard.

"Just promise me, no more funny business if I go up with you."

Is she alluding to last night? That was some funny business, yet, if I'm being perfectly honest with myself, I'd do it again in a heartbeat. But I have to respect Devon. She was right when she said it was hardly fair of me to kiss her like that, out of the blue. I've had all day to analyze why I did it, although my hangover didn't help, and I'm still none the wiser. All I know is that I really wanted to do it.

"I'll make you some tea. That's all."

We head up the stairs that lead into a bathroom—this house was built with surfing in mind. What this house wasn't built for was two people who don't want to see each other naked taking off their clothes and showering separately. Every single time I've come here since Sam moved in, I've asked him to put in some sort of partition so surfing guests—mainly me —could have some privacy. But my brother has other priorities. He's probably used the lack of privacy to his advantage many a time.

I scratch my head and stand there hemming and hawing.

"It's fine, Sadie. I've taken off my wetsuit and showered with strangers before. I just want to get it off me now."

"You go first. I'll wait. Or I'll use the bathroom upstairs."

"You'll drip all over the floors."

"I'll clean it up."

"Do whatever you want." Devon heads into the shower and starts taking off her wetsuit. She's an old hand at it—of course, she is—because it takes her less time to get out of it than it takes me to decide that I'll just wait. Before I turn away from her, my gaze is glued to the tattoo on the curve of her hip. It looks so delicate and intricate. Then I gather myself and give her some privacy while I stand there shivering in my wetsuit.

I start taking it off so I can hop into the shower as soon as she's done. When Devon transfers her suit to the bathtub to wash it more thoroughly, I take over the shower. I try to focus on soaping up and getting the salt off my suit.

I'm acutely aware of us both being naked. I don't notice her stealing covert glances at me, but I can't say the same of myself. My eyes are drawn to that tattoo on her right hip. It starts mid-thigh and runs all the way up the side of her hip. It seems to extend to her lower belly but she's not at a good angle for me to see. Only after she has submerged her suit in the tub, does she reach for a towel and wrap it around herself.

"Do you want me to wash your suit now that I'm at it?" she asks, making me feel caught red-handed.

"Hm. Sure. Thanks," I manage to say. I hand her my suit and there's no other way to do this than by turning more toward her. Is she looking? It's impossible to tell. Do I want her to look? I might need to have a thorough and honest conversation about that with myself later.

By the time I've showered, Devon has taken care of both of our suits and hung them up to dry.

"You're such a pro."

"Your dad taught me how to take care of a wetsuit so it will last for years."

I can only nod. There was never an inch of negotiation room with my dad when it came to surf gear care.

"What are you in the mood for?" I ask when we've made it up to my bedroom and I open my closet.

"Oh my god." Devon's instantly drawn to the window. "This is what you wake up to?" There's one last sliver of orange sun visible on the horizon and the ocean is a patchwork of deep purple and blood red. "Fuck."

"Sam's the lucky bastard. He lives here." I stand next to her and enjoy the view. My house in Malibu has an ocean view as well, and maybe the ocean is the ocean, but it's different here in Clearwater Bay. This is the stretch of ocean I swam and surfed in as a kid. The place I gravitated toward when I was feeling sad and happy. It was on the beach I'm looking at now that our dad told us that he didn't think our mother was going to come back, ever, and he tried to explain why. None of us listened to that explanation—we would need a lot more time to even begin to accept it.

"Wow," Devon says.

I glance down at the cove. Most of the surfers have left now that darkness is falling. This beach is also the very spot where Devon tried to kiss me that afternoon.

"You're welcome here any time," I say, tugging the towel around me.

"I've been to the house before." Devon keeps staring out of the window. "Suzy had her birthday party here last year around the time she started working for me."

Another family party I missed. I tried to make it up to Suzy by flying her down to Malibu and hiring someone to cook us a lavish dinner, but things like that have never really impressed my sister. Even though we had a lovely weekend together, I could still tell it hurt her that I couldn't make it to her party in our hometown on the day that it mattered to her.

Another thing I need to get Leslie, my agent, to negotiate when my *King & Prince* contract is up for renewal. Enough time off to properly celebrate family birthdays.

I gaze into my closet and imagine which item of my clothing would make Devon look the most dashing. Something with color, like that orange top she wore at my birthday party. I find a green T-shirt and a pair of jeans.

"Here." I hold them out to her.

"I won't fit into a pair of your jeans."

"Leggings?"

"Yes, I'll try on some of your Malibu chic athleisure." She stands there grinning.

I reach into my stack of overpriced leisure wear and hand her a pair of yoga pants. "Bathroom's over there."

Still smirking, Devon heads into the en suite. I'm not sure what's so funny about all of this.

CHAPTER 18

## Devon

I couldn't say no to Sadie's invitation to come to the house. I wanted to surf to clear my head, and it helped, but only to a certain extent. Undressing in front of Sadie hasn't exactly helped my mindfulness about pretty much everything. But as long as she's here, for the following two months, I'm just going to have to go through whatever this thing is that I'm going through with her. Maybe the time has finally come to process all my emotions, to put it behind me once and for all, because, clearly, I haven't yet. But that's okay. The past catches up with us all the time. Then we deal with it. I know from my training as a life coach that there's nothing I can't deal with and once I've dealt with Sadie and what she still means to me, once we've comfortably settled back into whichever form of friendship is available to us, I'll be just fine again. She'll go back to LA, and I'll have someone to call if I ever feel like introducing Finn to the Malibu waves.

It's all good, I think, as I sink into a lounge chair overlooking the ocean, which is so soothing at dusk, it almost lulls me into feeling too comfortable. Not that I have a bone to pick with Sadie, because who am I to blame anyone for inad-

125

vertently trying to kiss me? But we do have to address it, just so that it doesn't turn into something bigger than it needs to be.

She comes out looking ravishing with her wet hair combed back and a loose-fitting pale-blue shirt over a pair of tight jeans, carrying a tray with a teapot and two cups.

"It's herbal so it shouldn't interfere with your sleep." Sadie pours the liquid into our cups.

"It would take some very strong coffee to interfere with my sleep tonight."

"Surfing tired you out?" She sits opposite me and draws up one leg onto her chair. *Christ*. With the light like this and her hair wet like that, mug cupped between her hands, Sadie looks like she's about to be photographed for some glossy magazine.

"I didn't get much sleep last night." I find her gaze.

"Right." She just nods.

"How about you? Suzy implied you and Sam went on a bit of a bender. What happened to his booty call?"

Sadie shrugs. "We ended up at the bar for a bit of a twins heart-to-heart."

It's like the ocean doesn't even exist anymore, or it's no longer as beautiful compared to what I see when I look at Sadie—she's even more gorgeous than when I fell in love with her, more mature and much more of all the things that make women so irresistible.

"It's nice that you can talk to him about, um, things." Did she tell her brother about kissing me?

"I never told him about... *you know*." She looks at me over the rim of her cup. "He did ask why you and I suddenly stopped hanging out when we were inseparable before, but I never told him."

"Why not?"

"It didn't feel right, and I had already reacted so badly."

"Let's not dwell on the past." Maybe I should thank her for keeping my secret, for not forcing me out of the closet and making me a potential victim of high school homophobia, but I'm not going to do that. Who would I be thanking, anyway? The Sadie of twenty-four years ago? That hardly seems appropriate. "Let's just dwell on the not-so-distant past for a minute. About last night, Sadie. I know I said that we should pretend it never happened, and I do stand by that, but, as it turns out, it's all I've been thinking about all day long."

"You and me both."

"There isn't something I'm missing here, is there?" I have to ask. I have to know.

"Like what?" Oh, great. Still playing coy. At least that's good to know, because I won't be going there.

"About a possible other reason why you and Mike divorced..." I'm done beating about the bush. I need her to come out and tell me.

"Oh." She seems genuinely surprised. "Oh. No. I'm not suddenly into women, if that's what you're asking."

"Yet you kissed a woman."

"I kissed you, Dev. It's not the same."

"I'm still a woman. Always have been."

"Well, yes, but... You're not just a woman to me. Maybe I can't call you my friend, yet you feel like one. I love being around you. I love surfing with you. I love talking to you. I love... this. Sitting here with you. It just feels right."

"But what am I supposed to do with that?"

"You're right. I shouldn't have kissed you. I can see that now. It confuses things."

"You think?" I scoff. "Surely you have other female friends. Do you go around kissing them?"

She shakes her head. "They don't make me feel the same way that you do."

"It's wonderful that being around me makes you feel so great, but I have feelings, too."

"Of course. I'm sorry if I made you feel used or anything else like that."

"I don't feel used, but..." How can I explain this without putting any ideas in her head—or my own? "I'm a lesbian, Sadie. When a highly attractive woman that I happen to be very fond of kisses me... well, you know. I'm not made of stone. It does something to me. Something that you might not be able to feel yourself, because it doesn't mean the same thing to you."

"Yeah. I'm sorry. It was unfair."

"It's also hard not to see the irony in it, after what happened when we were sixteen and I kissed you." High time for a chuckle. "Maybe all it meant was closure. We've come full kissing circle."

"Maybe that's a good way to look at it." Sadie puts her tea down and gets up. She goes to stand by the railing, looking into the swiftly falling darkness.

Instinctively, I join her. Dark or not, I could look out over this deck for a few good hours to come.

"Oooh," Sadie groans. "I love this song." She pulls her phone from her pocket and turns up the volume of a well-hidden sound system.

I recognize the intro and nearly melt into a puddle. "Oh my god. Me too." It's a bit of a lesbian anthem but maybe I shouldn't point that out to Sadie right now.

We enjoy the song in silence while we gaze out onto the blackening ocean. It's a surprising duet between Lana Lynch and Isabel Adler, both out and proud singers, and it's so powerful, so sexy and gorgeous, it takes my breath away.

Standing here with Sadie, next to the ocean—our very own little part of it since we were children—is as perfect a moment I've experienced in a long time.

"I guess it figures that you would like that song so much." Sadie's first to break the silence after the tune ends. "You being such a lez and all."

"What's your excuse?" This is how I like us best. When we banter and joke and say all the things that are much harder to express in a serious conversation.

"As if I need an excuse to enjoy a really banging tune. It's just beautiful. With Lana Lynch's raw rasp and Isabel Adler's delicate voice. It's the contrast between them. And the lyrics. Admittedly, they're quite hot."

"Hot?"

Sadie looks me square in the eye. "The song's called 'I Should Have Kissed You.' Of course it's hot."

I shake my head. "Fuck you, Sadie." I'm beginning to think she's playing the song on purpose, to bait me into something. Or to create another 'moment.'

"What? Why?"

"I feel like you're playing me somehow. I'm not a big fan of games like that. I can't do that with you."

"Dev." She tilts her head. I can barely make out her eyes. "I don't know what you're talking about. Surely, you've enjoyed plenty of duets between a man and a woman and considered them hot. The gender of the singers doesn't matter."

"Sure."

"I'm not playing you. I promise." She brings a hand to her chest. "Why would I do that?"

"Seems to me you don't have much of a clue why you do anything these days."

"Only when it comes to you." I can't read the expression

on her face. There's a tiny wrinkle between her eyebrows as if she's confused, but her gaze is clear and direct. "Sorry. I shouldn't have said that. Fuck. I really need to check myself around you."

"You shouldn't have to. We're friends now, remember?"

She huffs out a breath of air. "I'm just... You've grown into such a gorgeous person and, half the time, I don't know what to do with myself around you. I guess that..." She looks away. "I am attracted to you. When it comes down to it, that's the very simple reason I kissed you last night. I couldn't help myself. You are so beautiful, not just..." She looks at me again. "Not just how you look, but how you are. How gracious you've been with me. How loving you are with your son. How utterly cool you are out there." She points at the ocean. "No wonder I'm confused."

She's confused? She should have a look inside my head right about now.

"Sadie," I say on a desperate breath. Why is she saying these things? She's not into women but she's into me. She's attracted to me and that's the 'very simple' reason she kissed me? None of this makes any sense to me. "Fuck."

"I know." She scoots closer to me until our elbows touch. "It's unfair, but it's how it is." She gazes at my arm. "Those tattoos are to die for, by the way."

"I'd never have taken you for someone who would be into that."

"Turns out I'm into a lot of things I didn't know I was." She's close enough for me to be able to make out the glint in her eyes. She's shamelessly coming on to me. After the conversation we've just had, that's very audacious. Maybe the surf got her high—no Japanese whisky can be blamed for anything untoward tonight. She removes her elbow from the railing, turns to me, and runs a fingertip along my forearm, along the stem of the flower that is tattooed on my skin there. "In case you hadn't noticed, I'm totally into you."

"It's kind of hard not to." What am I supposed to do when Sadie comes for me like this? Keep my wits about me? No chance. She wants this and so do I, even though I know I need to protect myself. But protect myself from what? Maybe Sadie is the one-night stand that will break my dry spell. Maybe it can only be her as long as she's in town. "Therefore..." I inch closer. I look into her eyes; she gazes back at me. A small smile plays on her lips. Who cares if she's been playing me or if she's genuinely confused? Right now, the only thing I care about is feeling her lips on mine again.

I lean in and I kiss her, like I did all those years ago. But everything is different now. We're women instead of girls. And this time, she kisses me back. She pushes herself against me and kisses me as though she has hungered for this kiss as long as I have—which would be impossible, but that's what it feels like. Like our desire for this is matched. Like the impossible has happened.

Her tongue slips into my mouth and she groans a little, making me go weak at the knees. I grab a fistful of the shirt she's wearing and pull her as close as she can get. She brings her hand to my neck and the cool touch of her fingers undoes the last of my doubts.

We turn fully toward each other, just the sides of our hips touching against the railing now. I curl my arms around her. I inhale her flowery soap scent from that shower we took earlier. I let her kiss me again and again. I give my sixteen-year-old self everything she ever wanted—and my current self as well.

CHAPTER 19

## Sadie

I'm dizzy with desire for Devon. I meant every word I said earlier. From the instant I saw her again last weekend, I've felt something. I've wanted something like this to happen. Now it is and it's divine because Devon is divine and sexy and I sure hope she knows what she's doing because I don't have a clue. Although that makes it extra thrilling when my lips find hers again, when our tongues dance together. Everything about her is so soft, so accessible, so everything I expect it to be—as if my body has been waiting for this somehow.

Her hair is still wet and my fingers get tangled up in it, but it doesn't stop us from kissing more. As if we're making up for lost time. Like this is what was meant to happen all along.

But then, inevitably, we break from kissing and hesitation takes over. Kissing her is all well and good—and utterly delicious—but where do we go from here? Maybe Devon was right when she said that there are certain things that she might feel that I can't. The way I feel right now, though, I'm thinking she was quite wrong about that.

"Fuck," she whispers—again. "So much for pretending last night's kiss never happened."

The slant of her head is so inviting. Her gaze on me is so enthralling. Her lips are so infinitely kissable. And I'm sure of one thing: I don't want her to go. I want Devon to stay with me here tonight. I want her.

"Will you stay?" I ask, my heart fluttering in my chest.

She huffs out some air, as though that's the last thing she expected me to ask. I understand that she's surprised. "Are you sure?" She hooks a fingertip under the waistband of my jeans and pulls me closer to her. It lights a fire under my skin.

"Very."

"What about Sam?"

"Sam has his own bedroom."

Devon chuckles. "Thank goodness for that."

"He's at the bar. God knows when he'll be back. Let's just pretend Sam doesn't live here. Just for now."

"If you're sure." She leans in again but instead of kissing me on the lips, she goes for my neck. Her breath is hot on my sensitive skin there. She kisses a moist path to my ear. "I'll stay," she whispers, ratcheting up my desire for her another notch. "But give me a minute to call Hunter and check on Finn. I don't want him running home and not find me there."

Devon walks to the end of the deck to make the call, but I can't help but hear her side of the conversation. She tells Hunter she won't be home till late, without giving any further detail, and I can picture him, and Bobby with him, dying of curiosity about what she's up to. When she's done, she walks back toward me.

"Let's go inside." I take her hand and lead her up the stairs to my bedroom. Just in case, I lock the door behind us.

"I've been wanting to unbutton that shirt for a while

now." Devon's not pulling any punches. All the hesitation, all the prudence she displayed before, seems to have gone out the window now that she has taken this step. Now that she has kissed me. Now that she has decided to stay. There's no room for ambivalence in this bedroom—not tonight. She pulls me toward her again and undoes my shirt buttons. When she opens my shirt, I delight in how her eyes go a little wide. "No bra," she whispers, her voice barely audible.

She slips her hands underneath my shirt, along my sides, and my breath hitches in my throat at her touch. I haven't slept with anyone since my separation from Mike, and with no one else but him for seven years prior. To be touched by someone else entirely, someone new—and a woman, no less —is more than enough for my heart to slam itself against my ribcage with sheer anticipation of what might follow.

This isn't just any other person or just any woman. This is Devon Douglas. It could only ever be her, that I'm certain of somehow. As certain as I am about kissing her again. Her lips are already reaching for me. Her hands travel up my back, her fingertips light as a feather. My breasts press against the T-shirt she borrowed from me. I want to get it off her as quickly as possible. I want to see that tattoo on her hip again. I want to see where else she has hidden treasures on her skin. I want so much. I want it all.

Devon's tongue delves deep into my mouth, claiming me, with zero trepidation. She's not treating me like some delicate flower, like a woman who has never done this before. We're doing this together. I made it happen. I instigated it; there are no two ways about it. But I had to tell her how I feel. Under Devon's gaze, now that we're both forty, there's just no other choice. How else was I going to make her kiss me again? How else was I going to make her erase the dreadful memory of our very first kiss? It's time for new memories and for plenty of new kisses.

I hoist up her T-shirt. I've waited long enough. She has to let go of me and she does so reluctantly, our lips connecting for as long as possible, until she has to withdraw and reach up her arms. She's not wearing a bra either—I suppose I could have lent her one but the thought didn't even occur to me earlier.

I swallow hard at the sight of her naked upper body, although she doesn't look nearly as naked as I feel, because her skin is covered in tattoos. A black line curls up from under her leggings and snakes around her belly button—it must be the extension of the tattoo on her hip. The rest of her belly is porcelain pale. Her nipples are small and hard and waiting for me to take them into my mouth. I take a good look at her arms first. Both of them are completely covered in ink, from the shoulder down to the wrist, and it looks like the most breathtaking work of art I've ever seen.

Devon smiles her close-lipped smile before hooking her finger underneath my jeans again. She flips open the button and unzips me. Her mouth does a little tilt when she sees I am wearing panties—I know she's not wearing any. I know that when those leggings come off her, she'll be completely naked. And although I saw her naked earlier when we showered, this nudity is entirely different because of what's about to happen.

She slides my jeans off me and crouches down, like she does so effortlessly on a surfboard. I step out of my jeans and stand in front of her in just a flimsy pair of panties.

"You're so fucking gorgeous, Sadie." She sounds as though she means it from the bottom of her heart—like not much has changed for her since she fell in love with me when we were sixteen. Before she comes for me again, she looks me in the eye, and says, "No regrets. Okay?"

"None." I sound more resolute than all the times on set when I've had to chase a criminal-on-the-run and yell at the top of my voice, "Hands up, motherfucker!"

She gives me a nod, then slides the leggings off her gorgeous legs. As if she knows it's what I want to see, she turns her tattooed hip to me as she puts the leggings away. I can't help myself. I scoot closer and run a finger over it. My limited knowledge of botany doesn't allow identification of the flower I'm tracing a finger over, but I'm sure I'll have plenty of time to learn the details about her tattoos later.

Now that she's fully naked, a new kind of determination glints in Devon's eyes. She walks me to the bed and we lie down side by side.

We look at each other and take a few breaths to adjust to the situation before things get out of control again. When she touches me next, a fingertip running softly along my side, there's so much tenderness in her gaze, it floors me even more than when we kissed earlier. I can't claim to love Devon, but I do feel something for her—a lot, in fact. Otherwise, I wouldn't be here.

Her finger dips lower, following the waistband of my panties. She traces a circle around my bellybutton, and long-dormant parts of me awaken. Her finger skates down but her touch is featherlight. Yet, when her fingertip reaches my clit, even with the fabric of my panties as a barrier, I feel it everywhere. But she's just teasing. She slides her hand back to my hip and pulls me in for another kiss. It's hungry and grows more desperate as the minutes pass.

I run my hands over as much of her skin as I can, until I cup her delicious ass cheek in my palm. The soft roundness of it surprises me again, but I have no time to recover from all the tiny shocks being delivered to my system. Devon pushes me onto my back. She's taking control.

Just as I can't claim I love her, I can't claim this is something I've dreamed of forever, because it's not. It's something that's happening to me as a direct consequence of seeing her again, of seeing something in her—of suddenly seeing the two of us together. I might not have dreamed of this, yet it feels like a lot of my dreams are coming true. Because who better to do this with, to get back into the swing of things after a divorce, than an old friend? Someone as gentle and wonderful and capable as Devon.

Her hand has slipped in the direction of my panties again. Her lips are on my neck, kissing their way to my chest. She stops the descent of her hand just above my panties and lets it rest there while her mouth finds my nipple.

I let out a low throaty groan—a sound I didn't even know I had in me—as Devon swirls her tongue around my nipple. I bury my hands in her hair and give myself to her. I let her devour me and take away some of the loneliness that has settled deep inside me since my divorce, that unsettling feeling you get when you are supposedly adored by millions of TV viewers, but go home to an empty house that only reminds you of how much you failed at something you really wanted to succeed at. After the divorce came through—it was all handled swiftly and almost too neatly by a battery of overpaid lawyers—all I did was surf and every time I went out there, board tucked under my arm, a little piece of Devon, of the best surfing buddy I ever had, took to the water with me.

She lavishes her attention on my other nipple and while she does, she cuts her gaze to me. While her tongue circles my nipple she looks into my eyes and in that moment, I think I might very well come to love her. If not her, then who could I love? I certainly love how her hand is traveling lower again, her fingertips digging underneath my panties. Oh god. My clit stands to attention. Every cell in my body burns for her. Why am I even still wearing these? Is that some sort of lesbian thing? In bed with Mike, my panties were always the first thing he disposed of. But Devon is not Mike. She's the opposite of him with her long hair and her feminine touch. Mike was a gentle, thoughtful lover, but this is something else. It's incomparable. It's a unique experience in my life. Devon's touch, though gentle, is also full of determination and tenderness and intent.

I need to feel the air on me everywhere. Every last inch of my skin needs to breathe. I get a feeling I'll need the oxygen. I push my panties down. Devon narrows her eyes, pulls her lips into a lopsided smile, then gives me a hand. She tosses my panties somewhere in the room behind her. Then, I spread for her. The intimacy of the action revs up the intensity of what we're doing. It makes things very real for me.

She slides up next to me and gazes at me while her finger traces complicated figures on my inner thigh. It inches closer to my throbbing center, but not nearly close enough.

Her gaze still firmly on me, her brown eyes full of desire, Devon withdraws her finger and brings it to her lips. She sucks it deep into her mouth and I feel myself grow even wetter—just like that finger she just licked.

She sinks her teeth into her bottom lip while her wet finger travels back between my legs. Oh god. Here we go. She circles it around my clit and the extra lubrication surely wasn't necessary because I'm already wet like a river—like the ocean we love so much. Waves of lust crash through me and I wish I could ride them like I do on my surfboard. I wish I could slip inside the tube of this particular wave and ride it out as long as possible. But I'm already being pulled under by the sheer force of it, by the sheer force of what Devon's finger on my clit is doing to me. But Devon doesn't let me crash into the waves just yet. Her finger slides down, lower, through my wetness. With her mouth slightly agape, as though she's feeling everything I'm feeling, she pushes her finger inside me.

I exhale sharply. "Oh, fuck," I say. "Oh, yes."

Devon moves her finger while she leans in and kisses me again. Her tongue in my mouth and her finger inside me are driving me completely nuts. I'm caught in a current so strong there's no point in putting up a fight. I want to go under. I want to surrender to this wave of all things Devon. I want to drown in this sea of lust and desire.

I'm not sure how she does it—it must be some sort of secret lesbian trick—but as her finger slides high inside of me, she plays with my throbbing clit in such a way that my resolve is no longer a match for all this masterful skill. Although, when I open my eyes as we break from our kiss, and I look into Devon's delighted face, I know very well this isn't a matter of skill. That it isn't just Devon playing some magic lesbian voodoo on me. It's her, making love to me. It's Devon Douglas making me come with the force of a tidal wave that's impossible to ride. A tsunami that you see coming from a mile away that washes over you because there's no other choice. So that's what I do. I let go and I come at Devon's divine fingers.

CHAPTER 20

## Devon

Sadie has never looked more beautiful to me than she does right now. She's still too shocked to return my smile. Her body's still coming down from that cloud I sent her to. She's entirely unselfconscious—the way she is when she attacks a wave and there's no time to second-guess herself—and deep in the arms of pure joy.

When a smile does break on her lips, it's the most glorious smile I've ever witnessed.

All I can do is bow down to her and kiss her again and again. I guess we haven't come full kissing circle just yet. She throws her arms around me and pulls me close, as though she's seriously considering never letting go again.

"Fuck, Dev," she sighs when I give her back the use of her lips. "I didn't know I had that in me."

It seems to me that alongside coming home, Sadie has gone on some wayward journey of self-discovery as well, and she's coming across all sorts of things she didn't know about herself. Tonight, I'm more than happy to be a conduit to this deeper knowledge. I have to give myself this gift, this means of closure, also. I'll deal with the consequences tomorrow.

"Maybe it's because you turned forty. Maybe..." I'm just babbling—spouting nonsense, really. "This is not something you could do in your thirties."

Her body convulses against mine as she laughs.

"Maybe my body also couldn't do this." I don't know where she gets the strength so soon after that climax, but she topples me off her and slides on top of me.

Because of her sudden movement, I'm hit with a hint of trepidation. "You don't have to, um, do this, you know."

"Do what exactly?"

For crying out loud. Am I going to be bashful about this now? Yet, I feel like it needs to be said. "You don't have to reciprocate. I mean, I realize tha—"

Before I can continue, she presses her lips against mine. She trails a path to my ear and whispers, "I never accepted the orgasm gap when I was married to a man and I'm most certainly not going to accept it now that I'm in bed with a woman."

"How very woke of you," I reply, secretly relieved because I'm about to explode with desire.

"There's nothing woke about it." She pushes herself away from me a fraction and I can see her face again. "I want you like you can't believe."

Music to my ears, but I can't help but tease her a little bit, despite the growing pressure between my legs. "Who are you? You vaguely look like how I would imagine Sadie Ireland to look after a world class orgasm, but you don't sound like her at all."

"Let's see what you sound like when Sadie Ireland has her way with you."

"I'm all ears."

"And tattoos." Sadie peers at my hip, at my magnolia

tattoo. "This looks so incredibly sexy and cool on you." She traces her finger over the outline again.

Instead of thanking her for the compliment, I pull her near me and kiss her again. I will never get enough of kissing Sadie. I lose myself again in kiss after kiss, as if to assuage the sixteen-year-old who still lives inside me and was denied something crucial. I cup Sadie's cheeks in my hands. As much as I want her lips to travel elsewhere, to discover more of my body, I simply can't stop kissing her. Every time she tries to pull away, I draw her back. I just can't get enough. But I'm not the only strong-willed woman in this bed and there comes a point when I need to let Sadie have her way.

I let her trail her lips along my neck to my collarbone. I watch as she gazes at my breasts before lowering her mouth down to them. And then, I'm engulfed by the exquisite sensation of Sadie Ireland's lips clasped around my nipple. Instantly, my body turns into nothing but desire. The entire expanse of my skin turns into an erogenous zone, and the places where she presses against me seem to light up with the most powerful of sparks. Maybe I've been waiting for this for twenty-four years. I lived most of my life without her, without my former best friend and the girl I once loved, because I had no choice, but something deep inside me latched onto her with such a tight grip, only this can loosen it. This very action of Sadie and I in bed, of her tongue flicking along my nipple, her hands roaming across my skin.

I fully expect her to repeat what I just did to her, but Sadie surprises me. She kisses her way down to my belly button, then trails the tip of her tongue along the curl of my lower belly tattoo and follows it to my right hip.

To have her linger there, her breath hot and moist on my skin, is almost too much to bear. I've been simmering with increasing desire for a week now—since the return of Sadie, my enduring weakness. And then, she surprises me even further.

She settles between my legs. Really? She's going to do that? She's going all the way this very first time for her with a woman? My skin lights up even more with anticipation. Maybe I should tell her, again, that she doesn't have to do this, but fuck that. She's only doing it because she wants to. Because she wants *me*. Out of all of this, that's the hardest to believe. But Sadie's lowering herself toward me now. She kisses my inner thigh, again and again.

I'm about to lose it already. How many women around the world have dreamed of a moment like this? Sadie Ireland seconds away from going down on them. I'm sure many have, but none of them have had the dream for as long as I've had it. None of them have known Sadie as long as I have. None of them have spent hours and hours with her doing nothing, just hanging out, talking about boys as though that was even something I was interested in.

She digs her fingertips into the flesh of my behind and the next thing I feel is her tongue on my clit. The warmth of it is magical. Her touch is mind-blowing. Sadie takes me into her mouth, engulfs me with her hottest heat, with this incredible amount of intimacy, and all the barriers I've held up, all the tears I've held back since she no longer wanted to see me, crash through the very last of my resolve.

I cry and I scream out her name and I clasp onto whatever part of her I can grab hold of as I give myself to her. To Sadie Ireland. The girl I've always loved.

I'm elated and destroyed at the same time. I cover my eyes with my arm because I'm not sure I should have so much emotion on display. I'm supposed to be the cool chick with all the tattoos and all the wisdom.

"Hey." Sadie clambers up to me quickly and curls her

fingers around my wrist, trying to remove the arm that's covering my teary eyes. "Dev. It's okay," she whispers. "I know this is emotional."

I try taking a few deep breaths, stealing a little bit of time before looking at her again.

I lower my arm and peek through my fingers. "I'm sorry. I —" I kind of lost it just now, I think, but I'm not going to tell her that.

"This is a lot." She slides my hand away from my face and intertwines her fingers with mine. "I get that. I do."

This is exactly what I meant when I said even just kissing her could trigger a whole slew of emotions inside me that I might not know how to deal with—and that would be impossible for her to reciprocate. Maybe that was why I was so cautious earlier when I assured her she didn't have to make me come. Maybe part of me already knew how much it would undo me, because undone I am. Because this is Sadie and, despite all the years that have passed and all my best intentions, I don't know how to deal with that.

All I can do is pull her near me again, hold on to her, take comfort in her warm skin against mine.

"I don't have a lot of words right now," I manage to whisper in her ear after a while.

"Words are not required." She wriggles free from my clasp and smiles at me before kissing me ever so gently on the cheek. "We can just lie here. Fall asleep together."

"I have no energy left for anything else." It's been a day and a half, what with processing last night's kiss, surfing with Sadie, and then this. "Thank you for not kicking me out."

"Why would I do that when I have you exactly where I want you?" She sounds as though she means it.

"Oh, Sadie," I groan. Even more to discuss, to pick apart and determine what it all means. But not tonight. My sudden tears have left me more exhausted than all the other things we did. "For now, I'll happily take falling asleep in your arms."

"Come." She settles next to me and opens her arms. "There's a spot for you here."

I shuffle closer and nestle myself in the crook of her shoulder. I sling an arm around her waist and hold on tight.

"Just a heads-up," she says, her muscles shifting underneath me. "I'm going to have a bone to pick with you when you wake up tomorrow."

Damn. Is she regretting this already? I push myself up to get a look at her face.

"You wore my leggings without panties and effectively ruined them."

Relieved, I erupt into a chuckle. My brain's too exhausted for a comeback, but I have all night to think of one. I lie back on Sadie's shoulder and settle in her embrace. Whatever the future might bring, I will always have had this moment.

---

When I wake up, the bed is empty. Before I panic about that, I think about Finn. As soon as I can find my phone, I'll text Hunter to check in. Then my gaze is drawn to the window. We never did close the curtains. The ocean is bright and blue and oh-so inviting.

I hear noises downstairs. Last night, it was very convenient to forget this is Sam's house. Damn. Last night. I remember how I fell apart. Even in the bright morning light, with all my wits about me, I can hardly blame myself for that.

I glance at the empty spot in the bed next to me. Nothing new there, of course, although, a lot of weekend mornings when Finn is with me, I wake up with him next to me. But what I feel now is nothing like waking up to an empty bed at home. I'd best get up and face whatever's coming.

The small bag I carry when I go surfing with my house keys and phone is probably downstairs. I need it if I want to text Hunter.

I reach for the leggings Sadie lent me and I can't help but smile as I do. How spoiled of her to suggest they're ruined just because I wore them commando. She probably hasn't done her own laundry in a while. Truth be told, I don't much feel like putting them on. I saunter to the en suite bathroom and find a robe, feeling kind of like a naughty teenager as I do.

Just as I'm about to exit the bedroom, the door opens. Sadie walks in with two steaming mugs in her hands.

"Ah, damn it. I was going to wake you up with the divine aroma of coffee drifting up your nose."

A huge smile breaks on my face at the sight of her. I take one of the mugs from her. "Thank you. This place has excellent service."

"Earth-shattering orgasms at night and damn good coffee in the morning." She walks to the window and opens it. "Do you want to drink it outside? Just a word of warning. Sam's up and already milling about downstairs. With a bit of luck, he'll go for a surf soon, but he knows I'm not alone, and well, he saw your wetsuit downstairs, so..."

"Right." I sigh. "I need to find my phone. I really want to text Hunter."

"It's in the den. Shall I get it for you?"

"It's okay. I'm a big girl, Sadie." It's endearing that she would want to spare me from seeing Sam, or maybe she's trying to spare herself from something. "What did Sam say? When he put two and two together?" She could have told him anything. I could have just stayed the night. Then again, this place must have at least five bedrooms, so why would I have slept in Sadie's room—as if we were having a teenage sleepover.

"Nothing much. He's probably saving it for after you've gone." Sadie walks to the door. "I'll go downstairs with you." She slides past me and sends me a smile as she does. Before allowing me to leave the room, she stands in front of me and kisses me on the lips. "Good morning, by the way. I tried to wait until you woke up, but you just kept on sleeping."

"Someone exhausted me last night."

Her smile turns into a grin. "Just so we're clear. No regrets."

"No regrets," I reply, although I get a feeling I might come to regret saying that.

"Good." She kisses me again and I'm already melting once more. What she made me feel last night was so powerful, my skin is still ultra-reactive to her touch and my mind is already angling for a repeat performance. But no. This is the tomorrow I never wanted to come. It's here. Time to deal.

We go downstairs and I try to sound as casual as possible when I say, "Hey, Sam."

"Devon." He pulls a face, but I'm too keen to find my phone to say anything back. Besides, I don't owe him an explanation.

I spot my bag on the coffee table. I make quick work of texting Hunter, telling him I'll be home soon, and to kiss Finn for me.

"Sometimes being neighbors with the father of your child is almost the same as actually living together." My voice sounds strangely high-pitched, like I'm not myself.

Sam sits there smirking.

Sadie has spotted it as well. "Stop that." She throws a cushion in her brother's direction.

"Stop what?" Sam catches the pillow easily. "I haven't

done anything. I just live here. And I kept my part of the bargain. I've brought zero women home since you arrived." He cocks his head as if to say, 'not something that can be said of you.'

Sadie rolls her eyes at him. "Let's go outside." On her way to the sliding doors to the deck, she throws another cushion in Sam's direction.

"Tell you what, ladies." Sam jumps up. "I'll be the gentleman that you know me to be and make myself scarce."

As soon as we're on the deck, I forget all about Sam. I've only just sat down with my coffee, casting my gaze over the brilliant ocean, when my phone beeps with a message back from Hunter. It simply says:

*I'm drawing some conclusions here...*

"I'm really going to have to reset some boundaries with Finn's dad. We're way too up in each other's business."

"Hm." Sadie's dressed in last night's jeans and blue shirt. She looks every inch the relaxed TV star on vacation. "We should probably talk, shouldn't we?" She looks through the open window, probably to check whether Sam made good on his promise and left, then draws up a chair next to me.

"At some point, I guess we should." I lock my gaze on hers, my heart all over the place, because I have no idea what she's going to say and all I want to do is kiss her again.

CHAPTER 21

## Sadie

My gaze keeps drifting downward, into the cleavage created by the robe Devon's wearing but hasn't secured tightly around her body. I need to focus, but it's hard because even though we should talk, I don't know what to say to her. I can't define what happened last night. I don't really know what it means.

"Um," I start. "Do I need to take you out on a proper date?" It's only meant as a sort-of joke.

"Do you want to take me out on a date?"

"We can go to The Bay. Sam already knows, anyway."

"He knows we've slept together. As far as I know, that's all we know as well." Devon's lips are tighter than I'd like them to be—no hint of that seductive smile this morning. "What do you want, Sadie?" Her eyes are still as kind as ever, projecting that she's willing to understand whatever it is that's going on inside me. If only I knew what that was myself.

"Going with my gut... and with the memory of last night..." Can I put my hand on the patch of thigh peeking through the slit of her robe? I'm not sure. Since I'm trying to go with my gut, I do it anyway. "Last night was amazing. I'm

151

not pulling an oh-my-god-what-was-that straight-girl-with-remorse act on you. Just so we're clear."

"Okay."

"I know it sounded like a joke, but maybe going on a date is exactly what we should do." I press my fingertips into her flesh. "We should probably do it here and not go to a restaurant. I'm not sure I'm ready for that. Next week might be a little crazy and I was hoping to keep a low profile."

"Because of the season finale?"

"Yes. Even though it's only a TV show, people can go a bit batshit over things like that. All the usual unwritten rules of respecting my privacy in this town might not apply for a while."

"I don't have a problem staying indoors with you." The croak in Devon's voice is so sexy, I have to keep myself from kissing her again.

But before I do that, I need to take a little time and ask myself what this is. What I'm doing here. I need to take Devon's feelings into account, perhaps even more than I do my own.

"I'll cook you dinner," Devon says.

"Tonight?" There's no other way I'd rather spend my Saturday night than with Devon in the privacy of her house.

But Devon shakes her head. "It's Hunter and Bobby's date night. Finn's with me and I can't cancel on them this late in the day."

"Is it a problem that Finn's home?"

"It might be." Devon does smile now.

"I get it. Sunday? Monday? Tuesday?"

"Suzy's organizing a viewing party for the *King & Prince* season finale on Tuesday, in case you hadn't heard."

"I hadn't. You know more than I do about my sister and my schedule." My hand slides up Devon's thigh. "We're having an Ireland family dinner on Sunday, so... how about brunch right now? I can't wait until Monday or whenever else I might see you again."

Devon just blows some air through her nostrils. "I want to enjoy this without ambivalence. I really do, but I don't know what to think, Sadie. I don't really know what to make of this. Truthfully, I had kind of expected you to tell me it was all a mistake come morning. Instead, you're asking me out on a date and it's what I want, but I'm not sure it's mine to want..." Devon pauses. "As a hard rule, I don't date straight women. Nothing good has ever come of that. And I know we have all this history between us and this spark that seems to be driving us a little crazy, but none of that changes that I might get very hurt here, because you're not just a one-night thing to me. You can't be. There's too much attached to you still. Last night made that crystal clear."

"I hear you, Dev. I really do. But all I can offer you right now is a date and to tell you that I felt it too last night. Maybe not everything you felt because how can I possibly get inside your head to know what you're feeling? But I felt so many things. And I like you so much. As you said, there's still so much between us. So why not try?"

Devon scoffs. "Because you're here on vacation. You'll be going back to pick up your life in Hollywood in less than two months and..." She shakes her head. "Okay, I'm sorry. That was extremely lesbian of me. Thinking too long-term like that."

"Whatever this is, whatever this will or will not be, all we can do is take it one step at a time and be completely honest with each other." I find Devon's gaze. "My cards are on the table. I don't want to walk away from you. I want to see where this goes."

"I'm not going to make myself utterly miserable and say no to that, but I need a little bit of time to gather myself."

"That can be arranged." On the beach below, I see Sam heading into the water. A potentially brilliant thought occurs to me. "Do you think Finn would be okay with the most awesome babysitter tonight? Staying at a swanky beach house while he's at it? Sunset *and* sunrise surf included?"

Devon follows my gaze. "You mean Sam?"

I nod.

"It's Saturday night. I'm sure your brother has far more exciting plans than minding my son."

"You know what? I'm not so sure of that. I think spending time with Finn is the biggest gift you can give Sam right now." Even though I was quite tipsy, I remember very well what Sam told me the other night about wanting a family of his own. Some more time spent with an actual child might be exactly what he needs. "If you trust him with Finn, of course. That's really not for me to decide."

"Let me think about it. And ask Finn how he feels about it. I'll let you know."

"If we do end up dating tonight at your house, you have to let me cook for you."

Devon pulls up her eyebrows. "You? Cook for me? Don't you have a chef? Do you ever even do any cooking?"

"I do when I'm on vacation and I want to cook for you."

"Make a mess in my kitchen?"

"We could cook together, if that would make you feel more comfortable. Or..." Another lightbulb goes off in my head. "I'll hire us a private chef and wait staff. We can pretend we're in a top-class restaurant but enjoy the privacy of your home."

"You can make that happen? For tonight?" Devon looks genuinely impressed—it's a look I like on her.

"All it takes is one call to my assistant."

"Ah, so it's your assistant making it happen."

"Making things happen for me is kind of her job. She's got two months off while I'm away. Being paid handsomely to take care of my house."

Devon chuckles. "Okay. I won't say no to a taste of your lifestyle. You talk to Sam. I'll talk to Finn. Then you can woo me all night long."

"I can't wait." I scoot my hand a little higher up Devon's thigh again.

"I don't think I can get out of this chair." Devon peers at the ocean.

"Still tired from last night?" I ask, as she clasps her thighs together, denying me further access to her upper thigh.

"No. I slept really well. It's this view. I can't tear myself away from it.

I get up and wiggle myself between her and the railing. "This view, you mean?" I straddle her lap and look into her eyes.

"That view's not too bad either. A bit like watching TV on a Tuesday night."

## CHAPTER 22

# *Devon*

"Where's Finn?" It's always my first question when I arrive at Hunter and Bobby's.

"Bobby took him to the farmers market." Hunter pulls back a chair for me, as if I'm suddenly the Queen of Sheba. "Which is superb timing for this little chat you and I are going to have."

I sink into the chair and he must already be able to read it off my face. That smirk I sent Sadie after I kissed her goodbye earlier is impossible to get rid of. I shake my head because part of me still can't believe what happened last night.

"It was like magic," I utter, probably not making much sense. "And now I don't know what to do with myself."

"So, you and Sadie." Hunter waggles his eyebrows.

"We spent the night together." It even feels magical to say it, but I sense the danger of it as well. Sadie can break my heart into a million little pieces again, only this time, I'm forty years old and I have a five-year-old to take care of. I can't afford to fall apart after she's done with me.

"Oh my god." Hunter's doing a more than adequate

impression of Bobby's theatrics. "Like in, actually, you know?"

"Oh, yes. We slept together and it was... out of this world."

Hunter does a sharp intake of breath. "I knew this was going to happen. I knew you would do more than kiss on the back porch. I could sense it. There's something between you."

I'm not in the mood to call his bullshit right now. And maybe there was something palpable in the air the other night when we all had dinner together. "There's so much between us."

"Wow. I'm a bit stumped for words." Hunter drums his fingers onto the table. "What was the morning after like?"

"Pretty amazing." I'm already smitten—or smitten all over again, with a ghost from my past. "Sadie's amazing. She's..." I huff out some air. "I can't fall for her. I won't let myself."

"Maybe you shouldn't spend the night with her then." Hunter says it as though it's already a foregone conclusion that I've fallen for Sadie. Maybe I already have—or maybe he's just as besotted with her, albeit in a platonic way.

"She asked me out. She wants to hire some fancy chef to cook us dinner tonight." I look into Hunter's clear blue eyes, hoping to find some wisdom in them, or at the very least a little bit of temperance—a few moments of respite from this turmoil in my heart. "I need to check with Finn if he's okay with Sam babysitting him."

"If he's not, Bobby and I will take care of him," Hunter is very quick to say.

"It's your date night."

"Trust me. If I tell Bobby we're having Finn tonight because you're on a date with Sadie Ireland, he might just roll out a red carpet for her on the street." He taps his finger against his morning stubble. "Or maybe we can keep Sam company. Either will work for Bobby. And me." He gives a determined nod. "You're free as a bird tonight. Okay?"

"Thanks, but..."

"No, buts." He waggles his forefinger at me. "None, Dev. I mean it. Do this for yourself. Don't go thinking it to death. Just enjoy it."

"But what about..."

"That was a 'but.'"

"She's only in town for two months." I ignore his admonishment.

"Yes, and you know that. You know what you're getting into. You both do. Just be honest about what it can and can't be."

"Meaning?" It's always useful to get someone else's opinion on a matter of the heart like this.

"I know you have history, and I also know that, um, many a straight woman is ripe for the turning a bit later in life, say post-divorce, but don't go ruining this by getting your hopes up about anything too romantic. It pays to be realistic about these things."

"I'm not sure I can be very realistic when it comes to Sadie." Anyone else, maybe, but not Sadie.

"Look at it more as a vacation fling than a possible lesbian U-Haul situation."

I chuckle despite myself. "You tell that to my poor little heart."

"You're not sixteen anymore, Dev. You're a grown woman who is very capable of making informed decisions. You're a frigging life coach. Coach yourself. Apply your precious model. Do the work. Do whatever it takes, but don't deny yourself this. Just be very aware that it's temporary."

"Could you do that?"

"Of course, I could."

"That's easy enough to say. Besides, you're a man."

"You don't have to say it as though it's a deadly disease." Hunter treats me to a well-deserved eye-roll.

"You know what I mean. It's different for men. Less feelings are involved."

"It's not about not feeling the feelings. Feel them all. Gorge on them. Fill your heart with them. Just don't go expecting the impossible. That's all I'm saying."

"I suppose I could give that a try."

"You should, because what's the alternative? That you pretend Sadie's not here for the coming two months? That you ignore your night of hot lesbian passion together? Would that really be an option?"

I shake my head. All I want is to be with Sadie. To wake up next to her and head straight into the surf with her. To shower together after and tumble back into bed. To have a short-lived whirlwind fairy-tale romance with her. That much might be in the cards for me, but Hunter is right. It would be downright foolish to hope for anything more.

"Once Sadie's gone, we will still be here, darling. Finn, Bobby, and me. Your family will still be here. Your mom and dad. Your friends. Your clients. The ocean. Your life will be there to return to. But just allow yourself to be a little crazy for a while. To be that wild chick you once were. Live it up with Sadie Ireland. Look at it as a much-needed vacation for yourself as well. A vacation from your regular life. We all need a break. And you know Finn's safe with us."

As if on cue, I hear Finn's voice in the distance. He's reached that age now where he no longer rushes to throw his arms around me in the tightest of little-boy hugs after a night at his dad's.

"Hi, Mom," he just says and goes into the kitchen.

Bobby looks at me as if Madonna herself is sitting in his living room, like an apparition from the queendom of gay divas. As though all he and Hunter have done since I texted last night is speculate wildly about Sadie and me. They probably have.

## CHAPTER 23

## *Sadie*

S am joins me on the deck. He gives me a bottle of water. "Don't forget to rehydrate," He smirks at me as though he thinks he already knows everything.

We let a silence fall, although it's never really silent when you live this close to the ocean and its soothing roar.

"Do you want to talk about it?" he asks.

If not with my twin brother, then with whom? "I've asked her out on a date."

"Okaayyy."

"Which reminds me." I send my brother my sweetest smile. "How would you like to babysit the coolest five-year-old in town tonight?"

"Finn? Oh, sure. I think I can manage that. I'll get someone to cover for me at the bar." He perks up even more. "Do you need me to make myself scarce again?"

"No. The idea was to let Finn have the night of his life staying here with you. Maybe you can even take him out surfing tomorrow morning?"

"Devon's okay with that?"

"Yes, I think so. She was going to ask Finn if he was up for it and let me know."

"I know he's her kid, but she can be a little protective of him. Especially when it comes to surfing. Never mind that I was already teaching kids how to surf when I was only eighteen."

"I think I've managed to convince her that you are trustworthy."

"I am, you know." He suddenly sounds serious.

"I know you are." I send him a grin. "Maybe turning forty has changed us both. Maybe it's a twin thing."

"For your information, I haven't suddenly developed feelings for another man. I wouldn't have an issue with it if I had, but it hasn't happened to me yet."

"Bobby will be very sad to hear it," I joke.

"Tell him maybe once I turn fifty." My brother enjoys flirty attention from females and males alike.

"Maybe I'll just keep that to myself." I bump my heel against his shin. "Thanks for agreeing to babysit Finn tonight."

"He will have the night of this life. Make sure to tell Devon that her son might express reluctance to go home on Sunday."

"She'll be delighted to hear that, I'm sure."

"So..." he says.

"So?"

"You asked Devon on a date. It wasn't a one-off, then?"

"How could it ever be a one-time thing with her? It feels utterly impossible. She's just... so amazing. She's so cool, oh my god." I realize I sound like a teenager again.

"I don't want to play devil's advocate, but, um, could it be that you're caught in some sort of nostalgic trap? Like your mind has traveled back in time and you and Devon might look like you're both forty but you're acting like sixteen-year-olds?"

"Did you know that she was completely in love with me when we were sixteen?"

"I didn't, but it would explain a lot."

I figure I can tell Sam now. Not because I owe him an explanation, but because of what happened between Devon and me last night—and what might still happen.

"She was in love with me and, one day, she tried to kiss me. I was such a bitch to her." Even though Devon has explicitly said she has forgiven me, I'm not sure I've completely forgiven myself. "I slapped her across the face."

"Damn. What did you do that for?"

"Hell if I know. All I know is that I let it ruin our beautiful friendship."

"Poor Dev."

"So maybe what you just implied does have some truth to it. It is a trip down memory lane to be with her. But it's not just that... It's like I can't keep away from her. I'm already counting down the minutes to tonight and she's only just left."

"You had a lot of good times together. Part of you is probably remembering that. The part of you that's been reluctant to revisit that time in your life... Maybe, well, you know... Dad was great and he did his best, but it wasn't always easy growing up without Mom."

"Not only that she wasn't there, but that she clearly didn't want to be there. I think that messed me up most of all. Our own mother didn't want us. That's what it boils down to."

Sam goes silent the way Dad does sometimes.

"Look, Sadie," he says after a while. "I know I'm not one to talk. I know I've broken a few hearts in my time and maybe that's why I'm saying this, but, be gentle with Devon. Don't play her."

"I don't want to play her. I don't even know what it means to play someone."

"Don't just take what you can get from your... dalliance. Take her feelings into consideration."

"I will. I do. I *am* conflicted about this, but given the choice between thinking that I shouldn't pursue this just because I've always believed I'm straight, and simply going for it because it feels so damn good... it's not a hard choice to make."

"Maybe not for you, but stop to consider that it might be very different for her."

"I honestly don't think that what I feel for Devon is very different than what she feels for me."

"Really?" I understand the incredulity in Sam's tone.

"Yes. I can't explain it, and, at this point, I don't think I have to. I just want to feel it. I want to enjoy it. It's been a rough year and being with Devon is just so joyful and also, still, after all these years, strangely familiar. I feel safe with her. Like when I was young, and stayed at her house on the weekend when we were still friends and we had these sleepovers and I'd wake up in the night and it was so easy to pretend I had a mother again because Devon's mother was just down the hall."

"Sounds to me that has more to do with Mom than with Devon."

I shake my head. Maybe I've said too much but to my credit, I had to articulate this out loud for myself as well before realizing it might be true.

"The divorce has left you a little vulnerable. I get that. You wouldn't be in Clearwater Bay if it hadn't."

"What do you mean?" I know what he means. I haven't

come home nearly enough since landing the part of Leona King, despite Clearwater Bay being in California and not a million miles from Hollywood.

"You're hankering for some long-lost feeling of home," Sam says.

"Maybe."

"This is not a reproach. I'm glad you're here. Like really, truly, genuinely. It's so cool to spend time with you. Dad might not be the one to tell you in so many words, but he's very happy about that as well. And Suzy, well, she's Suzy, you know?"

"I'm glad to be here." I hope that in twin-speak it translates to 'I'm sorry I left.' "I've only been here a week and I can barely imagine ever going back to LA. I didn't know it was going to be so wonderful to be back here for a longer period of time."

"Apart from the fact that your siblings are awesome and the surf is always great, perhaps that has something to do with a certain Double D."

"Oh no." I bang my foot onto Sam's calf hard enough so he winces. "Don't call her that." Double D was a nickname the hormonally frustrated boys in high school gave Devon.

"I'm only reminiscing. Just like you."

All I have in response to that is another kick against my brother's leg because, of course, he's right about my stay in Clearwater Bay being so wonderful in a large part thanks to Devon.

---

The circumstances are not ideal just yet. I've had to ask Devon to retreat upstairs while I show the caterers I've hired around her kitchen. I don't want her to have to do anything but show up and enjoy herself.

The people my assistant has arranged to cook and serve us a first-class meal are nothing but professionals who have brought everything they need—and are much more proficient in figuring out how an oven works than I am.

"You can come down now," I yell up the stairs.

"I'll be ready in five minutes."

"I'm going to pretend I'm arriving in five minutes then." It's all a bit silly, and I was already feeling so giddy.

"Good thing you're an actor," Devon shouts down, making me chuckle.

I wait on the back porch because I'm not going to stand outside Devon's front door all dolled up for everyone to see.

Then, finally, we're ready for our date.

Devon walks out. She's wearing a pair of hip-hugging pants with an emerald-green top that makes her hair look like it's on fire. "Wow. Is that the real Sadie Ireland?" she says when she rakes her gaze over me. "You glam up quite nicely."

"Not half as much as you." I bridge the distance between us. Already, I want to kiss her. But I'm also pretending we're in an actual restaurant. Let's see how long I can keep that up.

"Meaning that I look quite shabby most of the time?" The lines bracketing Devon's lips deepen deliciously when she smiles like that.

"You could have turned up in your wetsuit and that would have been fine with me."

"It's not the most date-friendly." Devon takes a step closer. "Hi. Lovely to see you again." She kisses me ever so gently on the cheek.

"And you." I stare into her eyes for a split second. What I said to Sam earlier was the honest-to-god truth. I truly believe what I feel for Sadie is no less than what she feels for me, because how can she possibly have more butterflies doing somersaults in her stomach than me right now?

A server appears in the doorway. "Would you like to have drinks out here?" he asks.

"Sure." Devon's patio table is already covered with a linen cloth.

"I'd invite you to sit on the doorstep with me again," Devon says, "but who knows where that would end?"

I erupt into a chuckle. The flirting is well and truly on. I can only conclude that Devon's up for this as much as I am, despite the trepidations we could have about it all.

CHAPTER 24

*Devon*

S adie looks stunning in a low-cut blazer with what looks like nothing much underneath, I can't keep my eyes off her. She looks every inch the glamorous prime-time TV star—no longer the casual version of herself. She has dressed to impress—perhaps even to seduce.

I've turned over Hunter's words in my head and have concluded he's right. I need to take what I can get from whatever this is—an irresistibly sexy cocktail of teenage nostalgia and acute re-infatuation—and then be ready to move on. In my head, it makes perfect sense. I'm just not sure yet how exactly it's going to work out in real life, with a real-life Sadie sitting across from me, looking like the most beautiful woman on earth, with all her attention focused only on me.

I sip from the glass of champagne that's just been topped up by a waiter who walks around my house as though it's his own. The experience is a touch unsettling, but then I look at Sadie, and I forget about the chef and sous-chef in my kitchen and the sommelier decanting the wine he will serve us later that will match the dishes that are being prepared.

Earlier, when I dropped off a hyperactive Finn at Sam's,

a little trepidatious because Sadie's brother is a life-long bachelor without any childcare experience, he looked at me all funny again, but he couldn't say anything because of Finn.

"Has Sam said anything?" I ask.

"Sam has said many things." Sadie shoots me a smile. Maybe she forgot she's not in Hollywood tonight, because it's so dazzling I almost forget what I just asked her. "He's confused." Sadie does a one-shouldered shrug. "I can hardly blame him for that."

"I think everyone's a bit confused at the moment."

"Strangely," Sadie says, tilting her head, "I don't feel very confused. I feel excited and a little light-headed and as though anything is possible."

"Can we have a cards-on-the-table moment?" If I don't say what I want to say now, I fear I might become too swayed by Sadie's charm to mention it later.

"Of course." When she leans forward, I get a glimpse into her blazer. Is she even wearing a bra underneath? I'm getting a little hot under the collar already.

"What we talked about this morning. About taking things one step at a time and being as honest as possible with each other along the way..."

Sadie nods.

"I'm going to say a very big yes to that, because... Well, because I really want to. I want to do this with you, Sadie. I want to be on this date with you and I want to surf with you every day as long as you're here and I want to get to know you again. I want all of those things, but I'm also being realistic. For that reason, I won't involve Finn in this all too much. Because no matter what this turns into, you'll be leaving at the end of it and I'm perfectly willing to be your vacation fling, your summer romance in idyllic Clearwater Bay. I'm down for that, but I don't want Finn to grow attached to you in the same way that I might."

"Um, okay." Sadie glances away. When she looks at me again, she narrows her eyes. "So you're planning to grow quite attached to me?"

"There's a distinct possibility of that happening. You're quite hard to resist." I make eyes at her cleavage. "Give a girl a chance at least."

"This old thing." Sadie sits there grinning as though she knows very well what that blazer would do to me. "I wear this all the time."

"I bet you do." A server appears at the table, presenting us with some amuse-bouches. "That waiter must be quite beside himself by now," I say, once he's gone. "What if he secretly snaps a picture of us?"

"First of all, no one I hire is going to do that. We make sure of it. But, secondly, what if he did? We're just two old friends having dinner." To prove her point, she reaches for one of the fancy nibbles and pops it into her mouth. "Oh my god. This is so good."

"If Finn spoke with his mouth full like that, I would tell him off."

"Try it." Sadie has swallowed her food. "Then try to judge me again."

"I'm hardly judging." I eat the amuse-bouche while trying to remember what the server had to say about it, but too much of my attention was focused on Sadie. "Hm." I make a spectacle of groaning low in my throat.

"You sound a bit like you did last night," Sadie says.

She's not giving me a chance at all. The date has only started and she's already come out all guns blazing. I blame our history together. All the time we spent together as teenagers and the indestructible common ground that creates.

173

I might have been an only child, but there were times, before I fell in love with her, that it felt like I had a sister, that's how close we were.

"You're going there already?" Two can play that game. "That's bold." I had expected Sadie to be much more bashful about her first time with a woman—with *me*—but she talks about it as though it's nothing out of the ordinary.

"Where else am I going to go?" Sadie exhales deeply. "To reply properly to what you said earlier." She leans over the table. "I want to do this with you too, Dev. I want you. Do you think it can be as simple as that?"

"Fuck, no. There's nothing simple about it, but we're both adults. We can both acknowledge what this is."

Sadie draws up her eyebrows. "What would that be?"

"Two old friends… rediscovering each other."

Sadie nods. "Agreed, but earlier you spoke as though whatever might grow between us already has a definite finality to it. As though our friendship will have to end again when I go back to work. Why do you feel that way?"

"I'm not saying our friendship has to end. But what we did last night is not that common among people who are just friends."

"Very true." She sips from her champagne, but her gaze remains firmly locked on mine. "But I work in LA, not the North Pole. You can fly there in an hour."

"That might be so, but… what are you saying? What are we even talking about here?"

"Honestly, I don't really know. I just wanted to go on a date with you. To see what would happen if we did."

"And here we are." Maybe I shouldn't have brought it up. Maybe I should have been more casual about it as Sadie clearly is. Still, I feel like it's different for me.

"I sort of know what you're getting at," Sadie says. "I do,

but let's just go with the flow. Let's just enjoy ourselves, because I am enjoying myself. That's the thing. I always enjoy myself when I'm with you. Always have and I still do now."

Sadie really is pulling out all the stops, saying all the right things. If she keeps this up, I'll be completely in love with her again come tomorrow morning. Then how will I be able to remain realistic about the whole thing?

———

We've moved inside for the appetizers. My dining room looks almost unrecognizable as the backdrop for the bunches of flowers and carefully placed chandeliers that don't belong to me.

The champagne has gone to my head, as expected, but, that too, I will just enjoy. It gives me the courage to ask what I'm about to ask.

"Can we go back in time about twenty-four years?"

Sadie just nods, as though she knows that what I'm about to ask is not something she's going to be able to charm herself out of that easily.

"When I kissed you that day... I get now that it came as a surprise to you. That we were on totally different wavelengths, but I couldn't see that because I was too deep in the throes of my teenage infatuation with you. But, um, why did you slap me like that? It was quite the aggressive reaction."

"I know. I'm so sorry, Dev. I wish I knew, but I don't remember. I can only speculate as to why I responded so appallingly."

"Please, do."

Sadie huffs out some air. "There could have been so many reasons. Maybe... I wasn't even that disgusted by your kiss,

175

but I was disgusted with myself for not being disgusted with it. Times were different then."

I shake my head. I'm not buying what she's trying to sell. "Surely if that had been the case, you would have started talking to me again eventually." In the end, it wasn't Sadie's slap that hurt me the most; it was losing my best friend—and the girl I loved more than anyone else.

"My teens were not the easiest time. When I was sixteen, Suzy had just left home and even though she was only three years older than us, she did kind of take responsibility for Sam and me. She tried to mother us a bit in the absence of our real mother. Not that it's an excuse, but it was tough sometimes."

"You don't need an excuse for what you did, Sadie. I was just curious if you'd given it any thought over the years." I remember asking my mom where Sadie's mom had gone and, if she hadn't died, why Sadie no longer had a mom like all the other kids we knew.

"Not all that much, to be perfectly honest. I've come to accept it as just one of those things in life that happen, for whatever reason. I've wondered, though, how our friendship might have evolved if it hadn't been destroyed that day. Whether we'd still be friends now. What our twenties would have been like. We might have even gone to college together. Who knows?"

"Or to Hollywood."

"You'd make for a super sexy TV detective. All the lesbian viewers would go totally gaga for you and your tattoos. I can just see it now. You in one of Leona's leather jackets, sleeves rolled up, and a gun strapped to your hip."

"Packing heat?" Sadie probably doesn't get the double entendre. Oh, damn. Now my mind has gone there and I can see *that* happening.

"This is America."

"What's it really like, though? To walk around with one of the most recognizable faces in the country?"

"It's not too bad, although fame can be a pretty toxic by-product of being an actor. I love acting. I love disappearing into a character, becoming a different person for a while. But, of course, I'd be lying if I said I wasn't also a little addicted to the celebrity part of things. The money. The many doors that open just like that. Just because I play a character on a TV show. As if that makes me so special." A soft smile plays on her lips. "Mike and I used to talk about this endlessly. It was our go-to topic. It was also something we had in common. We grew into the whole thing together and it made for a lot of bonding opportunities before we got together. Even though I didn't want to be with him anymore, and the feeling was quite mutual, I did lose one of my best friends in the divorce."

I'm a little too familiar with that grueling feeling of losing a best friend, but I'm not about to start wallowing in the same old self-pity again. I want to hear more about Sadie and her recent bout of heartache.

"I was talking about this with Sam earlier," Sadie continues. "It's been a tough year, emotionally. Divorcing someone you once loved so very much is difficult and complex. Although I was relieved when it was finally all over, it also made me feel like a failure for not being able to make it work."

"Maybe..." This is what I do for a living and it's not something I can just turn off. "There's another way of looking at it." I take a moment to gauge Sadie's face, to check if she's receptive to me putting on my life coach hat. "Yes, it's painful. Life's painful sometimes. But what you consider to be a failure is not something you did wrong. It's just something that happened because of circumstances. Because of life. It's a by-product of living, like pain. That doesn't make it a failure, because what did you do wrong except live your life?"

"Are you *therapizing* me?" She paints on a smirk.

"I'm merely asking a question." I'm familiar with this kind of resistance. "Inviting you to take a different, perhaps more helpful perspective."

"You must have dozens of clients who are madly in love with you."

I can't help but laugh. Sadie does that to me. "I really don't think so."

"Oh, Dev. In that case, you have no idea of the effect you have on people. How can they not fall for you?"

"Most of them are straight women, so..." Again, I can't help but follow up with a chuckle.

"Touché." Sadie smiles back at me. "And I imagine that the majority of them weren't your best friend in high school."

"Correct." The spell of the moment is broken by the entrée being served. Grilled halibut with tomatoes prepared three ways.

"You only coach women?"

I nod.

"No men allowed?" Sadie asks.

"Men generally don't need deprogramming from the patriarchy's influence as much as women do. Although the patriarchy is harmful for men as well, because of all the toxic male supposed ideals they have to live up to." I don't want to launch into a rant against the patriarchy—god knows where that will end?—so I just look at Sadie, at how she spears a morsel of fish onto her fork and glances at it, but her gaze is pulled away, and it very much seems as though she can't stop looking at me either. When I'm with Sadie, the patriarchy and all the ways in which it has kept women down, might as well never even have existed.

## CHAPTER 25

# Sadie

"**W**hy did you become a life coach?" When we were growing up, I was always convinced Devon would become a professional surfer.

"A *feminist* life coach," Devon corrects me—always with that irresistible smile on her face, though. "Because women are suffering. So many women, even in the so-called liberal West, suffer from anxiety, not feeling good enough, imposter syndrome, mental health issues, because of how we're still, even in this day and age, being brought up and socialized to please and do so many things we don't want to do without knowing it. And I want to help. I want to let these women know that it doesn't have to be that way. That life can be amazing and rewarding instead of crippling and exhausting. And even more so, when something bad happens in life, which is pretty much inevitable, we can also handle that, because there isn't anything we can't handle. It's my life's mission."

The passion in Devon's words in infectious. She gets the same sparkle in her eyes as when she talks about Finn.

"Maybe I should sign up." I'm only half joking. My life could do with some serious coaching these days.

"You already get to sleep with me," Devon says, and I nearly spit out the sip of wine I just took.

"Do I?" I say once I've recovered from her forwardness.

"You already successfully seduced me once."

"Excuse me, but last night, *you* kissed *me*."

"It's not about who kisses who first, Sadie. It's about all the things you said about me. How kind and cool and sexy I was. And, not to forget, a much better surfer than you."

"Not a word of a lie except about the surfing." Devon is much better at it than me, but it's not a competition—and I've got my flirt all the way on.

Devon's phone beeps and something about her changes instantly. Her face becomes a little drawn and her entire body stiffens. She did leave her son in my brother's care.

When she looks at the screen, a gorgeous smile blooms on her lips. "Finn really is having the time of his life." She shows me a picture of Finn riding a wave close to the shore.

"Sam said you shouldn't be surprised if he doesn't want to come home tomorrow."

"I haven't always been fair to Sam. Probably because he's your brother." Devon quickly texts something back, then, visibly relieved, puts her phone away. "He's always been such a reminder of you. Even last summer, when Sam was still giving surfing lessons, Finn really wanted to take a few lessons with him, but I wouldn't let him. There was this resistance inside me that I couldn't get past. I can so clearly see now that it was still about you."

"I'm sure Sam will happily give Finn daily private lessons at no charge whatsoever."

"I'd only agree because it's always helpful to have more

than one teacher, not because any Ireland is better than me on a surfboard."

"That goes without saying." I glance at my empty dessert plate. The food and service have been excellent, but I hope the caterers leave soon. I want to be alone with Devon.

"Shall we go surfing tomorrow evening?" Devon asks.

"How about tomorrow morning?" I counter.

Devon pulls her lips into a lopsided grin and gives a slow nod. "I don't know, Sadie. I think I'd better ask you that again in the morning." She cocks her head. "That's only in case you were planning to stay the night, of course. I wouldn't want to assume." She peers deep into my eyes. "We haven't even kissed yet."

"I was waiting for the caterers to leave." It wouldn't exactly be like kissing in public. And maybe it would be good practice for when I do—if I ever kiss Devon in public.

"I get that, but I just want to put it out there that I'm more than ready to be kissed." She's taunting me. Even though I'm a little hesitant, I'm also very tempted.

"All right. You are the lady of the house and your house, your rules."

"Good to know." Devon pushes her chair back. "Come here." How did this escalate so quickly? We were just talking about her work, about her son, and now she's beckoning me over to her lap?

I get up and walk toward her, trying to block the hushed noises from the kitchen from my mind.

Devon holds her arms wide. I do as I did this morning on Sam's deck. I sit astride her legs.

"Hey," Devon whispers and brings her hands to the back of my head. "There you are."

A bomb could go off in the kitchen now for all I care and I wouldn't even notice. All I see and hear and smell is Devon.

My brain is flooded with memories from last night. I want to taste her again. I want her fingers inside of me again. I want to kiss every last inch of all those tattoos. There's no room in my mind to question why I want all of these things. There's only Devon, who's pulling me closer, who's about to kiss me again.

Our lips touch and everything else falls away. There's only the two of us and the memory of the wonderful evening we've had so far. Snippets of conversation. Images of her sexy, seductive smile on the back of my eyelids. Her fingertips press into my flesh. Even though we just had a three-course meal, Devon's still hungry—hungry for me.

When we break from the kiss, Devon looks up at me with so much desire in her eyes, I'm of half a mind to drag her upstairs already, but we can't just disappear on the people cleaning up her kitchen like that. Or can we?

Devon doesn't look as though she is preoccupied with any of this. Maybe because she isn't a famous actor presumed straight by the outside world—and perhaps also, still, for a large part by herself.

"I want you," she whispers and although her voice is low, it's full of purpose and lust. She pulls me close to her again. "I really, really want you, Sadie."

"I want you too," I reply. "But I should probably say goodbye to the caterers. Don't you think?"

"Of course." Devon's demeanor remains unperturbed. She looks so sexy, so in control of everything. It makes a shiver run all the way up my spine. "Just tell them to close the door behind them when they leave."

Maybe it's because we're at Devon's home, or because we had an actual date with all the foreboding and innuendo that comes with that, but tonight feels very different than last night, which was much more impromptu. Moreover, tonight, it won't be my first time with a woman anymore. I already know what it feels like now—divine, thrilling, and oh-so satisfying—and I most definitely want to do it again.

"I'll be right back." Before I go into the kitchen, I kiss Devon on the lips.

It does feel a little awkward when I find the person in charge. What am I supposed to say? We're going upstairs now, but thank you so much for all your work?

"We're ready, Mrs. Ireland." Now would not be a good time to tell him I'm no longer a Mrs. "It was a pleasure to cook for you and your friend."

As I say goodbye, I make a mental note to tell my assistant to include a generous tip when she pays the catering crew. Having to face them does give me pause, though, because how can it not? I might be all turned on and more than ready to jump into bed with Devon again, but none of it feels like it's part of the real world—of my real life.

My real life is in Malibu where I spend most of my time in my trailer on the *King & Prince* set, where I used to be married to my male co-star. Where my agent, Leslie, might very well have a heart attack if she finds out about what I've been up to during my vacation, even though it's none of her business—but that's easy enough to say. My image is her business. Although something has shifted in Hollywood since Ida Burton and Faye Fleming came out as a couple. Little did I know, when I saw that iconic picture of the two of them kissing at the premiere of the movie they made together, that I might find myself in a similar position one day.

"Is everything okay?" Devon has walked into the kitchen.

"Fine." All my doubts melt away at the sight of Devon. All those years ago, I might have slapped her—for a myriad of reasons that I'm sure seemed valid to me at the time—but Devon is no longer that girl who tried to kiss me. She is a grown-ass, breathtaking woman with a heart of gold and a glance so shimmering with desire for me right now, I go a little weak at the knees. So it's easy enough, like earlier when we kissed, to push any thoughts of my 'real life' from my mind and just focus on Devon and enjoy this, whatever it is, while it lasts.

"Come." Devon reaches for my hand and leads me upstairs. Minutes later, I'm in her bedroom again, but the circumstances are entirely different from last time I was here —when her son waltzed in on my hangover and I had no clue of what was happening. I know, in every cell of my body, what's going to happen in this room, in this bed, tonight.

Devon reaches for the top button of my blazer. She shakes her head. "How dare you show up for our date like this?" She undoes the button. "How am I supposed to react when you're not wearing anything underneath this jacket?"

"Exactly like this," I manage to say.

Devon makes quick work of the remaining buttons and in a matter of seconds, my blazer is sliding down my arms.

I hear her sharp intake of breath. It's been many years since I've had that effect on someone in the bedroom—that I've taken another person's breath away. The sensation fills me with even more desire, but also with a shot of confidence. With the feeling that, perhaps, I was meant to come back home and do this with Devon. The inevitability of it is becoming crystal clear to me.

I snake my fingers up her arms, along the flowers tattooed on her skin. Devon kisses me again and this time I'm naked from the waist up and my nipples grow hard instantly. Devon pulls back for a moment and takes the opportunity to hoist her top over her head. We're not wasting any time, then. I get it. If she's as hot for me as I am for her right now, there is no time to waste. Unlike last night, when things got a little emotional and we were exhausted after trying to best each other in the waves, tonight, we have all night. There isn't an inch of Devon's body I don't intend to explore tonight. I want all of her, all night long.

She unhooks her bra and I'm a little floored by the sight of her naked breasts again, by the vulnerability it injects into the air to stand half-naked in front of each other like this. She comes for my pants next.

"I need you naked," she whispers in my ear as she guides my pants down my legs. "Now." Devon hooks a finger underneath the waistband of my panties.

It doesn't take long for us to crash naked onto the bed. Devon's kisses are ravenous, her tongue demanding, her hands grasping for, it seems, all of me at once.

"I need you," she says on a desperate sigh, before kissing her way down to my breasts. Her touch is less gentle than last night, but it suits the mood—and it matches my own desire. As though she knows this is how it needs to be right now, after our delicious date.

The touch of her tongue on my nipple is soft, however, and exhilarating, and more than deft enough to light the entire expanse of my skin on fire. As her lips move across my belly, I know what's happening to her—because it's happening to me, too. She's overtaken with desire. It's consuming her like an unbearable thirst that can only be quenched by having me. By making me come. Competent and divine as they were, I don't think she'll only be using her fingers this time. I spread for her, for Devon, for this exquisite woman I might very well be falling in love with.

Her lips hover over my inner thighs already. The Devon who's always so collected and patient has exited the building —granted, it was a bit cruel to taunt her all night with only that low-cut jacket on and have her dream of what was hiding underneath, so close yet so unattainable, until now. She has all of me now and I don't mind one bit that Devon's patience has run out. I find her gaze. Her hair fans out over my hips. She looks like a lioness about to devour her prey. Then, her eyelids snap shut and the next thing I feel is her tongue between my legs and *my* breath is taken away.

Devon licks me, and I lose myself with every flick of her tongue. My body seems weightless and I give myself to her. I give her my body, my arousal, my climax, but also a little piece of myself I deemed inaccessible after the heartbreak of my failed relationship—I give her a little piece of my heart.

CHAPTER 26

## Devon

Sadie has just come for me and I'm a little beside myself. I got a little carried away peeling that blazer off her. Frankly, I don't remember all that much since the moment she bared her breasts to me. I do know her orgasm was more than adequate because of the tight clasp of her thighs against my cheeks.

She's smiling when I move up to her, when we lie face-to-face and I run a fingertip across her jawline. "Did you ask that chef to put something in my food?" I joke. "Some magic aphrodisiac powder or something like that?"

"Only to serve a delicious meal to a delicious woman." Sadie chuckles. "Damn, Dev. Phew."

"I got a little carried away."

"That's more than okay with me." She presses her belly against mine.

"You do something to me. I can't really explain it."

"You don't have to explain it." Sadie kisses the tip of my nose.

"I kind of feel like I do."

Sadie brings the back of her hand to my forehead. "Shut off your analytical brain. We're not here for analyzing."

"What are we here for then?" It's easy enough to comply with Sadie's wishes, but so much for protecting my heart—for keeping a realistic perspective on this. If I don't keep my wits about me, if I stop analyzing altogether and just start feeling things, then I'll start losing control of myself in the way that I did just now. I can't have that. Doing what I do, I know very well that control is an illusion and it most certainly isn't the solution to a lot of things, but with Sadie, I feel like I'm walking a tightrope and the ground beneath is very far away.

"We're here for this." She kisses my neck while she traces her fingertip between my breasts. My nipples stand to attention. Already, I'm more than willing to give up the very last ounce of control I might still possess. I want her with a desire —with a wish to abandon all the processes I need in place to protect myself—so fierce, it takes over everything.

She kisses her way up my cheek and finds my lips. I wrap my arms around her before letting my hand slide down to her luscious behind. We kiss and my clit throbs with lust for her, for us, for a never-ending repetition of nights like this. For endless date nights with Sadie. For arriving at the beach and her being the first thing I see, and my heart jumping all the way into my throat the way it used to.

She groans into my mouth a little, as though she never wants to stop kissing me. I hold onto her for dear life because it's not even midnight yet and I already know my plan has completely failed—perhaps because it was a foolish plan to begin with. Because I am already being realistic. This is real and Sadie all over me like this is all I've ever wanted. It will be real when she leaves, or when she realizes she's not into women—not into me—as much as she thought she was. Or when her agent comes calling and tells her it would be very bad optics to be seen with another woman all the time. Or whatever other reason she might find for breaking my heart again.

That will be very real as well and, maybe, I need another strategy for all this future heartache. Maybe I need to take as much as I can get from her now. At least then, I will have had it; I will have had her. Because I know she's all mine right now, at least for tonight. For that reason, I don't intend to sleep a wink. I will need every second to drink in all I can of Sadie. To make her come at my fingertips time and time again —and have her do the same to me until my body is so exhausted, so empty, I will have no choice but to take a break.

Her fingers have reached the apex of my thighs. They're so close to my wildly pulsing center I might very well explode if she doesn't touch me soon. But Sadie is a tease—maybe you have to be that way when you become an actor—and she lightly trails her fingertip around my clit. I can barely feel it yet it resonates all the way into the tiniest cells of my body.

"Please," I beg. Tease me all night long but give me this right now, I want to say, but my voice will surely no longer cooperate—too many words to string together for the state I'm in.

Sadie gazes at me and all I see in her face is awe, as though she can't believe any of this is happening, yet the fact that it is, is an utter delight to her. I wish I could take a picture of her face right now, to remember this moment forever. She's so beautiful but that's not all it is. It's as if she can read me some-how, as if she sees something inside me I have been unwilling to see for a long time.

With her eyes on me, Sadie's finger skates down, into my wetness, and something does change in her face now, into more an expression of wonder than of awe.

Yes, I want to scream, this is all your doing, but I need all my energy to keep it together. I don't want to fall apart like I did last night. I'm not ashamed of it and I can surely see the beauty in it, but I don't want that kind of heaviness for us tonight, nor what it might imply—that I've gone and fallen head over heels for Sadie already.

She slips her finger inside me. The corners of her mouth twitch. Her eyelids flutter. I can't stop watching her. Sadie's reaction to what she's doing to me is as much of a thrill as what her fingers are causing between my legs. Maybe she's acting right now. Maybe that's why she's able to keep looking at me in this most intimate moment, when she pushes herself inside me, but I honestly don't think so. I think she can't look away. Neither can I. Sadie's face has always been a delight to look at—a face needs something special, a certain *je ne sais quoi* and an undeniable watchable quality if it's going to star in one of the most popular and long-running TV shows of all time.

Sadie's face is the opposite of bland. The slant of her nose alone is enough to keep you guessing. It's not Hollywood-perfect. It's a little uneven, crooked even, and it lends her face so much character because it contrasts with the dark wells of her eyes, which are so fucking perfect, I'd like to drown in them right now.

Oh fuck. She slides out of me, leaving me breathless again —and wanting much more—and adds another finger. She drives her fingers inside me and her mouth opens as though she wants to say something. I'm waiting with bated breath, with all my muscles contracted, ready to relax for her, if only she will give me a sign. But Sadie doesn't say anything. She just flicks the tip of her tongue over her lower lip and because I've been staring at her so intently it's as though I can feel her tongue on me as well as her fingers.

Then my hunger for her becomes too much. I let go. I close my eyes and all I feel are her fingers inside me, pushing me to that blissful edge. Coming at Sadie's fingers is one of the biggest delights of my life so far. The climax shudders through me, leaving my muscles incapacitated for a while.

She gently withdraws her fingers and puts her warm hand on my belly.

There's not a hint of smugness on her face when I open my eyes. Only, I like to imagine, love. Although my brain, which is slowly coming to again, knows it's not love, but we're hardly friends with benefits either. My time with Sadie is way too intense for us to be qualified as that.

She nuzzles my neck, then kisses me on the cheek. "Jesus, Dev," she whispers. "I don't want to spoil the mood, but I think we're going to have to talk about our feelings sometime soon."

Then I show her how I feel about her—again—by pulling her close and kissing her firmly on the lips.

## CHAPTER 27
## *Sadie*

My muscles ache in places I didn't even know I had them. A faint headache pulses at the back of my skull. A clear sign I didn't get enough sleep last night—but I got plenty of other things in return. Devon all over me all night, exactly how I wanted her.

"Hey." She has only opened her eyes to slits and she's reaching for me again. "Have you checked the weather yet? Someone said she wanted to go surfing this morning."

"How about we catch the sunset surf tonight?" Devon's warm, soft body next to mine is irresistible. I press myself against her.

Devon pulls me close. "Sure. If my legs are not too jittery from all the times you made me come."

A warm glow blooms in my chest. I run a hand along her side but stop just before I reach her breast.

"I'm just going to check my phone to see if there's any news from Sam and Finn," Devon says.

I'm curious to talk to my brother later today—to see if his fervent family-with-child wish still holds up after some extended time with a five-year-old.

"Nothing from Sam. We're good." Devon collapses onto her back again. I push myself up on my elbows and look at her—I could do this for a good long while, just taking in every last detail of her face in the soft morning light.

I'm just about to kiss her again—because feeling her lips on mine is also something I can't get enough of—when her phone beeps.

Instantly, tension is visible on her face. Sam should really have a frank conversation with Devon before he decides to have kids—about the constant state of alert.

Devon reaches for her phone. "It's from Hunter." Devon reads the message. "I'll spare you the obscenities, but Sam has invited him and Bobby to brunch at his house. He's asking if we want to join."

In Malibu, I get invited to brunch or something like it almost every weekend, yet this spur-of-the-moment invitation feels so different. There's no hidden agenda—apart from Hunter and Bobby wanting to know all the details about what Devon and I have been up to, obviously. It's just family and friends gathering for an impromptu meal. Maybe that's what I've missed the most since Mike moved out—that feeling of belonging to something more than just myself. A clan. A crew. A tight group of friends. Family. Sam might tease me mercilessly when I see him next, but I wouldn't have it any other way.

"I completely understand if you want to see Finn," I say, even though it will probably mean Devon leaving much sooner than I want her to.

"About what I said last night." She brushes a strand of hair behind my ear and her finger lingers. "About wanting to keep you separate from Finn..."

"I get it." My heart sinks a little at the prospect of all of them having brunch together without me. "It's better for Finn."

"Maybe we should skip brunch." Devon's fingertip skates along the edge of my ear.

"That works for me as well." Sam will have plenty of opportunity to embarrass me at dinner with Dad and Suzy tonight—which reminds me that I should tell Suzy about Devon and me. This is a small town, and I don't want my sister to hear from Sam, or anyone else, that I'm sleeping with her boss.

"Maybe we should have that talk, because my body needs a little rest." She smiles up at me. The light hits her eyes and it's the most angelic sight I've seen in a long time, maybe ever.

"Or just hang out." I'm afraid if we do have a conversation about our feelings I might say something that I shouldn't, that is untoward somehow because of who she is, and who I am.

"How do you feel?" Devon asks.

"No regrets." I lower myself toward her, so I can kiss her lips again—I did get interrupted on my earlier try.

"Last night," Devon keeps talking instead of accepting my kiss. "You said that we should talk about our feelings sooner rather than later."

In response, I do kiss her, and of course she kisses me back. Our lips still touching, I play dumb. "Did I really say that?"

Devon nods. "You did."

"It's funny, because we'd already done so much talking by then. An entire date's worth of deep conversation."

"Flirting you mean." Devon pulls her lips into that glorious smile of hers. Her eyes twinkle with delight—or is it something else?

"I can't seem to help myself when I'm with you."

"Do you want to spend the day together?" Devon asks. "No pressure."

"I would like that very much." That sinking feeling from earlier has made way for one of pure joy at the prospect. "I just have dinner at my dad's tonight. Unless you want to come?"

"You want to take me home to meet your family already?" Devon snickers. "That's bold."

"Maybe it's a little soon. I should talk to Suzy first."

"You want to tell your sister about us?" Devon quirks up her eyebrows.

"I feel like I should. Sam knows and it's not that he can't keep a secret, but I know how these things can go. Does that make you uncomfortable because you work with her?"

"But, Sadie..." Devon squints at me. "What are you going to tell her?"

"That you and I have become... *rather* well acquainted again."

"I think she already knows that." It's hard not to notice how a hint of tension has crept into Devon's expression again.

"Do you think I shouldn't tell her?"

"That we're sleeping together?" Devon rakes her fingers through my hair. "You've only been back a week. Do you really want to ruffle all those feathers?"

"I hadn't thought of it that way. I just want to be able to have a conversation with my sister without hiding important things from her."

"I don't mind that you tell her, but news can spread fast. I'm not saying Suzy's going to blab and neither will Sam. But maybe you need to ask yourself if you can live with the news of us sleeping together being all over town—and it spreading from there."

That does take me aback. In that case, I'd need to tell Dad

as well. Or would I? It's nobody's business and gossip is just gossip. I've had lies printed about me on a regular basis for the past fifteen years. After a while, you just learn to live with it. The biggest difference is that news of my affair with Devon would not be a lie.

"Could *you* live with it?" I ask, stalling.

Devon shrugs. "Of course, but it's different for me. I don't have an image to uphold. Everyone knows I'm a lesbian."

"When I'm with you I don't much care about my image either."

"I don't care about your image either, Sadie, but I don't really know how these things work down in Hollywood."

"Trust me when I tell you that much dirtier secrets get swept under the rug every single day."

"I believe you..." Devon tugs playfully at my earlobe. "Is that what I am? Your dirty little secret?"

"It doesn't feel that way," I blurt out.

"How does it feel?" Devon's gaze on me is suddenly intense. She sure likes to know how I'm feeling.

"It feels like..." I can't lie, not to her, even though I might have some regrets about what I'm about to say. "I'm falling in love with you."

The corners of Devon's mouth twitch. "Oh, Sadie," she says and twirls a strand of my hair around her finger, focusing her gaze on the activity of her hand rather than my face.

"You don't believe me?" I'm a touch irked by her lack of verbal response. It makes me insecure because I haven't told anyone this in a very long time.

"I believe you, but..." Devon sighs. "Honestly, I don't even feel like arguing about what you just said, because it's exactly what I want to hear."

"Yet, you don't look very thrilled about it."

Devon purses her lips and does look me in the eye. "I am and I'm not, because... I can't look inside your heart or your head, but come on, Sadie. What feels like falling in love for you, might very well be something else entirely."

"Like what?"

"An emotional cocktail of post-divorce blues, the nostalgic power of coming home, being catapulted back in time with me... all of those things." She says it in a voice so level, so matter-of-fact, but also so kind and understanding, I'm almost willing to believe her. But I do know how I feel and I know what it is and what it isn't.

"All of those things you just mentioned might have something to do with it. They might enhance my feelings for you, but my feelings are real. They really are." Maybe it's time for that other million-dollar question. "How do *you* feel?"

"I think I'm victim to the exact same forces that are pulling you under. Like a current you'd be a fool to try and fight, but..." She gives me an unexpected little smile. "I'm crazy about you, Sadie, I think you know that. There's something between us that's so delicious, neither one of us can resist it and I don't think we should, because I don't believe in denying yourself something you want with all your heart, but we have to remain realistic about this, and starting to tell people about us might not be the smartest move."

"I agree, but Sam already knows, and Hunter and Bobby know. I can't leave my sister in the dark."

"I have no problem with that." Devon pulls her lips into a more convincing smile. "I'm trying to picture how she's going to react. There will be a lot of noise. Maybe take some earplugs."

"God, I've missed my family so much." I trace my fingertip over Devon's collarbone, secretly admiring her strong shoulder line. "Sometimes I wonder if it's all worth it."

"You're the one who said that LA is only a one-hour flight away. If you miss them so much, why don't you come home more often?"

"Damn. I didn't know I was going to get life-coached this morning."

"It's not coaching. It's an intimate conversation."

It's complicated, I want to say. But before I can gather my thoughts, Devon's phone starts ringing.

I hear a man's voice on the other end of the line that's not Sam's. "Bobby's going crazy," Hunter, says. "We're at Sam's house, which is fabulous, by the way, so we know Sadie didn't come home last night."

Devon rolls her eyes in the most exaggerated fashion. "The gays are going gaga," she whispers.

"I can hear you," Hunter says.

"Can I have the phone?" I push myself up and hold out my hand.

"With great pleasure," Devon says.

"Hi, Hunter," I say, my voice all peppy and full of charm. "This is Sadie. What is it that you're so keen to find out exactly?"

"Oh, Sadie. Hi. Um, morning. I mean, it's almost noon. Um, let me put on Bobby. He's the one who wants to know."

Devon is snickering beside me. After fifteen years of this, of having my face on TV being the only thing that sets me apart from any other human being, the effect that being a celebrity can have on people still amazes me beyond comprehension. As though we are a different species, while we are exactly the same as anyone else, with all the same hopes and fears and heartbreaks.

I hear muffled voices on the other end of the line. Devon's almost in stitches.

"Bobby speaking."

"Hi, Bobby. This is Sadie and I'm not sure you're ready to process what you're so desperate to find out."

"You can tell me anything, darling." Bobby sounds a lot more suave than his boyfriend. He'd fit right in if I had a star-studded party at my house in Malibu. "I kind of feel we're best friends already."

Devon rolls her eyes again. "Just tell him we're coming over."

I slant my head. Is she sure about this?

"Did I hear that right?" Bobby sounds much more excited than suave now.

"Just a second." I cover Devon's phone with my hand. "Are you sure? What about Finn?"

"Honestly, Sadie, I don't think there's any realistic way I can keep you from my son."

I assure Bobby we'll be there soon and hang up.

"That's a bit of a U-turn." It's a testament to how comfortable I feel around Devon that I can just come out and say that.

"It is." Devon doesn't explain herself and maybe she's right not to. Maybe it just is what it is—a person changing their mind about something. And I'll be the last one to complain about that.

CHAPTER 28

*Devon*

S adie and I walk to Sam's house. Like everything with her, it's like we're both something and the opposite at the same time. It's like we're a couple—or we might as well be—and it also feels like we're not—because we aren't. But I won't let confusion stop me from enjoying every minute with her—and that includes time spent with Finn, the most important person in my life.

Every single time I approach the ocean, my heart starts singing as soon as I set eyes on the water. It's a force much stronger than myself—a bit like being with Sadie.

"If your brother ever gets tired of his house, I'll happily take it off his hands," I joke. My business might be at a stage where I can hire people to help me, but a seaside property like Sam's is still something only Hollywood or tech money can buy.

"I can kick him out for you." Sadie bumps her shoulder into mine. Her fingers flit against mine but she retracts them quickly. "He can move back in with Dad."

"I don't want the wrath of Sam Ireland on me for the rest of my days."

"Maybe he'll find a woman to marry and have babies with in another town."

We're just chattering away, trying to defuse some of the nervous tension in the air.

"Shall we do this?" I briefly put my hand on Sadie's arm. It's difficult not to touch her, not to have some patch of her skin glued to mine.

"I have no problem with this. I know I'm the presumed 'straight' one"—she curls her fingers into air quotes—"but going somewhere with you doesn't faze me. It really doesn't. Besides, Sam's my brother, and Hunter and Bobby seem like good people, albeit a touch overexcited around celebrities."

I could kiss her again right about now. "Can we just, um, for Finn's sake, so as not to confuse him before I've had a chat with him, go easy on the public displays of affection when he's around?"

"That goes without saying." Sadie grabs my hand and pulls me to her. "Let me just quickly cop another feel now."

Giggling, I fall into her embrace and am once again reminded why, with Sadie, I never stood a fighting chance.

---

"Can I stay here again tonight?" Finn asks as soon as he sees me. "Daddy said I should ask you."

"You have school tomorrow, buddy." I gather him in my arms. He looks ready for a nap.

"Maybe next weekend?" Finn insists.

"He's a bit tired," Sam says. "We've been perfecting his bottom turn. He couldn't get enough of it. I needed all my powers of persuasion to get him out of the water this morning and, admittedly, a touch of bribery." Sam kisses me on the cheek as though we've been friends forever. He did take care of my son so I guess that makes us kind of family. "I had to promise we'd watch *Shrek* in the home theatre, which we have done and enjoyed a lot."

"Thank you so much, Sam. I bet he had an amazing time." I try to read his face beyond the goofy smile he sends me. "You must be quite exhausted as well."

"I was in bed by ten last night. That hasn't happened on a Saturday night since I was five myself."

From the corner of my eye, I see Sadie is almost sandwiched by Hunter and Bobby.

Finn is going slack against me. "I think I may put him down for a nap." I cup the back of my son's head in my palm. His weight against my shoulder is comforting and grounding.

"Sure." Ever so gently, Sam leans over and plants the softest of kisses on Finn's cheek "Sleep tight, surf champ." It's a gesture so tender and, in my eyes, so unlike Sam, it moves me to see him like this.

I carry Finn inside and up the stairs. I walk past Sadie's room, where it all began, and bring him to the room where I left his stuff when I dropped him off yesterday. All the bedrooms have an ocean view and it takes my breath away again. But not as much as putting Finn in bed, covering up his already limp body, and sitting with him for a few minutes, warmed to my very core by his soft, shallow breaths.

I will always be a mother first, but I will also always be so much more than Finn's mom. That's why I reversed my decision about keeping Sadie and Finn as separate entities in my life. I quickly saw through the illusion of that even being possible.

---

"Have you ever met Madonna?" Bobby asks Sadie. He has shown much more restraint in popping the question than I'd expected him to, although I'm quite sure it's been on the tip of his tongue for the hour or so Sadie and I have been here.

"I've been in the same room as her, but 'met' might be too big a word for it," Sadie says. "I went to one of her Oscar parties once."

Bobby's eyes grow wide as he gasps dramatically.

"It's his lifelong dream to be a guest at a Madonna party," Hunter says matter-of-factly. He has clearly regrouped since his mumbling session on the phone this morning. Hunter is more like me. He can easily see through the brittle facade that celebrity really is.

"I'm not sure I can make that happen for you," Sadie says. "Madge and I are not that close."

"How about Ida Burton and Faye Fleming?" Bobby exclaims.

"It's like everyone's gay these days," Sam says, earning him a few condescending looks from Hunter and Bobby.

"Sorry. I didn't mean anything by it." He looks at Sadie as he says it—as though she was the person he was really referring to.

"Look, Sam..." Bobby squares his shoulders. He might have gone overboard on the grapefruit mimosas. "You're very good-looking and all that, which, truth be told, lets you get away with quite a few things in my book, which is very un-woke of me, but it's remarks like the one you just made we don't need." He purses his lips. "In my opinion, it's really not that hard to be an ally and if we want things to change, we need A-list movie stars to come out of the closet, but even more than that, we need ordinary straight guys like yourself to just be chill about it and not say things like you just said."

Sam knits his impressive eyebrows together. He clearly doesn't have much of a clue about what he's done wrong.

"How dare you call my brother an ordinary straight guy," Sadie says, deflating the tension. "And for your information, Bobby, Ida and Faye are practically my neighbors."

Sadie has managed to capture Bobby's full attention again —and get her brother off the hook in the process. "Do you know them?"

"Not really, although we have the same agent... Truth be told, in the Hollywood pecking order, they're in an entirely different league than me."

"I thought TV was all the rage these days. All these movie stars are doing TV now, aren't they?" Sam asks.

"Hardly all of them," Sadie says. "And there's a big difference between playing a cop on a network TV show and, for instance, what Elisa Fox is doing in *Underground*."

"I don't think so, darling," Bobby says. "For me, it's just as thrilling to sit across from you on this fine Sunday." He fans himself with his hand.

"I'm hardly Madonna, though." It hits me how down-to-earth Sadie is. How she has come back to town as though she was working in the city as just any anonymous employee. I haven't seen her for a long time, but, at least in this stage of her life, she most certainly hasn't let her fame go to her head.

"There's only one Madonna," Bobby says wistfully. "She changed the game forever."

Suddenly, the door leading to the stairs off the deck opens.

"Well, well, well," Suzy says. "An Ireland party and I'm not invited." She finds my gaze. "For my own benefit, I'll assume it's one of their twin things."

"Suzy, hey." Sadie jumps up.

"It's not like that," Sam says. "This wasn't even planned. I was babysitting Finn last night and this is just his parents picking him up."

Suzy scratches her head, as though trying to put together a puzzle in her head, but missing a few key pieces. "*You* were babysitting Finn?"

"Yeah." Sam saunters toward her and throws his big arms around his sister. "But we're all very happy you're here."

"Hear, hear!" Hunter's already pulling up a chair.

"I just came to see my baby sister while she's in town." Suzy's clearly enjoying the attention being bestowed upon her. And her arriving out of the blue like this, which is what family does—I should be glad my dad didn't stop by my house this morning to spend some time with Finn—makes me see Sadie's earlier point about not keeping certain things from her sister.

As Suzy sits with all the airs and graces she can muster—and she has many—I decide she might have been the Ireland sibling most suited for a life in the spotlights.

CHAPTER 29

# Sadie

"Can we talk before we go to Dad's tonight?" I ask Suzy.

"We can talk any time you want," my sister says. "We can talk right now."

"Walk on the beach? Toes in the sand?" It's just the three of us left at the house. Devon has taken Finn home, and Hunter and Bobby had some errands to run—although, I got the impression, Bobby would have been perfectly happy letting Hunter do all of that on his own while he remained seated on the deck, sipping mimosas, grilling me about my life and the people I might know.

"Sure. As long as I don't have to go surfing with you again."

"Oh, come on, Suze. You used to love surfing."

"You know, Sadie, that's actually not true. I never loved it the way you and Sam do. You just remember it like that for some reason."

There are a lot of things I remember in funny ways for all sorts of reasons. We descend the stairs to the beach. As soon as my feet hit the sand, I feel the urge to grab my board and head into the water. Maybe later, as a reward for telling my sister that I'm sleeping with her boss.

"What's up?" Suzy asks as we start walking along the shoreline.

"Um." I've had a bit too much to drink at brunch and I haven't exactly prepared for this.

"Is it about Devon?" she asks when I take a little too much time to reply.

"Um, yes."

"Tell me." Suzy hooks her arms through mine. The afternoon sun is playing hide and seek with a couple of menacing clouds rolling in from the west.

"I—I think I might be falling in love with her."

Suzy stops in her tracks and looks at me. "While I was expecting you to tell me something was going on between you two, I wasn't expecting that."

I might have said a little too much too soon—not unlike this morning. I could tell it spooked Devon when I confessed my feelings for her, but I can't help how I feel and why would I lie about that to anyone?

"*In love?* Really?" She re-hooks her arm through mine and we start walking again. "How did that happen?"

"How did that happen? You invited her to our birthday party; that's how it happened."

"That's rich, blaming me." Suzy presses her hip against mine. She's my sister and she knows I'm playing. "If I knew you were going to fall in love with her, I might have thought twice about inviting her."

Suzy never thinks twice about inviting anyone anywhere, but this is not the time to get into that.

"We're spending so much time together and it's absolutely wonderful. It's like we have this connection that goes way back. This super-strong bond and all the time we didn't have together as friends, for all the wrong reasons, doesn't even matter. Like we want to make up for that now somehow. I can't get enough of being with her. I swear to you, Suzy, she's only just gone home and I'm counting down the minutes until I see her again."

"You don't have to tell me how great Devon Douglas is. Having her as my coach and working with her has been nothing short of eye-opening for me. It's as though, with her, I've finally found my thing. The work I want to do. My life's calling, if you want to call it that."

I chuckle at her silly wordplay.

"It did strike me as a little odd that you two suddenly became inseparable again like you used to be," Suzy continues. "Like we all went back in time and it's the nineties all over again."

I wish I could go back in time and do things differently. Rewrite mine and Devon's history. I'm not that big a believer in things happening for a reason. I certainly don't believe that aggressively rejecting Devon's advances that afternoon, although understandable from an insecure sixteen-year-old girl's point of view, was something I had to do to get where I am today—I'm not letting myself off that easily.

"That's how it feels sometimes. Like we've gone back in time. We used to be so close and, I guess, in a way, all that time I spent with her, made me feel like I belonged to..." I have to be careful not to step on my sister's toes. I will always be grateful for her being there for Sam and me after Mom left. But there's really only one way to say this. "To a family that wasn't broken, like ours."

"Hm." From the corner of my eye, I see Suzy nod. "Teenage friendships can get very intense. But that was then, Sadie. This is now."

I understand my sister's reluctance to talk about our

mother. I know that, as far as Suzy's concerned, the last word about her was said many years ago. I also appreciate that, unlike Sam, Suzy doesn't question my sudden attraction to another woman. She just accepts it as a simple fact of life, that sexuality can be fluid, and attraction to a certain gender can shift over time.

"I know, but what am I meant to do? Ignore how I feel?"

"Heavens no, but keep in mind you're away from your everyday life. What you're experiencing with Devon now might feel very real, but it's not your real life. That feeling you have right now, all those butterflies, they might disappear once you go back home."

*Back home.* Going back to Malibu, to my Hollywood life-style, doesn't feel like going home. Coming back here, to my family—and Devon—in Clearwater Bay feels like home the most. But I know Suzy has a point.

"I've only just arrived."

"All the more reason to give some serious thought to what it is you want to get out of this."

"Why, though? Why can't it just be what it is?"

"It can be what it is… if you even know what that is."

"What do they teach you in life coaching school?"

"For your information, Devon has taught me so much. I appreciate the hell out of her. She's gone through some dark times in her life and she's had to do a lot of work on herself— like we all have to. She's resilient and strong, but… clearly, you're her weakness. She has such a soft spot for you, Sadie. Any fool can see that. Just don't use her simply for your own pleasure. Just because you can."

"I don't feel as though I'm using her. It's all very mutual and…" I can't really tell my sister how much pleasure Devon's been getting out of our get-togethers, but the memory of it beats inside me like a heavy pulse. "We've talked a lot. We know where we stand with each other."

"Which is where?"

"We both have feelings for each other, but we also respect each other's circumstances."

"I'm not trying to talk you out of this. I'm happy you feel this way, especially after your marriage ended. But building a life with someone is something very different than what you're feeling right now. The elation. The butterflies. All the thrills that come with falling in love. Of course, you should enjoy it, because falling in love is one of life's greatest joys, but try to keep one foot lodged in reality. And try to remember why you came back home, after all this time, after only a few sporadic visits all those years. Remember that you're vulnerable and that, perhaps, you're looking for a bit of a whirlwind romance, something to take you out of your head, out of yourself—out of your life—for a brief moment or a few weeks or even a few months. But meanwhile, real life does go on and there will come a time when you have to return to it and this kind of escapist behavior will no longer make you feel so good."

"Is that really what you think I'm doing? Escaping my reality? Sure, the divorce has left me a little tender, but it's not like my life has suddenly turned to utter shit. And yes, I haven't been in Clearwater Bay for an extended period of time for far too long, but that's why I came back. I want to be here. I'm not escaping anything. I want to spend some quality time with you and Sam and Dad."

"And Devon," Suzy interjects.

"Well, yes. That was rather unplanned, but yes, with Devon as well."

"The work I've done with Devon," Suzy slows our walking pace, "is the most important work I've ever done.

She's the one who finally got me to accept that what our mother did had nothing to do with us—with me—but only with herself. It took me a long time, Sadie. It can still hit me out of the blue sometimes, but I'm good with it. I can deal with it. I no longer get so angry about it and I no longer blame myself or anyone else I love, like Dad. It's just how it is and it might have sucked big time then and it still does now, but I'm no longer trying to overcompensate for that. Like Sam with his flitting from one woman to another. Or you, hankering for our mother's love on TV. I was so restless for such a long time—since I was thirteen, really—but I've found some form of peace now. My own sense of belonging."

If Suzy can see right through me like this and Devon is her mentor, I can only guess at what Devon sees when she looks at me.

"Oh, Suze." Our pace has slowed so much, we're barely still walking. I hold onto my sister's arm a little tighter. "I'm sorry you had to go through all of that on your own. That I wasn't here for you."

"It was never your job to be here for me. I never expected that from you." She chuckles. "Look at Sam. He's always been here physically, and we're close, me and him, but I was never going to work through any of that with Sam or with you. It was my own thing to deal with, just as it is yours. And Sam's, for that matter."

"What about Dad? Did you ever talk to him about it?"

"Dad is a man of very few words, but the things he's said about Mom ever since she left still make sense. Of course it enraged us when we were in our teens and twenties, but maybe he was right... Would we rather have had our mother stay and be unhappy in her life, casting a cloud of doom over our youth that would have been very hard to crawl out from under as well—like so many so-called good wives do—or was it, with the benefit of hindsight, better that she left, even though it meant growing up without a mother?"

"That's an impossible question to answer."

"Not really. Maybe she knew what she was doing. Maybe she did it for us, because she knew we would be better off with just Dad. Because he's always been a natural at it and he did give us the best he could. He created this cocoon for us here in Clearwater Bay with all the surfing and all that time spent by the ocean and everything he taught us... Some might even call it idyllic." She lets her hands glide to my wrist. "I've never met anyone who can wax a surfboard as well as I can, and I don't even like surfing all that much." Her hand slips into mine.

Tears sting behind my eyes. All I wanted was to tell my sister about Devon and me. Instead, I got so much more than that. I wrap my arms around Suzy and, while the water laps at our toes, embrace her for a good long while.

# CHAPTER 30

## Devon

When I walk into my parents' living room, they're glued to the television. For a split second, I wonder if a major event has rocked the world and I've been oblivious to it on account of having my head way up in the clouds. But as soon as Finn walks in, my father opens his arms, and Finn rushes into them for a hug and kiss.

"That Beth Robbins is so watchable," my mother says, before turning off the TV. It's not the first time she's said it so it no longer takes me aback. And she's right. Beth Robbins is the only reason I ever flick to CNN, because whose brain can handle a constant barrage of bad news like that? "Glass of wine outside?"

I nod and follow her, leaving Finn in the safe hands of his granddad. They'll probably end up making cupcakes again and Finn will be so hyper later, especially after his lunchtime nap, that the only way to calm him down before bed will be some vigorous sunset surfing. I suppress a smile at the prospect of heading into the waves with Sadie.

"How was your weekend?" Mom asks.

That smile I managed to hide earlier can no longer be

kept at bay, because my weekend was nothing short of spectacular. But I can hardly tell my mother about that—she's never been Sadie's biggest fan.

"Goodness." My mother nearly pours the wine next to her glass, so entranced is she by my face. "I thought you said things didn't work out with Zara?"

On the way over, I pondered whether I should tell Mom about Sadie and me. If I were involved with anyone else, I wouldn't even think twice about it. I would have blurted it out already.

"God no." Zara was a mere blip on my romantic radar. I haven't given her a second thought. My head's filled to the brim with all things Sadie. "It's just, um, nice to have an old friend in town."

"An old friend, huh?" Mom's brow couldn't be more furrowed. "I take it you're referring to Sadie Ireland. I hear you've been spending a lot of time together."

My mother must have at least two extra sets of ears, what with how she always manages to hear about things going on in this town.

"How are *you*, Mom?" I try to deflect, even though she'll see right through it.

"I'm absolutely fine, apart from the fact that I'd really like to find out why my daughter has just walked into my house looking like a lovestruck puppy." She tilts her head and regards me intently. "That goofy look on your face reminds me of how you looked when you were fifteen and first fell in love with her."

Mothers and their damned maternal instincts. The number of times I've known what was going on with Finn just by glancing at him are countless, and he's only five. My mother has had forty years of practice on me. On top of that, she's not someone I lie to. I might have done so in my wilder years, when I was living it up in San Francisco, but these days, I only omit certain things. Besides, she can clearly read me like an open book.

"Oh, Mom... I know you're not going to want to hear this, but Sadie and I, we've..." We've what? Now that I have to explain it to my mother, it sounds rather impossible to describe. Unbelievable, even. Although it doesn't feel like either to me.

"What, darling?" my mother urges.

"It's hard to describe, but there's something between us and it feels very much like we're falling in love." There. I've said it. I know it's not rocket science I'm trying to explain here—although that's what it is, rocket science of the heart. The alchemy of what goes on inside of us when faced with someone so precious from our past. The ways in which our subconscious catches up with us, perhaps even plays tricks on us.

'Well, thank god it only feels like it." My mother's tone borders precariously on the edge of snappish. "And you're way too level-headed to go and fall for the likes of Sadie Ireland. Especially after what? How long has she been in town for? A week, is it?"

"Mom."

"Devon." My mother hardly ever uses my full name— only when she means business. "I'm your mother." Way to state the obvious. "You might be an adult, but I have to speak my truth. I wouldn't be a very good mother if I didn't set you straight right now. Because you clearly need it. You've waltzed in here with your head not screwed on right."

"Mom, come on. Give me a break. I'm just being honest with you."

"And I'm being honest with you. You're in cloud-cuckoo-land. It's clear as day. You've been like this all week and it doesn't seem to be getting any better."

"Can't you just be happy for me?" I've regressed to textbook teenage petulance already. Not a good look, but sometimes it's like that with my mother, especially when she talks to me as though I am still a teenager. As though it were only yesterday I came home heartbroken after Sadie slapped me in the face. I've lived so much life since then. I turned into my true self. I made a wonderful life for myself and my son.

"I wish I could, darling. I really do. I wish that you would meet a lovely, kind, spectacular woman who knocks your socks off and who falls in love with Finn too. Truly, I wish for it every day. But I don't think Sadie Ireland is that woman. She can't be."

"Why not?" As I ask the question, I can see my mother's point of view, but I'm not about to admit that to her—or to myself.

"I think you know."

"No, I don't. Tell me."

"She lives four hundred miles away, for starters." Not what I had expected her to begin with. "She was married to a man until quite recently." I can't argue with that, but it reminds me I should give my mother a little speech on the fluidity of sexual attraction. "And she hurt you, darling. She hurt you like no one else has hurt you since. I know it was a long time ago, a lifetime even, but it says so much about her character, about who she is deep down, that she didn't have an ounce of kindness in her back then. That she didn't even try to patch things up between you. That she simply deserted you, her best friend, because you were gay." Mom shakes her head. "I don't know how you can even consider being with her. How you can even stand to be around someone like that."

"Sadie's nothing like what you just described. She *is* kind and spectacular and, sure, a little wounded, but aren't we all? If I remember correctly, you felt very sorry for her for not having her mother around. You were always inviting her over, asking her to stay for dinner and spend the night."

"Doesn't that prove my point? I bestowed such kindness on her. Such compassion. I made her feel welcome in our home. I tried to make her feel like one of us, like part of an intact family. And that's how she repaid my kindness? By breaking my daughter's heart into a million pieces?"

I see what this is. This isn't about Sadie. This is about my mother. Sadie hurt her, too. "Maybe you expected a little bit too much of a confused, volatile sixteen-year-old girl without a mother," I say.

"Maybe," Mom says on a sigh.

My phone beeps in my pocket. I could do with a break from this conversation, so I take it out. My heart leaps into my throat when I see it's from Sadie.

*I can't make the sunset surf tonight. I need to do something for my dad. Talk later. xo*

"What's wrong," my mother asks. She must have read that off my face as well.

"Nothing." It's not really a lie. It's no big deal that Sadie's busy and we can't surf together tonight. That gives me more time and headspace to focus on Finn—and he can show me the tricks Sam has taught him. Yet, Sadie canceling on me is a touch unexpected after the weekend we've had. Maybe she just needs a little time. It makes perfect sense. Truth be told, I could do with some alone time as well.

219

"It's her, isn't it?"

"We were meant to go surfing tonight but she has to be with her dad. That's all."

"Uh-hum." It sounds a lot like "I told you so", or maybe that's how I'm making it sound in my head. Sadie has been driving me a little crazy and of course, as my mom said, my head's not screwed on right. My entire being is taken over by the sensation of falling in love, of all the glorious reminiscing, the beautiful surfing we've done together, the spine-tingling sex we've had, the endless, scintillating conversations we've engaged in. It's been quite the week and the rush of it, the avalanche of emotions it has created in me, is starting to catch up with me.

"Will you stay for dinner?" Mom's tone has softened. She reaches over and puts her hand on my arm.

"Sure."

"Hey." She gives my arm a little squeeze. "You've given me a lot to think about. I may need to do a bit of processing, but I'm not judging you, darling. I always trust you to do what's right for you and Finn."

"Thanks." I finally grab the glass of wine she poured for me and take a sip. I relax a little. I know my mother means well and I understand why Sadie is still such a red flag for her. And just maybe, I actually need someone to talk some sense into me.

# CHAPTER 31

## *Sadie*

I haven't seen Devon since brunch on Sunday, when we couldn't even say goodbye properly because of Finn and Suzy not knowing about us yet. We haven't acted as though we're together around anyone we know. Maybe we aren't even together. The things Suzy said to me last Sunday have given me pause. My sister made me contemplate the reasons why I've hurried into this impromptu affair with Devon. While it's true that all three of us stayed late at Dad's, until long after dinner had finished, I didn't have to stay for my father's sake—although he enjoyed having us all the house. But another romantic bout of surfing with Devon, forgetting where and who we were and melding into this blissful unit we seem to have become—and quite possibly ending up in bed with her again—didn't feel like something I should do. I tried to look inward, past the slew of butterflies that have set up camp in my belly, and ask myself what it is I'm really doing. I could only do that without Devon by my side.

For all those reasons, my heart is beating in my throat

when I ring Hunter's doorbell for the viewing party Suzy has organized for the season finale of *King & Prince*.

"It's you," Finn says when he opens the door. "Where's Sam?"

Hunter hurries behind him. "Finn, please. Manners. Say hello properly."

"Hi, Sadie." He smiles up at me sheepishly. He looks so much like his mother with his strawberry-blond hair and ultra-pale skin. I crouch down. "Sam had to stop by the bar, but he'll be here soon. I promise."

Hunter greets me as though I'm royalty, and Bobby's not far behind him. Suzy's mixing some sort of special *King & Prince* cocktail—whatever that might be—in the kitchen. There's no sign of Devon. She is coming, isn't she? Maybe I should have been in touch. Compared to all the times we've seen each other, and all the things we've done since, the past two days have felt more like a cold war than a simple little break.

"Is Devon coming?" I ask tentatively.

Hunter looks at me funnily.

"She's finishing a call with a client," Suzy says. "She'll be here soon."

Bobby walks up and curves his arm around my shoulders. "Anything you want to share with us about tonight's episode? Do we need to prepare for a shocking finale?" Bobby's heart might break when he sees Michael's character on the show die, but he's a big boy. He can handle it. It's only television.

"I wouldn't want to spoil your viewing pleasure. That would just be wrong."

"Here you go." Suzy hands out the cocktails she's been mixing. "And a virgin one for Little Mister Douglas." She gives Finn a glass as well.

"Little Mister Douglas is already past his bedtime,"

Hunter says. "Come on, buddy. If your mom finds you still awake when she gets here, we'll both be in trouble."

"But Sam isn't here yet," Finn says.

He looks up at me as though I'm the one who made Sam, his new hero, disappear forever.

"Why don't you get ready for bed and then we'll ask Sam to read you a story when he arrives?" I hold up my phone. "I'll tell him to get over here promptly."

Finn's eyes light up. "Okay." He looks around. "Come on, Spencer." The dog rushes to Finn and they disappear upstairs together.

"Sam did a good job," Hunter says, "but Spencer's a damn good babysitter as well."

"We've been thinking about asking your brother to teach us how to surf," Bobby says. "Just so we can keep up with Finn."

I can just imagine the scene. Bobby would be too mesmerized by Sam's abs to listen to anything useful he's got to say about how to approach the waves. "Finn's got Devon to surf with."

"Speak of the devil." Two people walk past the window. Of course, Sam has brought a date. To my surprise, his date is Cassidy. Maybe it isn't an actual date.

Bobby and Hunter make a big deal about welcoming Sam into their home, then Bobby takes him upstairs to tuck Finn in.

"Sam said it would be okay if I crashed your party." Cassidy has such a confident smile for an early twenty-something. Of course, she's more than welcome.

Suzy pours her a cocktail from the large jug she has prepared.

"It's such a treat to be able to watch with you, Sadic."

Some of the things I said to Cassidy that night I ended up

at The Bay come back to me. So much has happened since. I do remember her confiding in me about her crush on Sam and urging me not to tell him. At least I've kept that promise.

"Let's talk more after we've watched the show." The only person who knows my co-star is about to meet his demise is Devon, who's taking her sweet time to show up.

"I have a few theories," Cassidy says.

"Do tell." Suzy pats the stool at the kitchen island she's been hovering around. I haven't even told my own sister that Prince is about to meet his maker on the show.

"Hey." Hunter pulls me aside into the den. "Are you and Dev okay?"

"Um, sure. Yes, I think so."

"Okay." He squints at me. Does he know something I don't? But if he did, why would he ask me that question? It does plant the seed that I might not be the only one who has changed her mind a little about things, about slowing down and making sure no one gets hurt again. The biggest problem is that I see no reasonable way to slow things down with Devon. My skin itches to be touched by her again, my lips are pillowy with anticipation to be kissed by her again. It's the old battle between heart and mind. We should probably talk, but not before we watch the final episode of season fifteen of *King & Prince*.

"Five-minute countdown," Suzy shouts. She has clearly taken control of Hunter and Bobby's house even though she doesn't live here.

Devon still hasn't arrived and I'm getting antsy.

"Should I check on Devon?" I ask Hunter.

"Her call's probably running long," Suzy says. "It happens. But she'll be here. I don't think she'll want to miss this."

Sam and Bobby have rushed downstairs again, assuring

Hunter that Finn is fast asleep with Spencer guarding him at the foot of his bed. We all huddle in the couch and while it warms my heart to be here with my siblings—and Bobby and Hunter who are two lovely guys I wouldn't mind getting to know a whole lot better—it doesn't feel right because Devon isn't here. I wanted her to sit next to me, her hip glued to mine, while watching this.

The theme tune plays and Bobby and Sam hum along loudly.

The show starts and everyone cheers when my character appears for the first time. While it's still a little awkward to see myself on screen—like looking in a mirror but not quite— I've grown used to it after all this time. My colleagues in wardrobe and makeup always make me look like a million bucks. And those leather jackets do lend me a certain cool a bit like Devon with her tattoos.

When the first commercial break comes on, everyone— led by Bobby—claps.

"Oh, please. Come on." Not one of them seems to notice that Devon still hasn't arrived. "Nothing much has happened yet."

"Nothing much?" Bobby says. "What about you chasing the perp along Hollywood Boulevard? If I were so inclined, I'd be so turned on right now."

"Refills?" Suzy walks around with her pitcher of booze. Thankfully, Suzy's not Sam and she hasn't made her cocktail mix too strong.

"Should I text her?" I ask Hunter, feeling stupid, because surely I don't need him to tell me if I should or should not text Devon.

"Maybe, yeah." He nods then gets swallowed by the wild theories Cassidy, Sam, and Bobby are touting.

I send a text to Devon, asking if she's still coming over. Suzy squeezes into the spot next to me.

"Even though Devon taught me that keeping time with a client is essential for setting boundaries, I went over time with her more than once when I first started working with her. I wouldn't read anything else into her not being here. Okay?"

"Okay." I suppose it's not that big a deal that Devon's not here—she's probably helping someone who really needs it—yet something about it feels off. As time passes, it's starting to feel more as though Devon doesn't really want to be here with us tonight—because of me.

The commercial break ends and everyone, even Bobby, goes eerily silent. They're all glued to the screen and I force myself to, if not enjoy, then at least be aware of Mike's last scenes on the show that brought us together. To spare a thought for the wild ride we've been on. From wet-behind-the-ears co-stars to a well-oiled machine. From not knowing each other to understanding each other by the particular lift of an eyebrow or the slant at which we tipped our head. And then, to none of that any longer. From saying 'I do' to saying 'I don't want to be with you anymore.' From nothing to everything to nothing, again.

"Argh, Detective Prince is so hot," Bobby says on a sigh. "Oh, sorry, Sadie. You're not half bad either." He shoots me a wink.

He's right. Mike is a handsome man. He's always had his admirers, male and female. My phone buzzes and my heart leaps into my throat. But it's not from Devon. It's from Mike.

*Are you watching? You're about to blow my face off. ;-0 MM xo*

. . .

MM is what I used to call him in our better days. Maybe he's fallen victim to a bout of nostalgia, a feeling I'm all too familiar with, although not so much regarding him or our time together.

I don't really know what to reply. I'm still deflated about it not being Devon responding to my text. She's about to miss the biggest scene in the show's history so far. Antonio Prince is about to be shot to death, breaking hundreds of gay and straight hearts in the process.

I don't want to give Mike some deflecting comeback. Not right now, when the direct consequence of our failed relationship is about to be aired to America. Instead, I send him exactly what I was thinking earlier.

*You and I had such a thrilling ride together. We'll always have that. I wish you nothing but the best, MM <3*

I get a bit teary as I send it because this truly is the end of an era. I'm so glad I'm watching it here surrounded by people that I love in Sam and Suzy's case and whose company I enjoy in Hunter, Bobby, and Cassidy's case. That I'm not at some glamorous Hollywood gathering marking the end of what Mike and I stood for with a glass of champagne in my hand, smiling my TV smile because that's what people want to see. Anything else wouldn't fit the surroundings or the carefully curated atmosphere.

It's so quiet in the den. Everyone's on the edge of their seat. King and Prince are in pursuit of a presumed terrorist. The criminal has led them into an abandoned building. Leona and Antonio exchange glances. She's going after the terrorist while Antonio is going around the back. Leona enters the building. The perp reaches his stash of weapons. He grabs a smoke bomb and tosses it in Leona's direction. She covers her nose and mouth with the arm that isn't pointing a gun. She disappears behind the smoke. A shot is fired.

The audience sees how the terrorist is shot by Prince but Leona can't see. She's caught in a thick cloud. She hears footsteps. She yells for Antonio but her ears are still ringing from the bomb going off. She hears another bullet being fired. She makes out a moving body and one slumped to the ground. She believes Mike is hurt and aims at the perp. She shoots the standing man. He goes down with a thud she hears loud and clear.

"Antonio," she yells. "Are you okay?" She rushes toward the two men. The slumped one lowers his gun and falls all the way back. She's finally close enough to see that it's the terrorist. And the man she shot, who's chest is gushing blood, is Antonio Prince.

A communal gasp ripples through the den.

"Oh. My. God!" Bobby exclaims. "She shot him." He turns to me. "King shot Prince!"

"Ssshh!" Hunter swats him on the knee and we all watch how Prince dies in King's arms—how Mike dies in my arms. Then it goes to commercials again.

"Wow," Sam says. "A heads-up would have been nice, sis."

"Sorry," I mouth, feeling strangely emotional. Maybe Mike is the only one who understands what I'm going through right now. *King & Prince* changed my life in so many ways. It made my acting dreams come true. It introduced me to my husband. It made me rich and famous. *King & Prince* might go on without Mike, as so many other TV shows have done before when one of the leads decided to leave, but it will never be the same again. I wish Devon were here. I wish I could lean into her shoulder, maybe even have her throw her arm around me.

It's utterly ridiculous that she isn't here for this. Or maybe I'm being too selfish. Maybe that's what starring in a popular TV show does to you. It all becomes about you.

"Where is she?" I exclaim, despite myself—despite knowing I may have come to believe I can have everything I want when I want it, but that isn't always true.

"Who?" Cassidy asks.

"Devon." I shoot up out of the couch. "I texted her and she hasn't even replied." Am I being unreasonable? Probably a little, but this night has proven emotionally more challenging than I thought it would be. It's not only relief washing over me, as I had hoped, but so many other, more complicated emotions as well.

Regret, for starters. A sense of failure for walking out on my marriage—the very last thing I ever wanted to do because it's what my mother did. But most of all, a sense of loss because of Devon not being here right now when Antonio Prince is killed by Leona King on prime-time TV. At this moment, I see a few things very clearly that haven't been obvious to me, and that tells me something that I really don't want to hear.

"I'm going over," I state.

"What? But Sadie, we still have to watch the final part," Sam says. I honestly didn't take him for such a *King & Prince* fan.

"Maybe you should respect Devon's privacy," Hunter tries. "She would be here if she could."

That's me told, then. I can't argue with that. I have to respect Devon's reason for not being here tonight. Perhaps if I had told her what a big deal it would be for me, she would have tried harder. But I didn't know it was going to be like this—that it would bring me to the cusp of falling apart. I've been way too busy developing feelings for Devon I shouldn't have to notice.

"Okay." I sink back into the couch. Suzy gives me a sisterly pat on the knee. "Damn, Sadie, that was emo as fuck." I assume she's referring to the TV show and not my erratic behavior. "Dad's watching this. You should probably call him after."

"You couldn't possibly have expected that both Mike and I were going to continue with the show?" I say on a sigh that sounds a little more exasperated than I would like it to. "We're divorced. It doesn't exactly make for perfect working conditions."

"Did he decide to leave of his own accord, or did you make him?" Sam asks.

"We talked about it, and he offered to leave. Fifteen years of playing the same part is a long time, no matter how iconic. I know what it's like to be called by your character's name everywhere you go instead of your own. He wants to play different roles so he decided to step back."

"What about you, Sadie?" Hunter asks. "Don't you want to play a different part some time?"

It's so easy to see why Devon would have chosen Hunter as the father of her child. His voice is all kindness and his smile so warm, I feel like crawling into his lap and crying on his shoulder.

"I decided to go for stability for now. For myself and for the show. For some reason, *King & Prince* remains popular. Mike leaving is a big deal." I can imagine the calls my agent is getting right about now—although it won't be anything compared to Mike's. "One of us had to stay. And I've had enough upheaval in my personal life as well lately, so."

"It's starting again," Cassidy says.

My phone buzzes again. It's from Leslie, my agent.

*Great work on that scene, babe. So proud of you.*

It was easy enough to steal the scene. All Mike had to do was pretend he was dying.

The last part of the episode deals with the fallout of the friendly-fire shooting. King is so torn up, she even sheds a few tears—not something her character is known for—and manages to deliver a heartfelt eulogy for Prince, her devoted partner throughout the years.

CHAPTER 32

## Devon

Even though Sadie told me Mike's character was going to die, I'm glued to my screen. Not only because it's so damn hard to keep my eyes off her, but because I'm afraid to move. When I move, when I extricate myself from the spell I've been under the past hour, I will have to face my cowardice.

I consider myself the opposite of a flaky person. I don't bail on people nor do I not turn up to events, no matter how small or casual, when I've said I would be there. But after my call ended, despite the minimal distance between my house and Hunter's, my body simply refused. My feet didn't want to take the few steps to get there. I always listen to my body—it knows so much more than my brain ever can.

Now that the finale is over, I'm getting an inkling my body might have betrayed me. That I might have been a bit too keen on allowing its resistance. That's how Sadie messes with my head. Ever since that conversation with my mother, and Sadie canceling on surfing, it's as though the spell we've been under has been broken. And now, after seeing her ex-husband die in her arms on TV, it's an even louder reminder of all the reasons we should stop doing what we've been doing. Now that I have my wits about me again, I should take some distance from Sadie. Which is exactly what I did when she texted me earlier to ask if I was still coming over.

I switch off the TV and sit in the dim silence of my living room for a while, checking in with myself—another activity I've banned since seeing Sadie again.

But all I can think of is Sadie. How she must be feeling right now. How she's holding up because this particular episode airing must have been cathartic for her. Ever since she kissed me on my doorstep, Sadie is all I've been able to think about and it's not healthy. It's too much of a good thing. I've lost myself in the nostalgia and this false feeling of connection I thought we had.

The truth is I don't know Sadie Ireland better than the next person. I know things *about* her—and I also know what it's like to feel her skin against mine, hot and slick from love-making—but I don't know her. I've let myself get caught inside this web we both created because I wanted to. Because of the illusion of her I've lived with for the past twenty-four years. But none of it is real. I can see that now. It's just been a crazy week full of self-fulfilling prophecies and making myself believe that, just because we were best friends a long time ago, Sadie could fall for me as well.

I don't begrudge myself for giving into it, but it has to stop now. We might have fooled ourselves into believing that our teenage friendship from back in the day was a good enough foundation to base this on, but it's anything but. There is no foundation; only quicksand. It's all make-believe. A kind of magical thinking we allowed ourselves to indulge in because it felt so damn good. It even felt right for a hot minute. But we only fooled ourselves.

I understand why Sadie did it. She's going through

massive change in her life and, probably without knowing, she has created a kind of buffer so she didn't have to feel all her feelings—only what she believed she felt for me, which was a lot more fun than dealing with who she is post-divorce.

I can only plead temporary insanity. Even though I should know better, because I live and breathe these teachings. I talk about this kind of stuff, about the way our brain can trick us and how our biology works against us sometimes, all the time, but I'm only human after all. And Sadie has been my weak spot for a very long time.

The silence is interrupted by noise coming from the back door. A soft knock follows.

"Devon." It's Sadie's voice. "It's me."

I can sit here until the sun comes up tomorrow and conclude Sadie Ireland is my biggest weakness, but that won't change anything. I need to confront her. I need to speak up, for both our sakes.

I open the door. She looks a little pale and her eyes are a touch watery. I need to steel myself against this. Already, all I want to do is throw my arms around her and say her life might be in upheaval at the moment, but everything passes. Given enough time, everything will be okay. But that's not for me to say. I don't exist to make Sadie feel better—besides, I think I've done enough of that already.

"Hey." My voice betrays my feelings for her. "Come in."

"I missed you at the party. Suzy said you were working late." Sadie sounds as though she doesn't really believe that.

"I had a call run late, but..." We stand awkwardly in the kitchen, hips leaning against countertops. "I had some thinking to do, Sadie. About us. About what this is. Not seeing each other for a few days has been eye-opening."

"Oh." She nods as though she might understand. Maybe

she had a similar epiphany, but it's unlikely. "Okay." She gestures at a chair. "Can I sit?"

"Of course." I pour us both a glass of water.

"Look, Dev," she starts. "I don't know what you're going to say, but I get a feeling it's not going to make me jump for joy and I'm already feeling so raw from watching the finale... I'm not sure I can do this right now. I just wanted to see you. Make sure you're all right."

"I'm fine." It takes all I've got not to take her hands in mine, to thread my fingers through hers. "I'm sorry I wasn't there even though I said I would be. That wasn't fair on you."

"I'll live—unlike Antonio Prince," Sadie jokes, but her heart is definitely not in it. Not even a hint of a smile reaches her eyes.

"Maybe we can get together tomorrow? To talk?"

The last of the sparkle dims in her eyes. Was she expecting an invitation to spend the night?

"Not even a kiss?" she asks, and my heart breaks a little.

"Sadie, if I kiss you, then..." Then I'm right back to square one.

"Then what?" She tilts her head and leans closer to me—not close enough to kiss me, though.

"When we kiss, the rest of the world might as well disappear."

"That's very much the feeling I'm after right now."

"But it's also the exact reason why we shouldn't do it."

"Are you sure?" She is leaning in now. All I have to do to touch my lips to hers is move forward a few inches.

Instead, I pull back. It takes everything I've got, but I pull back. If ever there was a time to prove to myself that my Sadie-insanity was truly temporary, it's now.

I nod. "I'm sure."

Sadie presses her lips together. Even with a facial expression like that, she still looks achingly beautiful. I can't just let her walk off after such a blunt rejection.

"We could hug," I offer.

"I would really love a hug." Her voice breaks a little.

I open my arms to her, and she steps into my embrace. Sadie buries her nose in my hair. I hold her close against me. Because there's a finality to our embrace, I'm not letting go of her any time soon. It's hard to fight my feelings—those treacherous little bastards wreaking havoc inside my mind—with only the power of rational thought. Reason doesn't stand much chance when I hold Sadie close like this, when I have her where I believed, for the longest time, she belonged —in my arms.

The tip of Sadie's nose touches against my neck. Her lips find my ear the way they have done a few times when we were in much hotter circumstances than this.

"Is this a break-up from a relationship we didn't even have?" she whispers.

My chin bumps against her shoulder as I nod. I'm glad that I can't see her face. "Are you going to be okay?"

She curls her arms tighter around me and rests her head on my shoulder for a few seconds. She exhales deeply, then extricates herself from our hug.

"I get it, Dev. I do. What we had... we were doing this for all the wrong reasons. Well, at least, I think I was and I can only speak for myself. Silly as it all is when you put it into perspective, watching that season finale made a few things clear to me. Things I've been running from." She reaches for my hand. "You're so easy to be around. So utterly delightful and addictive. But I see why we need to slow things down, maybe even end them."

A lump the size of a golf ball lodges itself in my throat.

I'm about to start crying now. I don't want to say goodbye to Sadie, but I know I have to.

"Let's talk more tomorrow," I manage to say.

"We'll see. Let's take some more time to process." She brings a hand to her chest. "I need some time. My head's a mess right now."

"Okay." I have to respect her wishes. "Let me know when you're ready to talk." Or surf. Or hang out. Or be the friends we could no longer be all those years ago.

"I will." She casts me one last glance. "Bye, Dev," she says.

After she's gone, as I stare at the door she walked out of, the door I wanted her to walk out of, I cry all the tears I've held in for too long.

***

Time without seeing Sadie passes slowly, but it does pass, as time always does. During the couple of weeks that follow the *King & Prince* finale, I'm acutely aware of her presence in town, even though, miraculously, I never run into her. Not even while surfing, which I do every day to clear my head and get in synch with my body again, now that it's no longer being touched by Sadie.

Life resumes as though Sadie and I never had that crazy week of thinking we were falling in love with each other, and as the days go by, the madness of it all becomes more and more obvious to me. It very much was a bout of temporary insanity.

Alongside my own foolish crush, Finn seems to have developed one on Sam. He's been nagging me since the night of the finale to spend another night at the beach house, but I can hardly drop him off there now.

Luckily, Sam is easy enough to find at his bar. When I

stop by for a coffee almost three weeks after I've last seen Sadie, he sits next to me on the deck overlooking the ocean.

"Finn misses you. It's driving Hunter nuts. I think it's hurting his daddy ego." I look into Sam's friendly face. He has the same eyes as Sadie, dark and brooding.

"I'm available whenever he wants, although I wouldn't want to get in the way of Hunter's daddying." He holds up his hands. "That's not my place."

"I know you don't officially teach anymore, but if your offer still stands of giving Finn a few special Sam Ireland surfing lessons, I'd like to take you up on that."

"Really?" Sam sounds as though I've just given him a winning lottery ticket. "I'd absolutely love that."

"The first few times, I'd like to... be there." I almost said 'supervise.' "But, yeah, I trust you with him."

"Just let me know when and I'll clear my schedule."

"You're very keen."

"Finn's a great little dude and I guess spending time with him in the ocean reminds me of when I was little. When my dad taught us how to surf. Mind you, I always had to share him with Sadie and, to a lesser extent, Suzy."

The mention of Sadie's name twists something in my stomach.

"The rare times it was just me and him out there. Pure magic." He grins at me. "Or maybe it's my memory playing tricks on me."

You and me both, I think. And then, I have to ask. I can't ask Suzy about Sadie because it would be unprofessional and I don't want to cross another boundary—I've crossed so many already.

"How's Sadie?" My voice is shaky. This time apart has given me ample space to think, but Sadie is still my weakness.

I still can't ask after her well-being without a croak in my voice.

"Good, I think. Yeah," Sam says. "She's making a board from scratch with Dad. They're both really into that, as you can imagine." His eyebrows do a funny little dance. "She's given me the broad-strokes version of why you stopped seeing each other, by the way. We're over-sharing twins like that."

"I'm so glad she has you. That she has this..." I gaze out over the ocean. "To come home to."

"Are you okay? With all of this?"

"I think so." I'm not entirely sure, although I know some sort of cooling-off period was required. Things got heated between Sadie and me too quickly. There was barely a simmer before it all came to a spectacular boil. "Maybe it will be easier once she's gone back to LA."

"I'm just a simple run-of-the-mill guy, I guess." Sam says it with such a twinkle in his eye, it's impossible to take him seriously. "Maybe I don't really get any of this stuff between two women, but, um, for a while there, Sadie seemed genuinely besotted with you." His expression has shifted to serious. "I may not know much, but I do know my sister."

"What are you saying?"

"It's none of my business, really, but..."

It's remarkable how Sam is like both his sisters. Sometimes, I wonder what their mother was like. I was only ten years old, like Sam and Sadie, when their mother left town—abandoning her family—and I don't remember much about her. But all three of them must be a lot like her as well.

"You and Sadie seemed so into each other," Sam continues. "Like, totally. It kind of reminded me of when Sadie and Mike just got together. I'll always be her twin brother and I'll always be able to read her better than anyone else. With you, it seemed to be something so strong, it could only be real.

Then Sadie tells me it wasn't real and I don't know what to make of that." He shrugs. "Sadie's doing fine, going about her life of leisure in Clearwater Bay, and I know she's still working through the aftermath of her divorce. The last thing Sadie ever wanted was to be someone who quits on a marriage, who breaks a vow she solemnly swore to another person."

He flicks away a tangle of dust that has gathered on the table. "It makes Sadie feel like some sort of failure, because she hasn't had to deal with much disappointment in her life yet— apart from the really big one shattering her illusion that life's all about happy families who stay and surf together and love each other forever."

It sounds to me as though Sadie's return home has made Sam do some soul-searching of his own.

"With Mike, she led this picture-perfect Hollywood life. Both of them on a hit show. Both of them gorgeous as hell, living it up in their Malibu beach house. Turns out, that was the greatest illusion of all." Sam pulls his lips into a grin. "Sorry. I didn't mean to get all philosophical on you. Or analytical about Sadie. My point is the first week she was here, she basically spent most of her waking hours with you and she seemed so much happier, so much more carefree, and simply satisfied with how things were. She could deal with everything better, if you know what I mean."

I know exactly what he means. Of course, it was easier for Sadie to face life while thinking she was falling in love with me.

"She has to deal with all these things on her own," I say.

"Does she, though?" Sam looks me in the eye. "Why go through something alone if you can share the burden?"

"That might be true for some, but... you have to see things from my point of view. I can't simply be a person she gets over her ex with. Or sleeps with to make herself feel better."

"Sadie got over Mike a long time ago. Months before they actually divorced," Sam says matter-of-factly. "I'm just calling it as I see it. I admit I was shocked when Sadie told me that she kissed you that night, but after the shock had subsided, all I could be was happy for her." He bumps his elbow into mine gently. "I know we Irelands are complicated folk. That life has screwed us up a little. And being single isn't all it's cracked up to be. I'm seeing right through the allure of bachelor life these days. It's not what I want any longer."

"Suzy seems completely happy being single." As was I, I think, although I have been longing for a special someone in my life who isn't my son.

"Suzy is a very special case. You're right. She is perfectly happy on her own."

Sam's right that Suzy's the perfect example of someone who has thrown off all societal expectations and doesn't rely on a romantic relationship for her happiness—something I admire her greatly for because resisting the way of the world is one of the hardest things to do in life.

"Sadie told me you're broody." It's time to lighten the mood just a touch.

"Yeah. My clock's ticking, Dev. I need to find me a woman."

"I'm sure you won't have too much trouble." I like hanging out with Sam. He's easy to be around, just like his sisters.

"I've been thinking about asking Cass out." Sam has lowered his voice. He looks behind him to make sure Cassidy isn't just walking out of the bar.

"Then do."

"She works for me, though. And she's good at her job. Reliable and hands-on."

"I hear what you're saying, but you run a bar, Sam. I think you can take the risk." It's not the same as Sadie having to work with Mike for another season on a TV set.

"Yeah, I might just do it. Thanks." He sends me his famous Ireland smile now—I'm sure Cassidy stands as much chance against it as I do against Sadie's.

"I haven't seen Sadie in the ocean lately. She's still surfing, isn't she?"

"Oh, yeah. I think she's been picking her time a bit more, um, strategically."

"Avoiding me, you mean."

"Yes." I do appreciate Sam's directness. "But don't worry. I'm kicking her ass in the waves, just as you do."

I wish I could run into the water now, board tucked under my arm, Sadie in tow. The two of us heading into the waves together, so damn certain we can master them, despite knowing that the ocean will always be far superior to any human being.

## CHAPTER 33
# *Sadie*

Even though it's been more than four weeks since the *King & Prince* season finale aired, I still get stopped and asked for selfies on a daily basis. It's like everyone in Clearwater Bay has suddenly remembered I grew up here and am staying for a few months—and they need to make the most of it while they still can. Instead of asking for a selfie—the new autograph—some people pretend to shoot me with a gun made out of their fingers. I much prefer the request for a picture.

The only thing I'm glad about is I don't have to hide Devon from the extra attention I've been getting. I could just see the headlines on the gossip blogs. *Sadie Ireland shoots Mike Morales to be with her lesbian lover*, or something preposterous like that. At least I don't have to worry about any of that.

I mostly hide out at Dad's place, spending as much time in his workshop as he does. We're sanding down a piece of wood that will become the first dad-and-daughter surfboard in too many years. The good thing about being with my dad all day is that I don't have to talk much. He doesn't ask questions I don't know the answer to. All he has said about the season finale of my show was, "I figured that was the only solution." And that was that.

He doesn't ask about Mike. He never alludes to my marriage and its breakdown. Our main topic of conversation is the weather, how it will affect the waves that day, and how the board we're working on is progressing.

My dad lets me do a lot of the hard graft. Maybe he senses, with his fatherly intuition, that I need it. That it's doing me a world of good to lose myself in making something that means something to us. Something that isn't easy but that I know I can do because he's the one who taught me. Maybe he senses that I need this connection between us that has existed since I was a little kid and I just watched him work, watched him do his thing. A connection that has always been there, but I have sorely neglected over the years. The beauty of Dad is we don't need to talk about it. We don't need to hash it out. We just need to do *this*. We just need to work side by side, be near each other, breathe in the same air for a bit—and ride the same waves once in a while—for us to be okay.

It's such a comfort to come home to this. To know, as I did in my bones when I made the decision to no longer spend the show's hiatus shooting some movie or traveling to a faraway place where I could forget who I was for a few months, that this is what it would be like. That I could always return to this no matter how long it took me to find my way back home.

It's been equally easy with Sam and Suzy because we grew up together, although they require many more words to be spoken between us.

My dad, so it seems, doesn't require anything from me.

He doesn't judge me. He always thinks the best of me, even if I haven't stopped by home for longer than a few days in years.

I take a break and wipe the sweat from my brow. I sit on the bench outside the workshop and look at him. He's in his element, doing what he loves. I can't help but wonder, as I have so many times in the past, how a woman can just walk out on a man like that. Or maybe leaving a husband she loved was the price she had to pay for not wanting to be a mother. Or maybe she didn't love him anymore. There are so many things I will never know and maybe I don't need to know. Maybe, so many years after the fact, things can just be how they are.

Dad puts his tools down and sits next to me. I hand him a bottle of water.

"She's going to be a beauty," he says, the way he's been saying since we started on the board. "You should take her home with you."

I am home, I want to say. Nothing has felt more like home to me in the past year than coming back here. Apart, perhaps, from my brief dalliance with Devon.

"Thanks, Dad, but I think I'll keep her here. To ride when I come home." I try to find his gaze but it's not really our thing. He looks away into the middle distance, to the tree-tops behind his house. "I plan to come home much more from now on."

"That's great."

"Yeah." We sit in companionable silence for a while. This is so much better than lounging in one of the designer chairs I have on my deck in Malibu. I can't even see the ocean from here, but I see the surfboard we're making, and Dad's workshop, and the house he's lived in forever—the house I grew up in.

"Hey, Dad..."

"Yes, kiddo."

"For a while there, when I just got back... You know, for our fortieth birthday party." I can't rationally explain why I'm doing this. All I can think of is that I'm so comfortable in this moment, in my father's calming presence and his utter inability to judge me, in the safe space he's managed to create for all three of us, that I want to tell him. I want him to know this very private thing about me.

"Hm," he hums, the frequency of it as familiar to me as the roar of a perfect incoming wave.

"I truly believed I was falling in love with Devon Douglas." It's as though I have to say it. I have to give this thing between us, even though it's already in the past, a clear voice. I can't pretend it never happened and by telling my dad, I'm making it into something real. Because it was real. When I lie in bed at night, alone, I can still feel Devon's lips on me and even though I'm imagining it, I have a real-life memory to draw from—a most amazing real-life memory.

"You two were always so close," Dad says, his voice level as ever.

"We were and seeing her again, at this particular time in my life, did something to me. It opened something inside me. It genuinely made me feel as though I could love her."

"Could?"

"I guess I'll never know."

"Why not?" Dad sips from his bottle of water as though we're discussing the wax to use on the board instead of me falling in love with another woman. With Devon.

"It's, um... I guess it's not to be."

"Does she feel the same way?"

"She did." That much I do know, although I have no idea

how Devon feels now. Maybe she never wants to see me again. Maybe she has packaged up our little dalliance as a short error of judgment, a minor faux-pas, and has sealed off that box for good.

"Then what are you doing sitting here with your old man?"

I erupt into a nervous chuckle. "It's not a hardship for me to be here with you, Dad."

"I'm sure it's not, but that doesn't mean you should be here." He turns to me and does hold my gaze now. "I know, in my heart, that I did the best I could with you kids, but what I haven't been able to do is give you an acceptable idea of what a romantic relationship can actually be like." His tone is still even and free of judgment. "You're free to live the lives you want. Everyone is free to do exactly as they please. Your mother was. So was I. So are the three of you. But it can't be a coincidence that none of you is in a long-term relationship."

"I was married for seven years."

"Seven years is not nothing, but it's hardly long-term in the course of a lifetime."

"Maybe."

"I've had many years to think about this, Sadie. I might have been beaming with parental pride the day you married Mike because, for a moment, it made me feel as though I might have been able to instill something good and true about relationships in my kids. But I see now that it was a false feeling of victory. I got swept up by the romance of it all, too."

It's weird to hear my dad use the word romance, but not as weird as hearing him say all the other things he's saying.

"Your mother and I were together for almost twenty years and I know it didn't end well, and I never remarried or pursued much after she left, but I never stopped believing in the magical power of love. Not for you guys. It may sound odd, coming from me, but I mean it. Because I've always believed in family, despite what happened with your mother. You kids have been the greatest blessing of my life and it pains me that none of you have children or a family. That you don't know what it feels like."

"I think we do know what it feels like."

Dad shakes his head. "It's not exactly the same. It can't be."

"But, Dad—"

"As I said," he interrupts me, which is even rarer than him looking me in the eye like this. "You're all free to make your own choices and I'm not even remotely disappointed in you guys. How could I be when all three of you are nothing short of spectacular? But I just wish that one of you would be brave enough to take that leap. To just do it. Try it. Defy the odds you seem to so stubbornly believe in. Although I understand perfectly why you haven't." He shrugs. "Part of that is down to me. Part of that is down to things that simply couldn't be helped."

"Do you miss her?" I feel I can ask him now, when he's opening up to me in a way he never has before.

"Sometimes." He takes a deep breath. "I was devastated when Deb left. I know she needed to, but it took me a long time to accept that. But then I look at you three and I see her independence in Suzy, and her easy way with people in Sam. And you, you have her drive and her determination to live life on her own terms." He smiles. "She's still here in a way."

Have Suzy and Sam been on the receiving end of this speech? Am I only getting it now because I'm home for long enough? Or is this a spontaneous father-daughter heart-to-heart that's been a long time coming?

"I'm just saying," he continues, "that you shouldn't be afraid to fall in love again. Because you never know what might come of it. It might wither and die or it might blossom into the most beautiful thing. Maybe even something that will last close to a lifetime."

I'm glad I'm looking into my father's face, otherwise I wouldn't be sure it was him talking. Maybe this is the stuff he thinks of when his hands glide up and down a surfboard. Maybe, because he's our father and he thinks about us all the time, he knows us better than we sometimes know ourselves.

"It's not that simple. With Devon, I mean."

"Of course, it is. It's dead simple. You just need to stop being afraid." He surprises me further by putting a hand on my knee. "I know it's scary and I know you've been through a lot, but no matter what might happen when you put yourself out there, you can take it. I promise you that you can. Because you're my daughter."

Tears prick behind my eyes.

"What do you do when you get pulled under by a wave?" He holds on to my knee.

"Get right back out there."

"Sam might have taken that advice a bit too literally." I'm grateful for his raspy chuckle.

"But Dad, this thing with Devon, it's... I've never had feelings for a woman before. It's all new to me, yet she feels so familiar. At the same time, it's the most confusing and the most comforting and exhilarating thing. But I don't want to use her or make her a promise I won't be able to keep in the end."

"Sadie." His voice has dropped into a lower register. "All you can do is try." He removes his hand from my knee and pats me on the shoulder. "Don't you think you've been hiding out here with me long enough? I appreciate your company, but it's time to get your ass back into gear."

"Maybe..." My brain starts whirring, as if my dad's words have unlocked something in it. "I should catch the sunset surf."

"I think you should." He gets up, then reaches out his hand to me. I take it and let him pull me up.

CHAPTER 34

## Devon

The waves are kicking my ass tonight. There's a strong wind from the east and I can barely stay upright on my board. But I need to surf. I need to give my body this distraction. Ever since my impromptu chat with Sam, thoughts of Sadie have been spiraling out of control again in my head. So much so that, on a couple of occasions, when getting out of the water, I've had to stop myself from going to the beach house and knocking on her door. I meant it when I told Sam that things might become easier once Sadie leaves town. When I no longer have to be aware of her being so close, yet unreachable to me.

She must also really need time to process, as she put it, because she hasn't been in touch. Perhaps it's a blessing in disguise, because I don't know what seeing Sadie again will do to me. Although a lot of the time, it doesn't feel like a blessing at all. A lot of the time, I just miss her.

I spot a belter of a wave approaching. Because of the weather, I have the ocean pretty much to myself tonight. There's no glorious orange sunset light setting the surface of the water on fire. There are only heavy clouds and this wind, which is bordering on too dangerous to surf in, but I've weathered much worse storms, in and out of the water.

I approach the wave but miss my turn completely. The wave swallows me and once released, I sputter like a novice caught off-guard by the power of the ocean for the first time.

I'm about to give up. Some days, even surfing is too hard. I'm off my game and this wind is a little too treacherous. I lie belly-down on my board and start paddling to the shore when I see a surfer approach the water. Another someone crazy enough to head out in this weather. *Hold on.* I would know that walk anywhere. I recognize the shape of that body as though I was looking at my own in the mirror. Sadie.

Either she's feeling cocky and wants to measure herself against the evening's wild waves as well; or she has given up on her strategically planned surfing sessions to avoid me—and she's here for me. She wants to surf with me.

I sit up on my board and watch her wade into the water. She stops and waves at me. It takes more than a little wind to keep Sadie from surfing, that much I do remember.

She hops on her board and paddles toward me. My heart beats in my throat as she approaches. And of course it's fitting that the first time we see each other again is here, in the water, where we've always made everything right.

"I thought I'd find you here." She slicks her hair back. Her tone is casual. As though the past four weeks haven't happened. Or maybe she's done all the processing she can. I wonder what the outcome is.

"The waves are crazy today."

"Oh, yeah. I just saw you take that tumble." She grins at me.

"Damn." I don't mind losing face in front of Sadie. Not anymore. An incoming wave carries us a little closer to the shore. "If I'd known you were watching, I would have tried a little harder."

"Sometimes the waves don't let you." She looks into my eyes and delightful as it is to see her again, to be with her in the ocean, part of me wishes that she wasn't looking at me like that. Because my pulse is picking up speed already—and not only because of that massive wall of a wave I see coming toward us.

"Oh, shit, Dev. I think the weather's turning quickly," Sadie says.

In the distance, I see someone hurrying out of The Bay, gesturing for us to get out of the water. It's Sam.

"If my brother waves his arms like that, we should really listen to him." Sadie starts paddling to shore. She looks back at me. "As much as it may pain us to have to listen to Sam."

We head to the shore and strut out of the ocean side by side.

"That's NorCal weather for you." I sneak a peek at Sadie's shapely behind in her wetsuit. "Looks like you suited up for nothing."

Sadie peers at the clouds, then lowers her gaze to the angry whitecaps on the waves. She nods. "Looks like it. No more surfing today." She turns to me and smiles as though she doesn't mind at all that she won't be surfing tonight. "Looks like I'll have to kick your ass another time."

Another time? What is she implying?

"I came to see you," Sadie says. "Maybe we should talk now. It's been a long time coming." When she speaks to me like that, her voice full of confidence and easy authority, I'd follow her anywhere. Damn it. I'd best get myself together. *Be aware of who she is to you*, I inwardly say to myself, like a mantra I have to repeat in order to preserve a modicum of sanity around her. *Your soft spot. Your Achilles heel. That's okay. It doesn't mean you can't be strong.*

"Do you want to come to the house?" Sadie gives Sam a thumbs-up.

He responds in kind, then heads back to the bar.

"Um, sure." Just like last time we did this, I don't have any clothes with me, just a little pouch with my house keys and my phone that I pick up from the same spot where I always leave it on the beach. It's hard not to remember how that night ended.

"I have plenty of expensive leggings left you can ruin." Sadie sends me a grin I have trouble deciphering. Is she flirting?

"Maybe I should go home first and change." And let Hunter know not to panic when I'm not home tomorrow morning? *No. Stop it.* How can this be? Us not seeing each other for an extended period of time was supposed to cool us off, not make me even hotter for Sadie.

"If that makes you more comfortable."

"I think it would."

"Would you like me to come to yours?" Sadie asks. "Does that make it easier with Finn?"

"He's at Hunter and Bobby's tonight." I'm not going to pass up an opportunity for a nightcap on Sam's beach house's deck. "I'll be back in half an hour." I will need that half hour to do more than shower and put on some clothes —I need all the time I can get to pull myself together already.

---

Sadie has escorted me to the deck, which offers the perfect view of the waves rioting in the wind. No surfer, no matter how experienced, wants to be out right now, unless they have a death wish.

"I'm surprised my dad let me go out there. He usually has a more accurate take on the weather than the weather channel." Sadie pours me a cup of tea.

"I guess even Jack Ireland can make mistakes." The pulling-myself-together part of my quick visit home hasn't really worked. It was a frenetic affair of finding the right jeans while trying to make my wet hair look as though it'd seen a comb in the past few days.

"It must have been the conversation we were having." Sadie cradles her mug of tea between her hands. "He opened up to me in a way..." She pauses. "He never has before."

"Really?"

"It was weird and absolutely wonderful at the same time." She peers at me over the rim of her mug. "Not unlike other things that have happened to me lately." The way she's looking at me, she can only be alluding to what happened with us.

"Did you, um, get a chance to process all your feelings?" I ask, sounding a little sheepish.

"Not all of them. I don't see how that's possible." Sadie puts her tea down and flashes her beautiful smile.

God, those lips. Something twitches in my stomach and in that moment, I know I will never fully get over her. That doesn't mean I don't have choices, however. We always have choices, no matter the situation.

"But my dad said a few things to me that kind of hit home," Sadie continues.

How I wish I could have been a fly on the wall in Jack's workshop during that conversation.

"But I don't want to bombard you with any of this. We should definitely talk and I have a few things to say, but I imagine that you do as well. But first of all, how have you been? How's Finn?"

Asking after my son earns her another point in my book. "I've finally got him some lessons with Sam. They're both over the moon."

"So I've heard." I wonder if Sam has related all of that conversation we had, them being twins and such. "You took the leap, so to speak."

I nod. "He's almost six. I can take it now."

"And you?" Her voice is soft as silk. "How have you been holding up?"

"Just going about my life. Lots of surfing. Although it's been weird going back to my regular life with you still in town. It made me a little apprehensive, knowing that I could literally bump into you at any time."

"I've been hiding out at my dad's mostly. Surfing at times when I knew you were busy, courtesy of my sister."

"Really? You had Suzy spying on my schedule?"

"Not really. Please, don't blame her. I just asked her for times when she was almost certain you wouldn't be out there."

I chuckle. "I don't blame Suzy at all. If that's what you needed..."

"I've missed you," Sadie says, her voice unwavering. "Maybe I don't have the right to say that, but I missed you as though we ended a much longer love affair."

Love affair? Did what we have, no matter how brief, qualify as a love affair?

"I missed you too, Sadie." *Choices. Choices*, I repeat in my head. *Don't forget about your choices.* I sense that whatever is at the core of my being, the very essence of my soul, made its choice a while ago. Probably when I first clasped eyes on Sadie Ireland again at The Bay. All it took was one split second to have her lodged all the way back into my heart.

"I came up with this crazy theory..." Sadie pulls her legs onto her chair and wraps her arms around them. "That maybe we got together for all the wrong reasons, but that we also ended it for all the wrong reasons. And maybe, those two wrongs can make a right somehow."

Even my skillfully coached brain has trouble untangling that, but maybe I don't want to get to the bottom of it. Maybe I like for things to be vague right now. Vague, but full of promise. Full of this extravagant sensation unfurling inside me, like the perfect wave, that maybe something more is possible between Sadie and me, despite all the obstacles in our way.

"In my experience, two wrongs always make a right." When Sadie looks at me like that, her eyes half-lidded and her smile gorgeously crooked, I don't stand a chance. I may not know the person she is now very well, but part of me has known her forever. Part of me still connects to her, is drawn to her like metal to a magnet—like a force of nature. All it took for me to find that out, once again, was less than an hour in her magical presence.

When she smiles like that, her lips curled up and her eyes soft with kindness, all my good intentions are out of the window. I have no more choices.

"Oh, Sadie..." I don't have any words that can tell her how I feel. I should try. I came here to talk, after all, but how can I possibly express what she does to me? What she has always done to me?

Sadie puts her feet back on the ground and leans toward me. "Dad basically told me I should go for it with you."

My eyes widen. She told Jack about us? And he said that in response? "Do you always listen to what your father says?"

Sadie shrugs. "Only when the advice is so good it can't be ignored."

If I only lean in a fraction, I know I'm a goner. A lost cause to Sadie Ireland. For four weeks, I've been trying to control this feeling, this unease in my blood when I'm not with her, this desire to catch a glimpse of her—I might have rewatched the *King & Prince* finale a few too many times.

"But I don't want to take any of this for granted, Dev. I want you or, at least, I want to try... with you." She swallows hard. "But I will understand if you don't feel the same way anymore."

"Sadie," I whisper. "It's always been you." Then, I allow my body to do what it wants, to express what's bubbling in my soul. I bridge the distance between us and kiss Sadie on the lips. Again.

CHAPTER 35

# Sadie

I could ask myself why it's like this with Devon. Why it's second nature for me to kiss her, to move my body toward her—to always be moving in her direction with all of my being—like I'm doing now. But I'm done questioning this and myself. It can't be more obvious that it's Devon I want, and that kissing her is the most divine sensation on the planet. Nothing compares to the sensation of her lips on mine. To that thrill when she lifts her tattooed arm and brings a hand to my cheek. To that instant desire to surrender everything when her tongue enters my mouth.

The only possible conclusion is that, sometimes, it's like this. Sometimes, two people who knew each other when they were teenagers meet again, and an invisible spark flares between them. And sometimes, like my father urged me to do, you just have to try.

I don't know what the future might hold for us, or if we even have one, but I'm damn sure of what's going to happen in the next few minutes and the rest of this evening. Already, I'm looking forward to the heavenly feeling of opening my eyes in the morning and Devon being the first thing I see. Of waking next to her and pressing my body against hers. But first, we have some time to make up for—again.

"Come," I say, when we break from our kiss. She takes my hand and I lead her inside, up the stairs. This time, I draw the curtains, wanting to shut out everything else. It reminds me of what Devon said on the night of the *King & Prince* finale. That when we kiss, the rest of the world disappears.

I don't want the world to disappear, but I want to make my own personal universe so small there's only room for Devon and me. For this thing that sizzles between us, this fire that seems impossible to extinguish. I want to lose myself in this sexy cocoon of just us, in our own tiny world of her alabaster skin and that sexy tattoo on her hip and those luscious lips that are always so reluctant to show off her teeth underneath.

I want to drown in all things Devon and see where it takes me.

She's hungry for me, pulling at my clothes. Her fingers are clumsier than I remember, probably made so by her desire for me—I know because I recognize the feeling. We start tugging at our own clothes. We can't get them off quickly enough. When Devon has stripped to her panties and she slides them down her legs as well, I follow her example. It would be rude not to.

She pulls me onto the bed, and I settle on top of her. My skin glides against hers and I revel in her warmth and the burst of heat it creates inside of me. Her hands roam across my backside; her palms cup the cheeks of my behind. Devon's not playing tonight. She's more ravenous for me than she's ever been. This is no longer exploratory. This is pure need. Acute lust. A thirst so big, it needs to be quenched now or else we"ll both wither.

We kiss and kiss and I try to open my eyes to get a good

look at her, but I don't have to. Every last detail of her face is etched on the back of my eyelids. When I close my eyes, all I see is Devon Douglas. And I want her, oh how I want her. I spread my legs and straddle her thigh. My wetness spreads on her skin. I'm so hot for her. It must be because she is the world's best kisser and because the way she's cupping my ass leaves no room for interpretation. Devon wants me as much as I want her.

"Straddle my belly," she whispers, when we break from our kiss.

I pin my gaze on her. My brain isn't at peak capacity.

"I want you like that," she says, her eyes blazing fire.

When she speaks to me this way, her voice ragged with lust, it's no longer a matter of understanding what she means. We're operating on instinct and desire is the only thing that guides us. I push myself up and spread myself wide, her belly beneath me.

She smiles up at me. I guess she has me exactly where she wanted me.

"You're so beautiful," she whispers up at me. Her fingers dart along my hips. Her gaze locks fiercely onto me, as though Devon has no intention of looking away any time soon. Her fingers reach the inside of my thigh, wasting no time crawling upward.

She slides a fingertip along my wet sex. The grin on her lips broadens.

"You're so wet." Devon's voice hitches in her throat, as though she can't believe how turned on I am. But I am. I'm crazy for her. She's everything I want. Gorgeous. Smart. Cool as fuck. Down to earth. And insanely good at kissing and... at what she's about to do next.

Her fingertip dives a little deeper. She drags it upward and circles it around my throbbing clit. It's a thrill to be looking down at her, to witness the tiniest emotion as it crosses her face, the most minute of her expressions as she's about to give me the greatest pleasure once again.

She draws a circle around my pulsing clit a few more times before pushing her fingers high inside me.

I moan low in my throat. It's a groan so guttural I can feel it vibrate all through my body. I bring my hands to her chest and I let go completely. I buck against Devon's divine fingers. I roll my pelvis forward and backward, following her movement, intensifying the motion, riding Devon's fingers. I'm wild and free and as beautiful as she just said I was. With Devon, I feel every last little thing.

I try to keep my eyes open, to catch glimpses of her face, but it's impossible as this wave of all things Devon catches up with me. I can't believe she's doing this to me so swiftly again. Like she knows my body inside out—like she knows *me* inside out—and knows exactly what to do to me. But it's not any secret knowledge that has Devon driving me to the brink of orgasm, it's the combination of the two of us together. All we were then and all we are now. It's not the history we share, and it's definitely not our broken friendship that we're trying to mend, but the promise of what we can become together.

CHAPTER 36

## Devon

I'm basking along with Sadie in her orgasmic afterglow. She's sprawled across me, her breath hot against my cheek, her body deliciously heavy on mine. I curve my arms tightly around her. This time, I'm not letting her go again.

"Do they teach you that in life-coaching school as well?" Sadie says between a fit of giggles.

"What?" Her laughter is infectious. Her body vibrates against mine.

"How to make unsuspecting straight women come like that?" She gives a full belly laugh that is loud in my ears and fills my heart with so much joy, I can barely contain it.

I push her off me and roll on top of her. "You have the audacity to mock my profession during this profound moment?" I grab her wrists and pin them above her head. "Clearly, you still have a few orgasms in you and my job is nowhere near done." I gaze down at her. I don't believe in perfection because it doesn't exist—it's the biggest illusion of all—yet Sadie's face, when she's fully relaxed like this, when she's fully herself, can only be described as perfect.

Her expression turns serious. She bites her lower lip as she returns my gaze. "I want you so much." She might as well have just slid a finger inside me, that's how her words turn me on.

"You took your time to realize that."

She nods, her features still pulled into a grave expression. "I know, but... you have to admit that what happened between us was a little crazy. A little destabilizing. It was for me."

I let go of her wrists and slip off her. I push my body against her side and put a hand on her belly. She clearly has some more processing to do.

"It was for me as well. Here I was, contentedly going about my life, then you show up and turn my world upside down."

"I never meant to do that." Sadie turns her face toward me. "It just kind of happened, and maybe that's what bugged me the most. I couldn't wrap my head around why I suddenly seemed to be falling in love with you, as though falling in love with other women is all I've done my whole life." She blinks. "For the record, I haven't. And yes, you are you. You are Devon Douglas, but still... It was hard to reconcile the person I was with you with who I always thought I was. Who I was with Mike."

"I imagine it's all very confusing."

Sadie gives a slight shake of the head. "That's just the thing. When I'm with you, it's so crystal clear to me. I want to be with you. Even after taking the time to really think about, to sit with it, as you would say, wanting to be with you is the only outcome."

"I'm here and I want the same thing." I slide my hand to her side.

"It must be confusing for you as well."

"It is, but the confusion doesn't weigh up to all the other things I feel."

"Which are?" The corners of her mouth curl upward.

"I'm hopelessly, stupidly, crazy in love with you, Sadie Ireland. It must be because your face is on TV every week. The irresistible allure of celebrity and all that."

"Oh, you're a fangirl? I get it. A lot of women of your persuasion are very fond of Leona King." Her lips have bloomed into a full-blown smile.

"They don't know the real Sadie, though."

"And you do?" She brings her face closer to mine, preparing to kiss me again.

"I've felt, kissed and tasted a lot more of you." I shuffle toward her until the tips of our noses touch. "And we've surfed together. You learn a lot about a person when you ride some waves with them." I pause. "You may think you're afraid of certain things, but how you are in the ocean proves otherwise. You're fearless. Maybe that's why you kissed me."

"You were a wave I couldn't bear to miss." Her nose tilts away from mine. Her lips are so near, I can almost taste them.

"You've sure done your best riding me." Part of me might have regressed to the teenager I was, lying in bed next to Sadie, not wanting her to go to sleep, feverishly trying to come up with more witty things to say so the night could be prolonged —so I could be with her longer.

"Argh," she says on an exaggerated moan. "I hope you're not considering a career switch to comedy."

I touch my lips to hers. She doesn't yield to the kiss immediately. She pulls back a little so we can look each other in the eye.

"I'm in love with you too, Dev." She swallows hard.

In response, I can only kiss her while every nerve ending in my body lights up with joy, with effervescent sparks of pure, unbridled happiness. Sadie and I are in love with each other. Just maybe, it's as simple as that and all we've done is try to complicate our way out of it. But love doesn't work that way and the heart wants what the hearts wants. My heart's been after Sadie for a very long time.

When we break from this kiss, Sadie pushes her hand into my hair and pins her gaze on me. "Let me show you exactly how much I am in love with you."

Over the years, after an episode of *King & Prince* in which she looked particularly hot, I've allowed myself the odd fantasy of ending up in bed with Sadie. But never in my wildest dreams had I expected it to be like this. That she would be so bold, so brazen, so deliciously forward and unafraid. Then again, Sadie has always been those things, so why shouldn't she be them now, when she's really in bed with me? When it's her skin I feel against mine, her tongue dancing inside my mouth.

"I want you in a certain way as well," she says.

"I'm all ears." Maybe, with a new lover who wasn't me, whom she doesn't have history with, she couldn't be this forward.

Her lips are so close, I can feel them move when she speaks. "I want you in my mouth while you sit on top of me."

It's tempting to tease her, but this time I don't, because desire overtakes me again and this moment calls for some gravity. I love that Sadie is so comfortable with me that she can speak her mind like that, that she can just tell me what it is she wants. It doesn't just say a lot about her, but about us as well. As unlikely a combination as we may be, all the early signs that this could really be something, that this could be the kind of love that only comes along once in a lifetime, are there. Or maybe I'm just delirious with lust for her, the way I was when my teenage hormones held me hostage and I couldn't help but kiss her that day. So, of course, I comply. I do exactly as Sadie asks of me. I offer myself to her, for her to take me in her mouth, and make all the stars in the universe explode underneath my skin again.

Her tongue swirls along my clit and I have to hold on to the headboard of the bed behind her. I stretch out my arms. From underneath hooded eyelids, I glance at my tattoos. Maybe it's time for a new one. My left hip feels awfully naked sometimes, and Sadie seems to be very into the ink on my skin. What's funny is that, a couple of times now, she has referred to me as cool, whereas I used to be convinced that there was no cooler chick on this planet than Sadie Ireland.

Sadie licks me in the same way she attacks a challenging wave, without a doubt in the world that she can deal with it, with all the gusto a person can muster, with all the swagger of someone who's been in bed with the ladies all her life.

When I climax for the first time, I don't ask her to stop, because when it comes to Sadie, I'm a bottomless well of so many things: emotions, memories, lust, and orgasms. She licks me and licks me, her tongue soft and slick and divine against my insatiable sex. I come at her tongue until my body is spent and my muscles tremble with exhaustion. Afterwards, she cradles me in her arms, draping a leg over my hip. I look into her eyes and wonder when all my wildest dreams started coming true.

## CHAPTER 37

# *Sadie*

As glorious as last night was, waking up next to Devon, with a clearer definition of what this is now, without the confusion of the first time rattling around in my brain, is the most divine sensation.

Earlier this week, I got sent the first scripts for the next season of *King & Prince*. I was curious how the writers would deal with Mike's departure and how Prince's niece would be introduced, but apart from that, thinking about resuming my life in Hollywood hasn't filled me with a great deal of anticipatory joy. At times, I've even wondered if I should have been the one to leave the show instead of Mike.

My reluctance to go back to LA is only increased by the gorgeous sleeping form of Devon Douglas next to me. It takes all the willpower I have not to brush that strand of orange-blonde hair away from her face, but she's perfect just the way she is. With skin bizarrely pale for someone who spends so much time under the sun, and the lightest smattering of freckles around her nose. Her mouth is slightly agape and her lips look so damn kissable, but I refrain from doing so. We have a few more weeks together to do all the kissing we want.

There's no need to rush it now—there's no need to wake her up just yet.

I could lie here forever, just looking at her. Thinking about all the things we've said and all the things we've yet to say to each other. In the end, we haven't talked all that much yet. It's hard when all you want to do is tear each other's clothes off. For that, too, we have time.

As though she can sense me looking at her, and she intuits that I'm on the cusp of having a slew of impure thoughts about her, Devon's eyes flutter open. Instantly, she bursts into a smile.

"What? No coffee in bed? Service in this place is deteriorating quickly." She pulls me toward her.

"You're getting a different kind of service this time." I press a kiss to her cheek. "Morning, gorgeous. You were out like a light."

"I did actually surf last night, while you chickened out," Devon says, a smile lurking in her voice.

"It must be that." I slide my leg over hers and push my knee between her thighs.

Devon curves her arms around me. "I don't mean to be a spoilsport, but some of us have to work today." She nips at my ear. "What time is it?"

"Time for you to kiss me properly."

I delight in the way her body convulses underneath me. "You're so bossy. Is that because you're used to having an assistant at your beck and call?"

I shake my head, our lips already touching. "It's solely because of the kissability factor of your lips." I gently tug at her bottom lip with my teeth. "Lips like yours should be illegal, really. They're too dangerous to be around."

"Did something happen to your brain? Did you lose a little of your mind overnight?"

"Must be because I wasn't allowed to stop licking your pussy until you'd come a dozen times." My body's convulsing along with Devon.

"Your exaggeration muscles have been flexed as well, I see."

"Just kiss me, Dev. Shut me up before I spout any more nonsense."

"Gladly," Devon says and the way she kisses me shuts me up well and good. It's impossible to tear my lips away from hers. I anchor Devon beneath my body. I want to spend the day with her. I want to compress the four weeks we missed into the time we have left. I want double time with her. I want to kiss her endlessly. I want to feel her fingers inside me again. Most of all, I want to throw the curtains wide and see if the weather has calmed down, because, by god, do I want to go surfing with her. To go out into the ocean with Devon is as close as I can get to feeling like my teenage self and my current self all at once.

The girl I once was and the woman I am now. All the life I've lived in between. The betrayals, the heartaches, the successes—all the highs and lows of life pulsing inside me. With her, I can fully be myself. Devon's seen the worst of me already, but she has also seen the best.

"Argh," she groans. "I really need to know the time. I have a thing I can't reschedule this morning."

"Just tell whomever you're meeting you couldn't resist the dazzling allure of Sadie Ireland. They'll understand."

"Your sister might quit her job if I use that as an excuse."

"Suzy will understand." I can't wait to see my sister and tell her about what happened, and all the things Dad said to me. "But I'll make you a deal. I'll go get you some coffee while you get ready."

"Say hi to Sam from me," Devon jokes.

I kiss her one last time, throw on some clothes, and tiptoe downstairs. With a bit of luck, Sam's still asleep or already out surfing. I might join him if Devon has to dash off to work.

"Coffee for two?" Sam's already up all right. His grin is smug and oh-so annoying.

"Yes, please." Next to the coffee maker, I spot two steaming mugs. Maybe he heard me coming down the stairs and wanted to do me a favor. But he doesn't give me the already prepared coffees. He reaches into the cabinet and grabs two empty mugs.

"Thirsty?" I head to the counter and eye the mugs ostentatiously. "Or are you back to your old ways?"

"Cassidy's in my room," he whispers.

"Oh, damn!" A rush of glee shudders through me.

"Shh. Don't make a big deal out of this. Try to play it a little cool, at least."

"I'll make my own coffee. You go back to your lady."

Sam grabs the mugs. "I know what you're thinking, but I really like Cass. She's not just a one-night thing for me."

"All right." If Cassidy's still as smitten with my brother as she was a few weeks ago, I hope for her sake that Sam's being serious. "In that case, give her my love. Tell her we can hang out later and I'll tell her all she needs to know about you." I blow him a kiss as he disappears up the stairs.

While the coffee drips, I look out of the window. All the clouds have cleared and the ocean is eerily calm—a bit too calm for my liking, but I know that can quickly change. Like so many things can.

I take the beverages upstairs. To my disappointment, Devon's already fully dressed.

"I'm so sorry, Sadie, but I have to run." She holds out her hands for the coffee.

"Surely you have five more minutes to spare for Sadie Ireland." I flutter my eyelashes.

"I can give you three."

"I can work with three." I move behind her. "Lunch later? Or dinner? I would also like to call dibs on your weekend."

"You've turned into such a lez already." Devon lets the back of her head fall against my shoulder.

"Only because you've turned me into one."

"I already know where I'm taking you this weekend and you'd better brace yourself." Devon turns around in my embrace. "Don't expect any of that Hollywood cutesy stuff to work either."

"Ooh. Sounds exciting!"

"I think it's time you sat down with my mother."

"Meeting the parents already. Who's being a big old lez now?"

Devon shakes her head. "You don't get to make a joke like that, Sadie."

"Why not?"

"Because you're not a lesbian."

"Says the woman whose pus—"

Devon holds up her hand. "Your three minutes are up." She gives me a quick kiss on the lips. "I'll call you later."

"Can't wait." Once she's gone, I take what's left of my coffee onto the deck. From the open sliding doors of Sam's room, giggles arise.

I sit and gaze at the ocean. I contemplate all the things that have happened since I've come back. Devon. Dad opening up to me. Feeling so much closer to my brother and sister. The work Dad and I have done on the surfboard. Watching the *King & Prince* season finale with people I never even knew before but have already come to care about nonetheless.

Inside my room, the new *King & Prince* scripts await. As much as I love the show and all it has done for me, all the doors it has opened and all the unbelievable experiences it has given me, I'd very much like to toss those pages right into the sea, let the waves take them, absorb them and make them disappear, so they cease to exist, and I don't have to deal with them any longer.

Because that nagging little voice that made me come to Clearwater Bay in the first place, is quickly transforming into a loud cry demanding that I stay.

## CHAPTER 38

*Devon*

On Sunday, my father takes Finn, Hunter and Bobby to a baseball game. Maybe my mother wanted him out of the house for Sadie's first visit since we were teenagers. Perhaps Mom doesn't trust her reaction when she sees Sadie again after all these years—twenty-four years of motherly loyalty has built into an aversion to all things Sadie Ireland. All I know is that when I asked her if Sadie and I could come round, she said yes without too much hesitation in her voice.

Still, nerves flutter in my belly as we approach the house. On the way over, a stranger pretended to shoot Sadie with a gun made out of his fingers. She was a good sport about it and shot him right back. Apparently, this has been happening quite a bit since the *King & Prince* finale.

My mother is in the backyard, a bottle of white wine in a cooler on the table. Three glasses are lined up next to it.

She kisses me first, then stands in front of Sadie. She puts her hands on Sadie's shoulders. "Sadie Ireland," she says, then huffs out some air. "Wow." She gives Sadie's shoulders a squeeze, as though testing the firmness of her flesh. It's probably a bit soon for a hug—not everyone can move at the lightning speed Sadie and I have been traveling at.

"Mrs. Douglas. It's so good to see you." Sadie has turned her TV smile all the way on. I told her my mother would see right through it, but Sadie said that we would have to see about that.

"*Mrs.* Douglas?" Mom shakes her head. "You're not sixteen anymore, Sadie. Call me by my first name, please."

"You got it, Brenda. How are you?"

"How about I tell you all about it over a cold glass of wine? I have a nice bottle of Chardonnay open."

"Lovely."

We all sit. "I'm sure you're used to vintage bottles from French vineyards, but Californian wine is nothing to sneeze at." I can tell Mom's a little nervous about this. It's perfectly understandable for all three of us to be a bit on edge.

"I'm not a wine snob." The corners of Sadie's mouth seem tugged up by invisible strings, that's how persistent her smile is. "You can pour me a crisp NorCal wine any day of the week."

My mother proceeds to do just that. She's the first to take a sip.

"How's Jack?" Mom asks.

"Dad's very well. He says hello."

"I hear Sam is teaching Finn to surf."

They continue to skim the surface with small talk for a while longer. It drains the tension from the situation a little. I wish my mother had given me a similar speech as the one Sadie's father gave her last week, but I'm fairly certain she doesn't want me taking any great leaps with Sadie just yet.

On the other hand, it would have been perfectly plausible for me to have brought Sadie home as someone I simply rekindled an old friendship with. But we all know that's not the case. Sadie is so much more to me than an old friend.

"I'm not going to give you the third degree about your intentions with my daughter," my mother says when she's halfway through her glass of wine.

"Great, Mom." I can't help a little snark. "Because this is not the fifties anymore and it's not really your place to do so."

"I know it's not, but neither one of you can deny that you have a sketchy history. I had a front-row seat to what happened back then. I was there to pick up the pieces, and there were a lot of broken bits that had to be put together again. So you must understand my skepticism at seeing you two together like this now, all of a sudden." She pins her gaze on me. "I'm hardly an outsider in your life, yet I'm having great trouble understanding this."

"We don't fully understand it either, Brenda," Sadie says. "All we know is that being together is what we want. And my intentions are nothing but pure. I have no hidden agenda. I just want to be with Devon."

I melt a little on the inside at Sadie's heartfelt words.

"But in a few weeks' time, you're headed back to Hollywood. To your life there. What happens then?"

So much for not giving Sadie the third degree. It's a logical question, although she is being a bit blunt about it, but I don't want to think about Sadie leaving just yet.

"LA is really not that far. It's a one-hour flight," Sadie says. Has she given any thought to what's going to happen when she goes back to work?

"But you don't exactly have a great track record for taking that flight."

"Mom. Come on."

My mother cuts her gaze to me. "It's not just you I'm thinking of. It's Finn as well."

"You're being a little hostile." I hate speaking to my own mother like this, but I feel like I have no choice.

"I'm your mother, Devon. I will always worry about your well-being. It's only natural."

"It's okay," Sadie says. "It's true that I haven't come back to Clearwater Bay very often. Shooting a show like *King & Prince* is very demanding and, um, well, I haven't always made it a priority to come home in my free time. I love my family to pieces, but... I guess staying away was how I dealt with certain things."

"I don't mean to rake up painful memories for you, Sadie." My mother's tone has softened considerably. She speaks to Sadie the way she did when she sat at our kitchen table, trying very hard not to cry into her dinner, because with every week, month, and year that passed, it was becoming clearer and clearer that her mother wasn't coming back. My mother and Sadie's mom were far from best friends, but they were well acquainted. I know my mother tried to contact her to no avail.

"I just want to say that..." Sadie clears her throat. She takes a quick sip of wine. "I'm not my mother. Obviously, I don't know what she's really like, apart from the fact that she's the kind of person to leave her children for... I don't know for what or what was so much better than being our mother. I'll never know. But because she left, I was raised by a wonderful father, who always put us first, and who taught us all the important things in life." Her voice cracks a little. "Don't ask me how he did it, but he managed to bring up three rowdy kids on his own, while dealing with losing his wife. But he did and he is the most beautiful person I know. I may carry half of my mother's genes, but I'm my father's daughter when it comes to most things." Sadie wipes away a quick tear. Under the table, I put my hand on her knee. "Except for my divorce, maybe, but I'm dealing with that."

"I'm so sorry, Sadie," Mom says. "I came on a bit strong. Fists up and all that. It's how I am when it comes to my family."

"I get it." Sadie covers my hand in hers. "I finally do. Coming back here has made me see how much of my family's life I've missed. I don't intend to miss much more of it." Sadie glances at me. I send her the warmest smile I can muster. *Wait.* What is she saying?

"I'm not asking you to predict the future, Sadie. I'm not that unreasonable—"

"You know what my dad said to me the other day?" Sadie interjects.

Mom shakes her head.

"He said that no matter what happens, I'll be able to take it, because he raised me so that I can. So that I can deal with life's unavoidable valleys as well as its peaks. And if I'm as crazy about Devon as I claim to be, I have no choice but to give it my all."

I might be squeezing Sadie's fingers to a pulp under the table.

"I can hardly argue with that," Mom says.

"Your dad should be a life coach," I say.

"He's just an old surfer dude who loves his kids to death." Sadie's voice trembles. "And I plan to spend as much time with him as possible now that I still can."

"Sounds like I need to have Jack Ireland over for dinner," Mom says. Sadie's little speech must have moved something in her.

"If you can get him to leave his house for something other than surfing, then sure." Sadie's million-dollar smile is almost back to full wattage. "Although I'm sure he'd be glad to come.

Just, um, maybe give it some time?" Sadie chuckles. "This has all been going so fast, no wonder I'm so dizzy half the time."

"Now you're going to slow things down?" There's the mother that I know so well and love to bits. The woman who trusts her daughter to make the right decisions for herself and her son. Being a mother myself, I know that particular leap isn't always easy.

"Touché," Sadie says. She takes a few more sips. "How about we finish that bottle, Brenda?"

"Maybe you are a woman after my own heart. I count myself lucky if Devon drinks half a glass with me."

"Mom, alcohol is the—" I start, but catch myself, because this isn't about the amount of wine we do or don't consume between us. This is about her bonding with Sadie.

My mother refills our glasses, then holds up her own in a toast. "I hope I'll be seeing much more of you as well, then," she says.

## CHAPTER 39

*Sadie*

Devon and I are walking on the beach. It's a beautiful Sunday and the weather's getting warmer. Small groups of people are strewn across the sand. We're huddled close together but to anyone who doesn't know us, I assume we could just be two friends out on a late afternoon stroll.

"So..." Devon starts. "You plan to come back to Clearwater Bay more?"

I nod. "For many reasons."

"On a plane every weekend? That's not very good for your ecological footprint."

"True." I have no solution for that. "I could take the train. That only takes about eleven hours, which should leave us a few hours for making out."

"For the most part, my work is location-independent," Devon says. "I can come to you as well."

"Thanks, but I don't expect that. I know Finn comes first."

"I'll just drop him at Sam's," Devon jokes. "And he has his

father and Bobby. I can get away for the odd weekend or even a week here and there."

"That would be lovely. Obviously, Malibu has nothing on Clearwater Bay, but the waves are not too bad." I want to take Devon's hand in mine so badly, it makes my fingers twitch. I glance around. Surely, someone must have clocked me. But what's the worst that can happen? Someone filming us and posting it online. The news spreading like wildfire. A picture of Devon and me walking hand-in-hand on the beach going viral. But what does it even matter? I'm not choosing to be with Devon only to hide her away. If I'm going to be with Devon, I'm going to be with her out in the open. I'm going to give myself the small pleasure of walking hand-in-hand with her along the beach of our childhood.

I brush my pinkie against hers. Once. Twice. Then I let it linger, until I hook my finger in hers.

She looks at me, eyebrows arched up. Devon doesn't say anything, but threads her fingers through mine. I don't know what it means to her that we're walking on the beach like this, but, to me, it's everything.

I wish I lived in a world in which I didn't have to care about my image, but I don't. No one does, I guess, but it's worse when you live under the Hollywood magnifying glass. My agent may disagree, but I completely fail to see how walking hand-in-hand with a woman can destroy my image. Granted, it may cause some minor disruption, but Leslie can deal with it. That's why she gets a generous cut of my earnings.

"If a picture of this gets out," Devon says, "a large percentage of the lesbian population may never recover."

"Too much for them to take? That Sadie Ireland is canoodling with a hot female stranger on a Northern California beach?" I slow our pace. Suddenly, I want to do so much more than just hold Devon's hand in mine.

"Can you repeat that bit about the hot female stranger?" Devon tightens her grip on my fingers.

"Though infinitely hot, she's far from a stranger to me." I stop and stand in front of her. "She's the opposite and her lips are the very stuff my dreams are made of." I lean in to kiss her and Devon's not the type to question whether I'm sure I should be doing this. Now that we've declared our feelings for each other, that we've decided to follow our intuition and no longer ignore how much we want each other, she trusts I know what I'm doing.

I touch my lips to hers and, instantly, not too far away, someone wolf whistles at us. We don't stop to look at who it is, because we don't care. Our lips are locked, in the most beautiful place on earth for us. What else could possibly matter?

"A kiss on this very beach from Sadie Ireland," Devon says. "I truly never thought I'd see the day."

"It's been a long time coming." I bring the back of my fingers to her cheek, to the spot where I slapped her all those years ago.

"Imagine if you'd kissed me back all those years ago," Devon whispers.

"I don't have to imagine." I slant toward her again and kiss her with all that I have.

"I think we should go to the house now." Devon's breath is ragged.

I take her by the hand and we start toward the house. Just before we arrive at the back gate, I find her gaze. "We might not know what the future holds for us, but I do have options. I'm not tied to the show for a set number of years. My contract is up for negotiation after every season."

"We'll see," Devon says. "But thank you for saying that."

"I—" I start, but my phone buzzing interrupts me. I check the message. "I don't believe this. Leslie's heard already. She must have some very efficient Google alerts set up for her clients."

"What do you expect? You are Sadie Ireland, after all." Devon flashes me a grin. "And I'd very much like to take Sadie Ireland to bed right about now."

"Thank heavens for Ida Burton and Faye Fleming," I reply. "After their spectacular coming out, me kissing a woman on the beach is a mere blip on the world's gaydar."

"Another thing we'll have to see about." Devon almost pulls me up the stairs. "Meanwhile, kissing you on the beach has unleashed something in me."

"A horny beast?" I rush after her, hoping Sam isn't home. He's probably at the bar with Cassidy.

"Let me make quick work of introducing you to this sexy creature."

"Maybe its image can be your next tattoo," I say, but don't get a chance to say more, because Devon's lips are all over mine, and the only sound I make is a groan of delight in the back of my throat.

## CHAPTER 40

## *Devon*

"I thought you'd stay out there forever," Sadie says. "Are you deliberately trying to miss my big moment?"

I wiggle out of my wetsuit and go through the motions of rinsing and washing it. "There's plenty of time, babe."

"After missing the *King & Prince* season finale, now you also want to miss the new season premiere?" Sadie's trying to look cross with me, but more than anything, she's ogling my naked behind.

"I wouldn't miss that for the world, and you know it. It's about time I experienced some Hollywood glamor. I've been putting up with you long enough."

"Oh!" Sadie playfully slaps my behind with two fingers. "You'd better take that back right now or I'll rescind your invitation."

"Hop into the shower with me." I grab the fingers I just felt against my skin. "I'll make it up to you."

"I need to get my face on. A dozen cameras will be pointed at it in an hour's time."

"Your face already looks perfect as it is." I tug her toward the shower.

"Easy enough for you to say. You just flash some tat and everyone goes gaga for you."

"No, Sadie, that's just you." I curl my arms around her. She runs a finger along one of the rose petals tattooed on my biceps.

"I'm pretty much addicted to you, so yeah, I won't contradict you this time." She leans in to kiss me. "I may also be a little nervous about my first red carpet event with you."

"You should have gone surfing with me. It works wonders for all sorts of affliction, red carpet nerves included."

"Please. As if I don't know why you're out there in the ocean all the time. You spend more time lounging on your board, trying to catch a glimpse of Faye Fleming and Ida Burton than actually surfing."

"How dare you question my surfer ethics. That I would put some celebrity spotting above riding the perfect wave is just preposterous."

"Sure, babe. Keep telling yourself that." Instead of leaning in to kiss me, Sadie reaches into her back pocket and shows me her phone. "Check this."

*Good luck tonight, Sadie. Ida and I are rooting for you. Let's get together some time soon. Faye xo*

My eyes grow wide. "No way."

"Hollywood lesbians have to stick together." Sadie grins. "And our little club is growing and growing."

"Faye Fleming texted you." I can't believe it. I know to take celebrity with a grain of salt, but logic and reason go right out of the window when it comes to Faye Fleming and Ida Burton.

"She didn't specify I should bring you to this proposed get-together." Sadie's grin widens. "You're going home tomorrow so it might be difficult to include you."

"Instead of teasing me, why don't you respond to Faye's text." Because Sadie has always been Sadie to me, the girl I was so in love with I risked our friendship by trying to kiss her, the notion of her being the kind of person exchanging messages with the likes of Faye Fleming and Ida Burton is still quite strange to me.

Since Sadie started shooting the new season of *King & Prince* four months ago, I've stayed at her house in Malibu a few times, but, apart from a few visits to the set, we haven't ventured out together all that much. Dating long-distance will do that to you and so far, my hunger for having Sadie all to myself in private has been far greater than my desire to go to some Tinseltown party. "I need to hit the shower if you want to make your red-carpet moment."

"I'll tell Faye we'll try not to upstage her and Ida's iconic kiss from the *A New Day* premiere."

"Tell her whatever you want," I say, before ducking into the shower, "as long as you also tell her your hot female lover needs to be invited too." I turn on the water and whatever comeback Sadie has for me is drowned out.

I may not be able to hear what she has to say, but all the words she has spoken to me the past five months still ring very clearly in my ears.

Tonight's *King & Prince* premiere will be Sadie's last. At the end of the season, King is leaving the show the way Prince did last season—although, perhaps, in a less violent manner.

Sadie wants to spend more time in Clearwater Bay with her family—and me and Finn.

She has been dividing her time between Malibu and our hometown, but Sadie's schedule is hectic and often unpredictable—time is always the biggest enemy of any Hollywood production I've learned since being with her.

We manage a weekend here and there, but it's not nearly enough for all the time we want to spend together. A few more months of shooting, and Sadie can come home. She wants to take a career break and see what comes up next— much against her agent's advice, but Leslie would say that. Sadie has been unassailable in her decision to not miss even more of her family's life than she's already missed.

"I'll become a master surfboard maker. Who wouldn't want a board made by the one and only Sadie Ireland?" she joked the other day.

"Paint it in the colors of the rainbow and all the lesbians whose hearts you've broken by quitting the show might buy one. It's an iffy business plan, but you never know," I replied.

"Good thing I'll be shacking up with a very sought-after life coach, then," Sadie said.

Since word about us has gotten out, coaching requests have exploded—as though me being with Sadie changes anything about my methods. But I get what it is that people want to buy, although it's an illusion I'm not selling—quite the opposite.

Although when I open my eyes first thing in the morning, and Sadie, bathed in the light coming off the ocean, is the very first thing I see, I sometimes do believe that fairy tales can be real.

## CHAPTER 41

# *Sadie*

"Sadie, come on," Devon says. "Let me hold JJ for a bit."

"No, babe. I don't want to risk you getting broody again."

"That's a good one coming from you." Devon rolls her eyes at me.

As if he can sense his aunties are fighting over him, little Jack Junior starts crying. It doesn't start with a soft whimper as a warning sign. This baby goes from totally quiet to full-blown wailing in a split second.

"How about I take him." Sam swoops in. "Unless you want to change his diaper."

"Sadie should do it," Devon says. "She could do with the experience."

Sam quirks up his eyebrows. "Don't tell me you're also thinking about adding to the Ireland clan."

"We're only forty-three. It's still possible," I say, not because I mean it, but just because I'm among family and I can say things like that here.

"You're a lady of leisure now," Suzy butts in. "You could

291

be a stay-at-home mom, Sadie."

"Excuse me. I just finished a movie. Give a girl a break."

"Didn't Faye Fleming and Ida Burton just adopt two babies?" Cassidy asks.

"They're hardly babies." A smile blooms on my face as I remember our visit to Malibu last week—I still have my house there for when I shoot in LA. "Leroy and Leesa are eight years old."

"A year younger than me," Finn yells, as though this is a huge accomplishment.

"Devon and Finn gave them some surfing tips," I say.

"Faye Fleming was very impressed with me. I reckon she's after some private lessons from yours truly as well." Devon may play it cool as a cucumber now—when she first met Faye and Ida, she was anything but.

"I have no idea who you're talking about." Dad sits there grinning. "But I'm about ready for my birthday cake." He eyes Finn. "Rumor has it you made it."

"I made it with my other grandpa," Finn says, as though my father is as much his granddad as Devon and Hunter's fathers. "But I did most of the work."

"I'll get it. Come on, Finn." Devon and Finn disappear inside the house.

Sam walks onto the deck with a newly happy JJ in his arms. Suzy holds out her arms for our nephew.

We've gathered at our father's house for his seventieth birthday. Since Sam and I celebrated our fortieth three years ago, I haven't missed a single birthday in my family—Cassidy's, my new sister-in-law, included—and I was here on the day my godson was born.

The moments I've had with my family, and with Devon and Finn, have patched up a lot of the remaining holes in my soul. These days, I shoot a movie once or twice a year, but the rest of my time, I spend here, at home in Clearwater Bay, with all the people I love.

I surf every day, whether in the morning or in the evening; sometimes with my brother, although he's often too busy being a dad now; sometimes alone, but mostly with Devon and Finn as company.

"Happy birthday to you," Finn sings, while precariously balancing the cake in his tiny hands. But the kid's got good balance—he's a surfer after all. Devon's right behind him, beaming with pride.

We all join the singing, celebrating my dad. The man who gave us everything we ever needed.

I look into his wrinkled, satisfied face. He still goes out into the waves every morning. He keeps on trucking away at his surfboards. More days than not, I'm with him in his work-shop while Devon's working. He's been teaching Finn about what makes the perfect board as well, about the time and dedication and attention to detail it takes. I'm sure little JJ will be on a surfboard as soon as he learns to swim.

I cast my gaze over my family, over all these people I love with all my heart. Then I glance at Devon, whom I love more than life itself. She's distributing pieces of cake, her gorgeous arms glistening in the sun. I wait until she looks at me and revel in the glow it ignites in me.

Even though this is one of these glorious afternoons with my family I never want to end, I can't wait for later. After we've dropped Finn off at Hunter and Bobby's. Devon will mistakenly assume we're going surfing. But I have other plans for the sunset tonight.

As the sun dramatically lowers itself behind the horizon, I will lower myself onto one knee, on the very beach where Devon once tried to kiss me, and I will ask her to marry me.

There's no doubt in my mind she'll say yes.

# Get Three E-Books For Free

Building a relationship with my readers is the very best thing about writing. I occasionally send newsletters with details on new releases, special offers and giveaways.

And if you sign up to my mailing list I'll send you all this free stuff:

1. An e-book of *Few Hearts Survive*, a Pink Bean Series novella that is ONLY available to my mailing list subscribers.
2. A free e-book of *Hired Help*, my very first (and therefore very special to me) lesbian erotic romance story.
3. A free e-book of my first 'longer' work, my highly romantic novella *Summer's End*, set on an exotic beach in Thailand.

You can get *Few Hearts Survive* (a Pink Bean Series novella), *Hired Help* (a spicy F/F novelette) and *Summer's End* (a deeply romantic lesfic novella) **for free** by signing up at www.harperbliss.com/freebook/ or scanning the QR code below

# About the Author

Harper Bliss is a best-selling lesbian romance author. Among her most-loved books are the highly dramatic French Kissing and the often thought-provoking Pink Bean series.

Harper lived in Hong Kong for seven years, travelled the world for a bit, and has now settled in Brussels (Belgium) with her wife and photogenic cat, Dolly Purrton.

Together with her wife, she hosts a weekly podcast called Harper Bliss & Her Mrs.

Harper loves hearing from readers and you can reach her at the email address below.

www.harperbliss.com
harper@harperbliss.com

Printed in Great Britain
by Amazon